# MATCHED

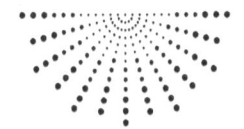

## S. E. LUND

ACADIAN PUBLISHING LIMITED

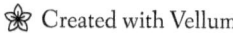

# CHAPTER ONE

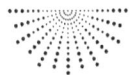

## INDIA

*TECHCRUNCH DISRUPT, San Francisco*

THE FIRST TIME I met Jon, he tried to pick me up. He almost succeeded. If he had, I doubt I'd be here at Tech-Crunch Disrupt today.

Picture it – one of my first beach parties of the year, Friday night before a week of midterms, and I'm with my best girl-friends. We're crazy in the way that only geek girls can be crazy – letting our hair down when we're usually buttoned up tight. Tequila shots, pitchers of beer, nachos. Music blaring, we're all half-drunk sitting on stools at the beach bar, and up walks this gorgeous hunk of a man I recognized from my English class.

I watch as Marina's eyes widen when he stands next to me.

"Hey, India right?" he says, his arm on the back of my chair.

"You're in my English course. Great name, by the way."

1

"Thanks," I say, used to getting ribbed about my name. "I recognize you." I turn to him, my drink in hand. "Professor Gardner's class. We're reading Tess of the D' Urbervilles."

"Yeah," he says and gives me a brilliant smile. "Or at least, we're supposed to be. I'm a bit behind. It's a romance, right?"

I shake my head. "Oh, it's not romance, believe me. More like a tragedy, and a warning about Britain's crumbling feudal system, the decay of the rural way of life due to industrialization and the oppression of women."

"Whoa." He makes a face of horror. "Deep. There was a movie made about it," he says. "With Nastassja Kinsky. Didn't Polansky direct it?"

"He did."

Jon nods his head thoughtfully. Then he smiles. "Wanna dance?"

Now, you have to realize that Jon Anders Thorson is perhaps the hunkiest hunk on campus. Not only is he a bit older than the rest of us, due to his having been in the Army for five years, he's beautiful in a masculine way.

That night, he wore a pair of swim trunks because he's been surfing and he's tanned and ripped.

He's gorgeous.

The three of us are sitting there, practically drooling over him, and he asks *me* to dance.

I glance over to the small space beside the DJ's table and sound system.

"There's no one dancing."

He holds out his hand, smiling. "Then we'll be the first."

"I don't dance very well," I say, making a face.

"Neither do I. We'll be a pair."

"Are you sure?" I hesitate, chewing on my bottom lip. "It might be more of a comedy routine than a performance..."

"Come on, India. Live dangerously."

2

That did it. It was something my brother Steven used to say to me when I was too afraid to try out new things when we were growing up together.

*Come on India. Live dangerously...*

Jon couldn't know that's what my beloved brother used to say to me before he died during a deployment in Afghanistan, but it worked.

I took Jon's hand and he led me to the middle of the small dance area where the two of us moved our bodies in ways that would worry a chiropractor and make Elaine Benes proud. He purposely danced like a robot and I couldn't stop laughing – partly from embarrassment and partly because he was hilarious.

And so uninhibited.

He was fun in addition to being swoonworthy with that sun-bleached dark blond hair and pale blue eyes. Square jaw, scruff and *built*. Six foot three or four, his biceps bulging and tatted.

I almost succumbed to his charms after several shots of tequila, bites of lime, and licks of salt. At the last minute, I came to my senses when he slipped his hand under my sweater and ran his fingers up my back during a blistering kiss in the dark behind the beach shack.

God... He was gorgeous. But he was dangerous. I could see that the first time I laid eyes on him.

I wasn't offended that he hit on me that first night. He tries to pick up every attractive woman who catches his eye. Marina calls him a manwhore. I call him a bonobo.

He prefers to think of himself as a woman's man.

*I can't help it if I love women.*

So, I knew the moment I saw him, he was not only out of my league, he was dangerous. With that easy smile, drop dead looks, and smoking hot body, it would be hard not to fall for him but he wasn't the type to see someone on a steady basis.

No. A quick hookup, great sex and then on to the next flower.

Not my thing. I'm all about meaningful and long-term so we were wrong for each other right from the start.

Still, he was a hard man to resist but I resisted him and that made all the difference.

HE STILL IS hard to resist.

Five years later, we're business partners. I'll be giving a talk at the Tech Crunch Disrupt San Francisco on the business we started with several other friends from Stanford.

Jon is CEO of Pacifica Technologies Inc. I'm CTO.

We're a spunky little startup that's challenging Lockheed Martin's dominance of the aerospace industry.

With my degree in Engineering, and our dual MBAs from Stanford, Jon and I, along with three other friends, built Pacifica from the ground up. Now, we've moved past the initial attraction to being great friends and business partners.

There's too much at stake to risk it on a night of sex, no matter how great it might be.

Still, there are moments when I look at Jon and wish we could get together. We're great as a pair, fantastic as leaders of our team. We have honest-to-goodness fun working together. I never get bored with him and always look forward to going to the office because Jon will be there, in the background of my day, making me laugh or challenging me to solve some problem.

Sometimes when I'm feeling lonely, I imagine what it would be like to be his lover, but most of the time, thoughts of Jon as a sex partner are forbidden. I do not permit myself to go there -- at least, not often.

We have a beautiful relationship. It's the envy of all our friends.

I won't let anything ruin it – especially not something as commonplace as sex.

But it's hard to watch him leave the clubs or parties with women he picks for a quick and dirty hookup.

Sometimes, I wake up in the middle of the night in the throes of an orgasm and it's always Jon who's involved, pumping away, or with his face between my thighs...

I really *really* need a man...

Marina, my best friend from grade school, is working on that for me.

She's a crackerjack coder, expert with algorithms and statistics and is working on a dating app that she plans on releasing this month, if the beta goes well.

Maybe, just maybe, she can find me a man.

It's been over a year since I split with my ex-boyfriend Blaine, who asked me to come with him to Manhattan and help him with his own startup.

When I asked him what I'd be coming as – a girlfriend or a business partner – he said the wrong thing.

*"Whatever."*

Not exactly the resounding endorsement of the depth of his feelings for me.

I couldn't just pull out of Pacifica and move to Manhattan as a whatever... So, I cried my eyes out and said goodbye to him.

One day, when Pacifica is big enough and my shares are worth enough, I'll cash them in and move to Manhattan on my own. I have ambition. I'm not hoping that Blaine and I will reunite or anything, but the future is not carved in stone and you can never know what lies ahead.

TODAY, Jon and I are at the TechCrunch Disrupt convention together waiting for our session.

"Ready?" Jon asks, standing up from his chair in the room outside the venue and slipping his laptop into a briefcase.

"As ready as I'll ever be." I grab my own bag and follow him to the main conference room, getting high-fives from some of the techies who are standing outside the door looking in.

We stand at the back of the room and catch the last few moments of the session before ours. Being claustrophobic, I need to see a clear exit or I get the heebie jeebies. But with Jon by my side, who was a paratrooper when over in Afghanistan, I'm brave.

He puts a hand behind my back and propels me forward, up to the front of the auditorium so I can climb the stairs to the stage to give our presentation.

It's wonderful what we have together. We won't let anything as crass as sex get in the way of our beautiful relationship.

Now, if only I didn't want him so badly, I might be able to get through this next hour and the coming presentation without imagining us together one more time...

Marina has got to come through with a match for me.

I need a man – badly.

# CHAPTER TWO

## JON

We fist bump before she walks up the stairs and onto the stage and she gives me that smile – the smile that says, *"I got this, Jon. Watch me blow their minds."*

That's my girl – India Louise Ward. Girl wonder at twenty-five years old. BS (Engineering) Stanford. MBA Stanford. My CTO – Chief Technology Officer. She's also my communications lead for the company. She's our public face, because why not put your best face forward and India is definitely Pacifica's best face.

She's beautiful.

We're at the TechCrunch Disrupt conference and India is the speaker, talking about our experiences as a startup and how we went from my parent's garage in Pacifica, CA to a hundred-million dollar tech business in Palo Alto. I'd be up there instead of India but I love seeing the audience when they realize that besides being smoking hot, she's smart.

*Really* smart.

You can see it in her eyes. They're hazel with flecks of green

7

and violet behind thick lashes. There's just so much going on behind them, besides being pretty.

Not that I'm obsessed with her eyes, mind you. But I'm a man. I notice those things.

Back to India – you have to be whip-smart to be successful in this business and she's practically a rocket scientist. She's one of the few women in a position of power in the aerospace industry.

Pride fills me as I watch her step up to the podium. There's polite applause, and the faces I can see in the crowd are all interested. They've heard about the girl wonder with the flaky name at Pacifica Technology, Inc. Now they can see her in person, and she's an eyeful.

*India.*

I mean, who names their daughter India?

Hippies, that's who. Her parents are old hippies, professors at Stanford, which explains India's brains. Her mom waited until she was forty to have children. Her father plays bongo drums, for fuck's sake. Her mother has all these crystals lying around their house and is into yoga and eastern religions and took India to Machu Picchu when she was eight. You'd think that being exposed to all that airy-fairy stuff would warp a young mind.

Not India's. She's a straight arrow. Workaholic. Capitalist straight down the line.

Her parents must be so torn. They're typical flaky humanities professors. As a result, India didn't go to regular schools. No, she went to Montessori. She went into Stanford's Education Program for Gifted Youth and was doing a fucking engineering degree when she was six-fucking-teen. India's beautiful and she's probably one of the smartest people in the room.

Today, she's wearing a knee-length navy skirt and a white silk blouse. Over top is a blazer that hides curves like you wouldn't believe. Her dark auburn hair is pulled back into a bun and she's wearing black-rimmed reading glasses and not much makeup.

It's her disguise, as she calls it. She puts forward a totally professional demeanor but underneath, she's as crazy and geeky as the rest of us.

Here's the other secret she's trying to hide: She's five-foot-five-inches of babelicious woman. You should see her in a bikini.

Scalding hot. I mean, burn your retinas hot. Curves that would make a man kill to grab onto them and pump hard.

I know that each and every one of the straight men in the audience want to bang her despite the disguise.

They all want her. Every straight guy I meet wants her.

Unlike them, I don't want her. I mean, sure, I *could* if the opportunity arose because she's sex on legs and beautiful, but it never does. On purpose.

I need her to do her job.

We need each other to be totally professional.

We're practically best friends and have known each other since our freshman year at Stanford.

I was an Army Ranger just returned from Afghanistan and was on the GI Bill, attending college to study business. Six-foot-three of hard-muscled killer. She was this pretty little brainy girl with a big laugh doing her engineering degree, and she stole my heart – in a brotherly-sisterly way – and put me in my place when I got too wild.

We took the same intro English class and the friendship began over coffee, and then beer in the student pub. We did our MBAs the same year. Now we're business partners.

I rely on her to run the technology department of Pacifica so I can focus on the financial side of things.

We're business partners and more importantly, we're friends.

People joke and tell us we should just give up the pretense and hook up, but no.

We don't go there.

I know what people think – they think I'm in love with India.

9

I'm not.

We're best friends. People say a man can't be best friends with a woman, and especially not a beautiful woman like India, but we are the exception that proves the rule.

She's not into relationships either. She looks up to me like the big brother she lost in the war. What we have is unique, and I'm determined to not let anything get in the way of our beautiful friendship, or Pacifica's success.

I listen with half an ear as she wows them with our latest roll-out, knowing her presentation on our latest satellite like the back of her hand. This one's destined for the military and will help soldiers on the modern battlefield. The contracts we're busy negotiating are huge. *Huge.*

Looking out over the audience, I can see the moment she finally wins them over and they're actually listening, their tongues rolled back up into their mouths. Behind her on the huge screen is her presentation, showcasing our technology.

I'm happier than ever. Stoked about the future. Going into business with India was my best idea ever, but if I'm honest with myself, there's this tiny smidgen of doubt in my mind about her. Lately, she's been distant – too busy for our usual chats, coffee breaks, and the occasional dinner out.

She seems preoccupied. I heard her talking about Manhattan and how she wants to move to the East Coast one day. Maybe open up another office there.

Manhattan is where her ex lives.

The jerk who broke her heart.

I thought she was over him, but I've heard a few of her girl-friends talk about how she hasn't had a date since they split over a year ago. I was glad to see the back end of him. He wasn't good for her. I knew that from the time they met until he left her, breaking her heart in the process.

The music flares at the end of India's presentation, startling me back to the present, and there's a huge round of applause for her. She smiles and bows to the audience, then leaves the stage, her face lit up, her cheeks flushed.

She's *amazing*.

We fist bump again. "You rocked it, girl," I say, a huge smile on my face as she steps behind the curtain, grabbing the bottle of water I have ready for her.

"I think I did," she says and opens the lid, drinking down half the bottle. "They seemed to like it."

"Listen to them," I respond. I take her by the shoulders and turn her around so she can see the audience through a crack in the curtain. I bend down so that my face is beside hers. "They loved you."

The audience is still clapping, because the presentation was a combination of technology and patriotism. It was stirring, talking about mission and performance and making the world a better place and *rah rah USA*.

When the applause dies down, I let go of her arms. "You deserve a cold beer."

"I deserve a fucking *keg* of beer," she replies, grinning up at me, a twinkle in her eyes.

That's my girl. Huge brain. Potty mouth.

I love her.

Not in that way, of course. In the brotherly, collegial, and proud CEO way.

"Let's go," she says and grabs hold of my arm, her fingers gripping my bicep. I flex it, because she's always kidding me about my workouts. I'm ripped. I work out daily – a habit I developed while in the service and I keep it up. No slacking off for me, even though I'm no longer in a combat zone.

"I'm starving," she says, gazing up at me with those eyes. "I want to stuff myself with a huge piece of steak to go along with that keg of beer."

"Your wish is my command, CTO of mine," I reply, but my mind substitutes *I want you to stuff me with that huge piece of meat of yours, Jon...*

I can't control that part of my mind.

Cut me some slack.

We walk out the side of the auditorium, my arm draped around her shoulder in a brotherly way. I'm no longer interested in the last speaker, so we leave the conference for a bar where we're meeting the rest of our team to talk about the conference and our latest contract. Then we'll go for dinner and I'll make sure she gets her big juicy steak.

Life is good.

*TWO HOURS LATER...*

LIFE SUCKS.

What the *hell?*

Marina Clark, India's best friend from Montessori, and from forever, is sitting with us and, as usual, she's frowning at me. She doesn't really like me. I don't know why, but she's always scowling at me like I've done something wrong. I check myself over. There's no food spilled on my crisp white shirt or silky blue tie. I run my fingers through my hair, which has a habit of falling into my eyes.

"What's your problem?"

She frowns. "You're working the poor girl to death."

"She's a big girl. She works herself hard. She's a winner."

Why Marina showed up at the bar, I'll never know. This celebration was meant for the team – not outsiders – even if she is India's best friend.

When India gets up to go to the bathroom, Marina leans closer to me.

"She's got a date tonight. Don't mess it up."

*What?*

"India has a date?"

I'm not the only one shocked by that announcement. The rest of my team members glance at me quickly, like they expect me to be mad. I frown when they lean forward, eager to hear the details. Marina fills us in on this guy she's matched India with.

As if India needs help finding men.

Besides, she doesn't want a man right now. She's focused on her career. I know, because she told me that when we met at Stanford, back when I thought there might be something between us. She wants to make a hundred million dollars before she ever gets serious about a man.

She's pure ambition – like me. Like the rest of us at Pacifica.

"She's lonely," Marina says plainly.

That hits me like a truck and I'm lost for words for a moment.

"How can she be lonely?" I say when I recover. I tip my beer up and take a long pull on it. "She's too busy to be lonely. She said so herself. She's focused on her career. India says men are superfluous. Those were her words, Marina, not mine. *Superfluous.*"

"You think she's going to admit to you that she's lonely?" Marina gives me this derisive snort and takes a sip of her own beer. "She comes home to an empty house and is so lonely that she sleeps on the couch with the television on because she hates being alone in her king-sized bed. True confession." Then she points at me, her eyes narrow. "Don't tell her I told you that. She'll kill me."

I frown and imagine India sleeping on her couch instead of her bed. I remember when she bought that bed – I helped her pick it out. I even imagined the two of us on it, but that's just an idle male thought. I'm as red-blooded as the next guy. But that was it. I imagined it one time, maybe twice. Less than a dozen times, for sure.

It's not like I think of sleeping with India often. I'm way too busy running one of the most successful tech start-ups in the past five years.

But speaking of her bed, it's hugely ostentatious with four thick posts of dark wood. Silk gray coverlet and throw pillows. In her huge master suite with the marble tile and expensive fixtures and the sliding doors that lead to her own personal deck overlooking the ocean.

She doesn't like sleeping in that bed?

I *love* that bed.

"She sleeps on the couch?" I say, still dumbfounded at the prospect that India's lonely and wants a date.

Marina nods. "Sad, right? So I've found this guy for her. I mean, he's right up her alley brains-wise. He teaches at Stanford, like her parents. He has a PhD from Harvard in Humanities. Philosophy."

"Philosophy?" I snort and make a face of disgust. "What the hell is that?"

"You know – 'what is the good life?' That kind of shit." She shrugs. "His name came up among my subscribers as a match. I figured he was smart enough for her. Plus, her family is big in the whole humanities thing. He's coming tonight." She glances at her watch. "Any time now, in fact. I'm sure India's nervous. She's probably in the bathroom throwing up." She wags her eyebrows in this most annoying way.

"Throwing up? What are you talking about? Why would India throw up because she's meeting a pencil-necked professor of philosophy?"

"He's not a pencil-neck. He's really handsome, in a professorial sort of way. She's shy, Jon," Marina says, and that's the second time tonight I'm struck dumb by something she says. "You should know that. God, what have you been doing all this time? Ignoring India? See, that's what I mean by 'you work her too hard.' You don't even know her."

"I know her better than almost anyone else."

I lean back, my blood pressure rising, my anger at Marina's meddling choking me for a moment. I sit steaming, unable to respond.

My India – shy? Nervous enough to meet some man that she'd throw up? I don't really even know her?

"This wasn't supposed to be a public event, Marina. This was meant to be a celebration for the team."

"India needs a man," she replies, shrugging like it's nothing. "I found her one."

"She doesn't *need* a man. She needs to focus on our business. On Pacifica. We have a big meeting coming up, at the Pentagon. I don't want her to be distracted by some flake from the Philosophy Department."

"No, *no*," she says and punches my arm. "She needs some, Jon. She's been out of circulation for way too long. You're always going on about how important sex is for human well-being. Isn't that right?"

I sit and glower at Marina for throwing my words back at me, but she doesn't seem to notice the hate I'm sending her way.

"Oh, here he comes," Marina says and sits up straighter. "Be nice."

*Be nice.* Like I'm not nice.

Into the bar walks this tall mother with dark hair and eyes, and a goatee. He's wearing a tweed blazer with actual leather patches on his elbows. And jeans. He must be forty if he's a day.

Old, in other words. There's actual gray in his hair at the sides.

"Him?" I say under my breath, giving Marina a glare. "He's an old man. Couldn't you find someone a bit closer to her age?"

"I did a really careful review of him, his values, his goals, his beliefs. They're a great match."

"I didn't know the app was ready..." I harrumph and lean back in my chair, taking a big drink from my bottle of beer. "I can tell just by looking at him he's not right for her."

"The soft launch is next month. We hard launch later, but I wanted to use India as a test subject. I've signed up about a thousand people to use as test matches. Most from Stanford and SFU. He ticks all her boxes."

I watch the dickhead professor of philosophy approach our table. I don't know who he is, but he's not the kind of man for India. That much I do know just by looking at him. How could he be? I can tell by the way he looks and dresses and walks that he's a stuffy old man. How could India be with someone like him?

"He's too old for her."

"Shush," Marina says and turns to the guy as he walks up to the table, all smiles. "Thomas! You made it. India's in the bathroom but should be right back."

"I did make it," Thomas says, his voice deep. "My flight from Boston was late but I managed to get an Uber driver who actually knows the fastest routes. I was giving a guest lecture at my old alma mater and we were late getting finished – I got swarmed by students wanting to talk after the lecture. I missed my flight but was able to get on the next plane out. Barely made it."

He gives us all a smile, his teeth white over his goatee.

I hate him.

Marina introduces him as *Doctor* Thomas McAllister. Professor of analytic philosophy at Stanford.

He's not a doctor. He's a professor. Doctors actually do important work in society, unlike professors of philosophy. I should know – my father was a doctor. I hate the way people call professors *Doctor* like they're something special.

"Pleased to meet you," I manage and shake the guy's hand,

squeezing extra firmly. "So, tell me, what does a professor of analytic philosophy do? I mean, when you're not giving lectures."

"We think about how to think. It's meta," he says, smiling like he's made a joke.

I don't know what the hell he means, thinking about how to think. What kind of lame job is that?

"Cool," I say, shrugging. "I already know how to think. Now I just make shit. Shit that helps the good old USA win wars."

I lean back in my chair, folding my arms, and smile at him.

Score one for the Viking.

# CHAPTER THREE

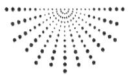

## INDIA

Marina insists that I meet the match she's found for me at the bar after the conference. She sprung it on me just an hour earlier. No warning.

Jon stepped out for a moment to talk to someone in the restaurant and so we're alone with the rest of the team.

"What's he look like?"

"Stop thinking about looks and think about compatibility," she scolds. "He's handsome. Tall, dark, goatee, well-dressed. I'd do him. Give him a chance. It's like he was made for you, based on both your answers."

The rest of the team are busy talking, so she scoots closer and shows me the pic on her cell.

Thomas McAllister, with a PhD in philosophy from Harvard. He's apparently right up my alley. He loves classical while my playlist features hits from the 70's. He cooks as a hobby

19

while I hate cooking. My kitchen cupboards are empty because I always eat takeout. While our music tastes clash, at least music is important to him.

I'm not so sure about the perfectly matched thing...

"You need someone stable. Someone who is strong, calm, and knows his own mind. And who shares your interests. He scores high on all those areas. You're a perfect match."

"I don't cook," I respond.

"You eat."

Marina matched me with him after I answered her questionnaire earlier this year. I'm one of her guinea pigs for the app she's working on with her friend Clint from Stanford. He's doing the coding and she does all the human stuff. It's called MATCHED and is in its soft release period, where they test it out to make sure it's ready to go before they do a full release with promotion.

I'm one of the first users and Professor McAllister is my first match.

In that moment, I wonder what Jon will think. He'll be merciless when he realizes Marina invited an outsider and that I have a date for the evening. Technically, I shouldn't have even invited Marina, but she's my best female friend.

Jon won't approve. I know that already. He thinks the business must come first, and it has. Believe me, I've devoted myself to the business for the past three years non-stop.

He's all business and no pleasure.

I need to unwind. I want someone to pamper me, to look after me.

Frankly, I want someone in my bed. I want to feel a man on top of me, and inside of me. I've woken up too many times in the middle of a wet dream with nameless faceless men.

"I need a drink."

"You need a hard dick," Marina says under her breath. "That's it. Plain and simple."

"Such a way with words," I reply. "Such deep analysis you have there, counselor. You did how many years of school to come up with that?"

"I speak the truth and you know it."

"I can't meet him now," I argue, panic rising in me that Jon will get pissed.

"If not now, when?"

I chew a fingernail and consider. "You really think he's a match?"

She nods, folding her arms. "I've got the questionnaire honed and perfected. It shows that he's definitely a match for you. You have the same interests, similar backgrounds. You have the same level of education and goals for the future."

"Jon won't like it if he shows up at the bar."

"Jon can go fuck himself. You watch. He'll be picking up some ditzy blonde before the night's over and won't think about you and what you're doing."

"He'll eviscerate Thomas."

"He'll try, but he does that to everyone. He's such a hardass."

Speaking of hardasses, Jon returns from the restaurant and sits down, taking his beer in his hand and saluting me with it. I smile back but then I get this feeling like I'm going to regret agreeing to meet Marina's match.

"Where were you?" I say, trying to make conversation to hide my nerves.

"Talking with a former colleague of my dad's," Jon says and he smiles softly. "He only heard recently and offered his condolences."

"That's nice," I say, my mind temporarily sidetracked from worries about my date by thoughts of Jon's father. He died very rapidly and very painfully from pancreatic cancer. Through it all, Jon was a rock, there for his dad every moment he could spare.

I went to see him before he died, and was shocked to see how

21

warm and affectionate Jon was with his dad. He held his father's hand and kissed him, talking softly to him as he lay in pain, waiting for the drugs to kick in and send him into a morphine-haze.

When he finally died, I saw Jon cry for the first time and it was hard to take. Jon is always such a joker, fun-loving and quick with a smile or laugh. We embraced that day when he returned from saying goodbye and I worried that it would turn into more, but at the last minute we thought better of it and broke the embrace.

I sigh and catch Marina's eye. She raises her eyebrows and points to her watch, a signal that my date will be arriving soon.

That sends my heart-rate racing and suddenly, I feel like I'm going to hyperventilate.

"Excuse me," I say and pick up my bag. "I'll be right back."

I practically run to the bathroom and close myself in a stall, trying not to panic. I take in a few deep breaths and recite my mantra.

Oh, *God*. What will Jon say? He'll be relentless.

I swear I spend more time with Jon than anyone else. Don't get me wrong – I love the guy. He's like my alter-ego. He's brave and fearless and a crazy man, while I'm shy and reserved and cautious. I need his fearlessness to accomplish anything, but this blistering pace at work is just wearing me down. I can barely remember the last time I was kissed – really kissed. Or the last time a man touched me intimately.

Actually, I can remember. It was Blaine, my ex, who left for Manhattan a year ago. I miss having a relationship. Sure, my last one ended badly with a broken heart on my part, but it was some-thing, at least.

I was in love with Blaine and I thought he was in love with me. We had a lot of sex. We laughed and watched movies together. It was real – or so I thought. But Blaine left for New

York and never looked back. I swore to myself when I watched him board that plane for the last time that, one day, it would be me leaving the past behind me and living the life I wanted.

So, I've put my head down and tried to focus on something besides the ache in the middle of my chest. And I've worked hard – harder than anyone else. Anyone besides Jon, that is. But I'm lonely.

I want someone deep and real. It might take me a couple more years to have the seed money I need to start my own company but I don't think I can face another two years without someone in my life.

That was why I did Marina's crazy questionnaire. That's why I agreed to go on a date with Thomas, but I had no idea it would be tonight.

After about five minutes, my pulse calms down. Then, my cell dings. I take it out and see it's Marina.

MARINA: *He's here. Get your ass out of the bathroom.*

INDIA: *Jon's gonna freak.*

MARINA: *Forget Jon. Get out here now!*

INDIA: *Oh, crap...*

MARINA: *Just come out. Thomas won't bite. He's really very erudite and cultured.*

INDIA: *It's not Thomas I'm worried about. It's Jon.*

MARINA: *Fuck Jon. No, I take that back. Fuck Thomas.*

INDIA: *Oh, crap...*

I put my cell back in my bag and leave the stall, washing my hands while I check myself out in the mirror. I pull my hair out of the tight bun and let it fall over my shoulders and down my back. I put my glasses away in my bag and run some gloss over my lips. I can't see very well without my glasses, but I can't wear contacts, so I'll have to squint.

I saw his picture. He's definitely handsome, in a rugged way.

I pull off my jacket and unbutton one of my buttons, showing a tiny bit more cleavage. Gotta use every weapon in the old feminine arsenal.

I paste a smile on my face and walk out of the bathroom and back into the bar.

Then I see the two of them sitting side by side – Jon with his arms crossed, his biceps bulging, his legs spread wide. His head is down and he's glaring at me. His handsome face – all square-jawed and scruff and perfect – is angry. His sun-bleached dark blond hair falls in his eyes in that sexy way, and his blue eyes are narrowed. I'd like to imagine that's jealousy in his eyes, but then I realize that it's really just contempt. His full lips are pressed tightly together.

He's pissed.

I feel his gaze move over my body, from my head to my feet and back again. He must have noticed that I've fiddled with my hair and unbuttoned my blouse.

I take a deep breath and walk up, trying to prepare myself for the onslaught.

"Thomas?" I say and extend my hand. "Marina's told me all about you."

For his part, Thomas stands up straight and takes my hand, kissing my knuckles gallantly. Beside him, Jon snorts and glances away, a muscle in his jaw pulsing. God, he's going to be a real problem.

What the hell was Marina thinking, bringing Thomas to this party? Of all times to have me meet a potential date. Jon thinks I'm some kind of machine, working sixteen-hour days and doing nothing but spending time with the team. He really doesn't think I'm a human – or a woman.

I'm just his damn CTO. That's all I am to him. A workhorse.

Well, I need some romance in my life. It isn't going to find me, so I have to find it. I realized that after Marina pointed out how much I work. How little time I get away from the team and Jon.

I intend to stop that at least a little tonight.

Thomas pulls out my chair and I sit down, smiling at him, pleased to be pampered just a bit. We talk for a while, and I feel everyone's eyes on us – especially Jon's eyes. I'm nervous and slightly self-conscious. Hell, completely self-conscious. People are smiling at us, their grins knowing. Pete, our software engineer, punches Jon in the arm playfully, eliciting a sneer from him. Jon's on his third beer and I can see a little bit of his wildness come out.

While I'm listening to Thomas talk about his course load with half an ear, I'm watching Jon, imagining him living in Norway back in Viking times. He's built, and he works out. He's gorgeous, if you like blond Viking gods. When we first met in freshman year, people joked about his background and called him Ragnar – *"Where's your boat, Ragnar?"*

Back then, he was totally ripped, his hair buzzed short. Former Army Ranger. Now, he looks like he belongs on the set of *Vikings*, all rippling muscles and longish hair bleached by the sun. Scruffy chin and jaw. Dark blue tribal tats on his body.

If looks could kill, Thomas would be dead.

I try to ignore Jon and focus on Thomas. He's nice, if a bit taken with himself, regaling us about his lecture at Harvard, how he was delayed because of the enthusiastic crowd of students mobbing him afterward. He tells us about his latest non-fiction book, *Philosophy and Star Wars,* that's being published this year and how he's going to do a book tour to promote it.

Yeah, he's handsome in a man-next-door sort of way, with dark eyes and hair, a touch of grey at his sideburns. A brilliant smile. Neatly trimmed goatee. He just doesn't do it for me.

There's no throbbing in my lady parts at the thought of being in bed with him.

Not the way they throb when I think of Jon but there's no

way I'd want anything to happen between us. I'd just be one more notch on Jon's belt and I deserve more.

Jon's a wild man, with enough looks and ambition to have whatever woman he wants for whatever he wants. Which is mostly just a hookup and nothing more.

That's not good enough for me. Jon doesn't do deep, unless it's Pacifica. His idea of meaningful is seeing that bottom line improve.

If he wasn't so damn sexy...

It's hell working for him, seeing him all day, every day walking around the office in his casually sexy way, muscle shirt and Bermuda shorts, flip-flops on his feet, his body tanned, his hair all messed from surfing in the early morning. It's hell, after a long day in the office, watching him pick up woman after woman at the bar for a quick meaningless fuck later that night.

Once we nail this new set of defense contracts, I'm out. I'll resign from Pacifica and I'm heading to Manhattan. It's been a dream of mine since I was a girl. After all these years of hard work, I'm ready to live my dreams. Start fresh.

Blaine said he'd be there if and when I decided to follow him to Manhattan, but he couldn't commit to being exclusive. And I couldn't give up what I had in San Francisco unless I knew that we'd be a couple.

So, for the past year, I've been licking my wounds and trying to recover. I'll be sad to say goodbye to Jon and the team at Pacifica, but I need to think about my future for a change, and not just the company.

There's more to life than your bank account balance.

Life has to have some kind of meaning beyond survival or success – else why be alive in the first place? That's something my parents have hammered into my head since I was a child. *Make your life meaningful.*

I watch Jon's face while I sip my drink. He's listening to

Thomas talk about his current course, teaching philosophy to first-year students. Jon's chewing on some nuts out of the bowl in the middle of the table. He keeps dropping them like he's not really paying attention, and I can tell he's bored by what Thomas is saying and pissed that Thomas is taking up all the oxygen in the room.

He meets my eyes across the table and his widen meaningfully, like he's sending me a telepathic message. *Is this guy for real? Is this really your date? WTF, India? He'll bore you to death.*

I realize that's me thinking it, of course.

Marina is so wrong about this guy. He's so not my type, it's almost laughable.

Sadly, Jon *is* my type, or at least my lady parts tell me he is even if my mind says stay away.

Marina seems to think Thomas is the man for me. If so, I don't see it. And, what's far more important, I don't feel it.

I promised her I'd give it a shot. She wants to test out their app and I agreed to be a guinea pig. Thomas is her first real test.

I think MATCHED is a flop, personally, but I'm willing to give him, and it, the benefit of the doubt.

Thomas finally looks my way after spending the last fifteen minutes telling everyone else all about his flight and his lecture and the person who was seated beside him and his terrible in-flight meal.

He smiles. "I have reservations for *Callandre* at eight. Shall we?"

Callandre is a top restaurant in San Francisco. It's all the buzz, so I'm pleased that at least I'll get some good food out of this whole venture.

He stands and holds out his hand, so I stand up and take it. Across the table, Jon frowns at us.

"Have a nice time," he says acidly. "Don't be too late. We have a defense contract to finish tomorrow morning."

27

"I'm aware of my responsibilities," I reply, miffed that he feels the need to remind me about something that I set up.

Thomas and I leave the bar. He escorts me to his car, which is nice – a sleek Mercedes – and we drive to Callandre, him talking the entire time about himself and his life and his car and his career. I barely get a word in edgewise during the drive, and try not to feel upset by how he monopolizes the conversation. Instead, I go all out, asking him about everything, and he seems just as happy to talk on about himself.

We arrive at Callandre, and I'm impressed as we walk through the doors. I've read about it in the dining section of the paper, but I'd never gone. It's all waterfalls and classy grey Zen décor, and we get a great booth in one corner of the dining room, next to the large bay window. Thomas seems to know the wait staff and they fawn over him like he's some big shot, but he's really just a professor.

He lets me sit first and then sits close beside me, smiling like he's the king of the world. He drapes his napkin on his lap and turns to me.

"You like it? Pretty impressive, isn't it?"

I glance around the restaurant and smile. "It is nice. I hear the food is really good. Do you come here often?"

"Weekly," Thomas says and then tells me all about how he knows the chef and how he's good buddies with some of the backers of the restaurant. I smile and listen, resting my chin on my hand while he tells me everything and anything about the whole business.

Not once has he asked me about myself.

Our food is great, and comes on delightfully presented plates. I eat with relish and listen while Thomas talks about the politics of his department at Stanford and how he's always the one who has to problem-solve when it comes to matters before the committee.

An hour goes by, and I keep him busy asking questions about his past, his education, his classes, his house on the cliffs overlooking the bay, his car, his family.

Finally, precisely eighty-six minutes after we arrive, our meal is over and we're drinking coffee and he turns to me after a pause in the conversation.

"So, enough about me. Tell me something about India. How did you get that name?"

I laugh, amazed that he's talked about himself for so long.

"There's not much to tell. My mother took a trip to India after she finished her first degree and fell in love with Kashmir. When she got pregnant after my brother was born, she liked the name India. They're hippies, to tell you the truth."

Thomas smiles and then launches into a fifteen-minute discussion of Eastern philosophy and how he's taught a class in London about how England's colonial history in India affected British culture.

So, in total, I get in three sentences about myself before he goes back to talking about himself.

Three frickin' sentences.

So much for Marina's questionnaire.

"Well, I guess it's time to go," I say and smile at Thomas after checking my watch. "I have to go back to the office and pick up some files, then it's working late at home for me."

"Oh, ending the date so early?" Thomas says, frowning. He checks his watch, which I notice is a Rolex. "I thought we could have a drink at my place."

"Not tonight, I'm afraid. I have a big presentation to prepare. Duty calls."

I give him a smile, fully intending to never see him again. I don't think there's anything else he can possibly tell me about himself. He's emptied it all out there.

"Well, if that's the case, I can drive you to your office. Maybe I

29

could come back to your place after and we can have a drink there."

I shake my head. "No more alcohol for me. I'll be up late working."

I stand and he follows me out of the booth. It's clear he figured he'd be coming back to my place, or me going to his, after this fancy meal, but that's his mistake. I can barely wait to leave his company, frankly; he's so self-centered, he has no clue that I'm so bored, I'd rather talk to my Uber driver than spend another moment with him.

But I don't. If he wants to drive me back to the office, I'll be happy to get rid of him there.

We leave the restaurant – after he pays the waiter and points out how big his tip is – and then we walk down the street to his car. I get in and he's strangely silent now, like he's busy thinking of what he can do next because of his disappointment that I'm not going back to his place for something extra.

I give him the address to Pacifica's office and sigh with relief when we drive up and he drops me off.

"Thanks so much for dinner," I say before I get out of the car. "It was delicious."

I get out and wave at him, glad that I'm finally free. He rolls down the passenger window and leans over.

"I'll call you," he says, his voice hopeful. "Maybe we can get together again some night when you're not working late."

"That may be a while, I'm afraid," I reply and turn back to the car. "We have this big defense contract coming up and I'm swamped." I shrug and smile, then give him an *I'll call you* hand signal.

Yeah, it was a *don't call me, I'll call you* kind of date.

Then I turn and practically run up the stairs and into the building where Pacifica has its executive offices.

Thank God I'm free.

I take the stairs to the third floor instead of the elevator, and go to the office door, surprised that it's still open and the lights are on. Someone must be working late. When I go inside, I find none other than Jon working in his office behind his huge mahogany desk. He glances up and sees me, and sits up straighter, closing his laptop.

"You're back from your date?" he says, his voice sounding surprised.

I go inside and throw my bag on his desk and plop down on the chair across from him.

"Oh my *God*, that man can talk about himself," I say with a huge sigh. "I thought I'd never escape."

Jon looks smug. "I could have told you he's not for you. I could tell that the moment I saw him. He's an old man, for God's sake. He must be forty if he's a day."

I shrug. "I have no idea how old he is. That's one thing he neglected to tell me, although he told me practically everything else about himself – his job, his family, his house on the cliff overlooking the bay, his credentials. I feel like his therapist or something."

"He sounds like a real blowhard."

I shrug. "He's just full of himself. I know a lot of men like that," I quip, shooting him a look.

"Not me," Jon says, sitting up straighter. "I'm all about other people. In fact, I've been told I don't reveal enough about myself and am a closed book. I think those were the exact words you used when you reprimanded me."

"My words exactly," I say with a laugh, because that's true. Jon is a total extrovert and can talk to anyone about anything. You truly feel his interest in you when you meet him the first time. Not only does he have this mind like a steel trap, remembering every face he's seen and hand he's shaken along with their name, he usually researches people he's going to meet and

31

knows some personal tidbit about them so he can show his interest.

I feel like I know everything about Thomas, but I feel like Jon knows everything about me. And everyone else in his orbit.

But none of us know anything really deep about him.

"I knew he was a jerk when I laid eyes on him," Jon says dismissively. "So much for Marina's dating app. I'd say MATCHED was a big failure when it came to matching you with someone."

"Don't tell Marina that. You'll break her heart. I promised to help her develop it and so did you." I pull out my cell to check for messages from Marina.

*MARINA: How did it go? Fill me in on the deets. I'm curious how my match worked.*

I text her back, not eager to rub her nose in her failure, but convinced that she needs to fix it. She'd been so sure that the questionnaire was honed to perfection. I'll have to set her straight.

*INDIA: Not good. He talked about himself the entire time. I didn't get a word in edgewise.*

*MARINA: What?*

*INDIA: I swear he asked me about myself once and I said three sentences. That was it.*

"Who are you texting? Marina to let her know how much of a failure her app is?"

I glance up at Jon, who's leaning back, a huge grin on his face like he's won some battle.

"Yes," I reply. "I'm telling her she needs to work on the ques-tionnaire."

"That's an understatement."

I frown at him. "Hey, she's my BFF. Be nice. So, the question-naire needs work. Usually, she's a genius at matching people up. There was Grant and Mona. They were like two peas in a pod.

And then Elaine and Chris. Even you have to admit those were perfect matches."

Jon shrugs, not ever wanting to admit defeat. Marina's skills at matching people are legendary. That's why we all backed her efforts to start the app. I even gave her some seed money, I had such faith in her and her coder.

INDIA: *Maybe you better do some more work on the questionnaire. It sure matched me up with the totally wrong guy. I mean you couldn't have matched me with a worse date than Thomas.*

MARINA: *That's so strange. I usually have such a great instinct for people who belong together. Oh, well. I'll run your questionnaire again and find someone else. I'm having a party next weekend at the cottage so maybe you can come and meet who I match you with.*

INDIA: *I don't know...*

MARINA: *You know you want to. Trust me about this. I know what I'm doing.*

INDIA: *Thomas isn't very good proof of that.*

MARINA: *One mistake. Let me try again.*

INDIA: *Okay. Talk later. Jon's here and no doubt he'll work me until the wee hours.*

MARINA: *He's a slave driver.*

INDIA: *Don't I know it... Later.*

MARINA: *Later.*

I put my cell away and glance up to see Jon staring at me, his eyes curious.

"What did Marina say? Is she crushed that her app failed to find you the man of your dreams?"

"She's hosting a party at the cottage on Saturday and wants me to come and meet another match she has for me," I say and raise my eyebrows, exhaling dramatically. "We'll see how well it does this time."

"Why do you bother? MATCHED obviously failed. I could have told you that before you even saw him."

"She's usually so good at this. I trust her instincts."

He sits forward and opens a file on his desk. That's the signal he's going to start working and I should as well.

I stand and pick up my bag. "I've got work to do before tomorrow. How late are you staying?"

He glances up, his mind already elsewhere. I can tell by the way his brow is furrowed. "Until it's done."

"Of course." I leave his office and go to my own, plopping down behind my own much less ostentatious desk. I look out at the dark sky, the lights of the city down below us twinkling. I wish I had met someone good, someone I felt interested in. I would have preferred being truly torn about telling the guy I had to go and work instead of being glad to escape my date.

For the next two hours, until almost midnight, I work on the presentation, checking facts, getting the flow of the slideshow just right, all the animations working properly and all the main points of our business highlighted. I run it through one last time and am pleased, sure that it's polished and ready to go.

Jon pokes his head into my office, his bleached-blond hair falling in his eyes in that sexy way, his scruff framing his square jaw.

"How's the presentation?"

"Good," I reply, then correct myself. "Great. I think it's ready to go."

"We can run through it in the morning." He checks his watch. "It's almost midnight and I'm exhausted. I'm going now. Do you need a ride?"

"Sounds great." I gather up my things, my cell and my notebook, stuffing them in my bag.

We leave the office together and he arms the alarm and locks the door, walking beside me down the stairs to the main floor exit.

Out on the street, a few cars down, is his SUV. He walks close beside me and we talk about my failure of a date.

"He talked the entire time about himself?"

"Yeah, I think I said three sentences other than 'Oh, really? Is that so? Amazing!' He was totally clueless."

"What a blind jerk," Jon says and laughs, and we bump together as we walk to the vehicle. "He doesn't have the first clue about how to get a girl to like him. He should have been asking you a million questions and showing you how interesting you are instead of the other way around."

"Is that what you do?" I say, smiling at him when he opens my door for me. "Is that how you get all your many women?"

He grins and it's boyish and sexy at the same time. "It is. I read *How To Win Friends and Influence People* ages ago and I live by it. I always put it into effect when I meet new people, whether they're business contacts or potential fuck buddies."

I laugh and can't help but wonder what he's like in bed, but at the same time, it would be the very worst thing I could ever do. It would ruin our wonderful business relationship and threaten my future.

I'm smart enough to know that once you sleep with your business partner, it's all over except the crying.

# CHAPTER FOUR

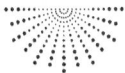

Jon

I DRIVE INDIA HOME, and on the drive, I ask her more about her date with Thomas. I wanted to find out why she's bothering with this whole dating business. I pull up to her house and hop out to open her door before she can gather her bag and do it herself.

We walk to her front door, laughing about something Thomas said, and she turns to me before unlocking the door.

"He actually said he's been told he was a great conversationalist." She rolls her eyes. "Can you believe it? He's one of the worst I've ever met. And I've met a few."

"He's an idiot," I say and lean my arm against the wall beside the door. "Be glad you know that now. No harm, no foul. But Marina better get her questionnaire fixed if she wants to be a success. She needs real results."

"She will," India says with a sigh. "Thanks for the ride."

She's smiling at me, her eyes soft, and without thinking I lean in and kiss her – like kissing her goodnight is the most natural

37

thing in the world. She stands as still as a statue, and when I pull back, her expression is one of shock.

"What was that for?" she asks in a tiny voice.

"You deserved at least a kiss goodnight after your bad date," I say, my voice husky for some reason. "I took pity on you, I guess."

An expression of pain passes over her face. "I don't need your pity, Jon."

Oops.

She turns and enters her code on the keypad to open her door, and I can see right away that I've pissed her off.

"I didn't mean that," I say quickly, hoping to recover. I stand up straighter, my brain working furiously to find a way to salvage things between us. "I meant, I felt affection for you after what you'd been through and it just came naturally. Not pity. Sympathy."

"Yeah, right," she replies and opens her door. Even in the low light of her front porch, I can see the blush rise on her cheeks. "I don't need your pity or your sympathy."

She's embarrassed that I felt sorry for her.

Crap. What a dope.

"Seriously," I say, trying to make things right between us. "I don't pity you, India. You know that. I wanted to be your partner because I admire you. I don't feel sympathy for you. I felt your pain. I've been on bad dates before. Believe me."

"Keep saying it and maybe you'll convince yourself," she says and closes the door in my face.

Damn.

Not a good end to the night. Here I was, trying to make her feel better by kissing her affectionately and I ended up hurting her feelings and embarrassing her.

To top it off, she's mad at me. We need to be simpatico on things. We need to be on the same page and cool with each other.

This was not good for our working relationship.

I exhale in frustration, leaving the front porch and returning to my car. Before I drive off, I text her.

JON: *I don't pity you. I pity the poor sonofabitch who's such a boring idiot that he didn't know what a gem he had on a date and blew it. I care about you, India. I want to see you happy. That's all. Don't take it the wrong way.*

Then I drive off, making my way down the curving highway and back to my own loft apartment in an old converted warehouse near the waterfront. I park the SUV in my spot and climb the stairs at the back of the warehouse loading dock, then take the stairs to the top floor where I live. I have the entire floor to myself and did all the work. It's a great space with huge windows on every wall and an open concept, all brick and exposed ductwork and hardwood floors. I love the open feel of the place and how it affords me a view of the San Francisco bay.

I strip my clothes off and have a quick shower, thinking while I scrub myself clean that I hope India gets over her hurt feelings.

Usually I'm good with words, and can finesse my relationships with people. I tend to get a bit defensive with India because she's so important to my life and my business and future. I want to protect her from hurt and from harm, so when I saw how disappointed she was with her bad date, I wanted to comfort her, but blew it.

The kiss – a mistake.

She doesn't want a pity kiss from me. She wants a business partner and friend.

That's what we've always been, and that's what I'm determined to ensure we stay.

I can't deny that I felt real affection for her when I kissed her, though, and for just a minute, my mind goes there – me on a real date with India, taking her home after, fucking her into mindlessness. So, there I am, standing in the shower, my hands soapy and

39

my mind on India, and I start to stroke my rapidly hardening dick.

Before I know it, I'm beating off to thoughts of India. I can't help where my mind goes when I'm in that moment of lust. Images of India in her tiny bikini when we go surfing together come to my mind unbidden. I can't help but think how delicious her curves are. She has great tits and a nice shapely ass. The kind a man wants to grab hold of and pump hard while he fucks her.

Yeah, I go there.

I shouldn't and I know it, but I'm just as red-blooded as the next guy, and India is a hot beautiful woman with curves that would drive any man wild with lust.

I stroke until my eyes roll back into my head, imagining her coming around my cock. That sends me over, my orgasm starting, pleasure spiking through me as I come. I groan, leaning one hand against the wall as the pleasure peaks and my cock pulses in my hand.

Finally spent, I wash off, and leave, wishing I had someone real with me at that moment instead of visions of India. I imagine what we'd do if she was my lover in addition to my partner. We'd probably dry each other off and go to the kitchen to get something to drink before hitting the sack together, falling asleep in minutes because we were both spent.

I kick myself mentally. Our partnership will only work if we keep it clean and professional.

Like an idiot, I broke that wall down tonight by kissing her.

It won't happen again.

THE NEXT DAY, it's a bit awkward when I show up in the board-room at the office and she's there alone, waiting for me so we can go through the presentation and do any last-minute changes as needed before our trip tomorrow.

"Hey," I say and take my place at the head of the table. She's sitting beside my chair and has the computer fired up and the projector running.

"Hey back at you," she says and forces a smile. Is she feeling that freaked out over the kiss and my stupid comment about pity? I hope she gets over it, and fast.

I lean back in my chair, putting on my glasses so I can see the screen at the end of the room. "Be my guest," I say, and motion to the projector.

She starts the slideshow, and runs through the presentation, talking about the company and how it was founded and grew to be the multimillion-dollar company that it is today, competing with the biggest corporations for contracts. She's good, has it down pat, and I have no quibbles with it. But she's a perfectionist and rearranges a few slides so she can spend some time focusing on the history of our latest product – the Heads-Up Display system we developed for the Army. She's really proud and I can see she loves to talk about it and the integrated coms system we developed to augment it.

While I listen to her describing the new communications satellite, I catch myself staring at her. Damn, she's so smart and attractive... If I were to marry some day, it would be someone like India. Someone with brains and looks and who knew how to have fun. I'm sure she's also good in bed. Just looking at her suggests she'd be fucking hot.

The presentation's great, but of course, I think about how the military types in the meeting will respond to having a woman give the presentation. I know what they'll be thinking: They'll be wondering what's under her dark blue suit and beneath her knee-length skirt. They'll imagine stripping off her clothes and warming her up with their tongues and fingers before filling her up with their hard cocks.

Or maybe that's just me.

41

*Damn.*

I breached the wall that separates us and now I can't stop going there.

When she's done with the presentation, I'm still imagining her with her hair down, her body naked and spread out beneath me.

"What do you think?"

I blink and try to focus. What do I think? I think I want her so badly that I'm going to have to go into the executive washroom and beat off before I'll be able to get any work done.

"Great," I say, nodding, a pencil in my hand, my glasses practically fogging up from the steam coming out of my ears. "I think we're good to go. Now all we have to do is get on our plane to Washington and deliver this sucker."

"What time's our flight?"

"Eleven thirty-five a.m. Two first-class seats on Virgin."

She makes a face, raising her eyebrows. "Not business class?"

"I got the seats upgraded. Perks of being an executive member."

She nods. "Will we be staying at the Hilton? I forgot to check with Cyndi."

"The usual."

She packs up her laptop and turns off the projector. "Well, I better get to it – finalizing the presentation." She checks her cell and must have a message. "Marina wants to know whether you're going to her party on Saturday."

"I wouldn't miss it."

"Good. I'll let her know." She texts something back and then stands. "I'll probably work all day today and the presentation should be in the can by supper. Should I meet you at the airport tomorrow or will we drive there together?"

"We can drive together. I have a car picking me up."

She smiles and leaves me alone in the boardroom, which is a

good thing because I still have an erection despite the talk about flights and hotel rooms. I want it to die down to at least half-staff before I head to the washroom to relieve myself.

Before I can, I get a text from Marina.

MARINA: *I want you to redo the questionnaire for me before the party on Saturday. I'll match you with someone.*

I frown. I don't need an app to find sex partners. I find them on my own quite well.

JON: *I don't need a date, Marina. Seriously. I have my fill of women when I want them.*

MARINA: *I know, I know. But I made some tweaks to the questionnaire and want to test if I can match you up with someone perfect for you. You're the hardest nut to crack, Jon. Seriously. If I can find someone for you, I'll know the app will be a success. Pretty please with probably a great fuck out of the deal?*

I sigh.

JON: *Your app didn't do a very good job with India. In fact, I have it on good authority that it was a total flop.*

MARINA: *I know. That's why I need your help. You did promise to help me revise the questionnaire.*

Even though I know she won't stop pestering me, I can't stop myself from arguing.

JON: *I don't do relationships. I'm too busy to get mixed up with anyone at the moment. I don't have time for anything more than sex. We've gone over this before.*

MARINA: *Jon, just because you got one 'Dear Jon' letter when you were in the Army doesn't mean all women are unfaithful. Some women are totally faithful. You have to learn to trust again.*

JON: *Okay. I'll redo your damn questionnaire. But I don't promise anything about going on an actual date.*

MARINA: *Thanks so much! I'll send the link to the online form right over. I promise you can back out of any date I arrange for you if you don't feel it.*

*JON: That's my price. If I don't like the woman, I won't go on a date.*

*MARINA: Agreed. Fill it out and submit it. I'll run it through the system and we'll arrange a meeting with the lucky winner. How does that sound?*

*JON: Fine. But I'm only doing it because you're India's best friend. You understand that, right?*

*MARINA: I do. Trust me on this. I'm sure I can find you the perfect match.*

*JON: There is no such thing, Marina. That's for fairy tales.*

*MARINA: Okay, old man. Shake your cane at me. I still believe in love.*

*JON: Later.*

I read over our texts and smile to myself. The woman is a born romantic.

The perfect woman for me doesn't exist. I thought I'd had one. Dee. When I went away to enlist, she promised to wait for me to return. It wasn't even six months before I got the Dear Jon letter and learned she'd hooked up with an old friend of mine who stayed behind.

I go to the executive washroom, locking the door behind me, and beat off, thinking about India the entire time.

That's twice in the space of twenty-four hours.

I need a vacation.

BEFORE I LEAVE THE OFFICE, I open the link and fill out the online questionnaire. It asks dozens of questions about interests and preferences – nothing I haven't seen before on the kind of interest inventories they do in business school.

If it wasn't the fact that Marina is India's best friend, I'd never even think about doing the questionnaire.

It's all BS.

As to perfect matches, there's no such thing as perfection. If you hold out hope of meeting the perfect woman, you'll be sadly disappointed. People settle. That's it. They screw around until they get lonely or bored and decide they want to play house. They look around at what's available and pick one.

That's all.

People who use the dating apps?

They're at that stage of wanting to settle. The app merely finds them someone at the time. In a decade, maybe even in five years, they'll be different people, and they'll stick with their partner out of guilt or because it's easier than getting a divorce.

That's not the future I want for myself.

I submit the questionnaire and put it out of my mind.

THE TRIP GOES WELL. We fly on Virgin Atlantic, first class to Washington. We both keep to ourselves the entire flight. I'm busy reading financial reports. Beside me, India goes over the presentation. By the time the plane lands, it's after eight and we've barely said a dozen words to each other, each of us lost in our own preparations for the morning meeting.

On the drive to the hotel, we're both on our cells, reading messages and responding to texts. We arrive at the hotel and I check in for the both of us, handing India her key before we take the elevator up to the floor.

Since we ate on the plane, I say goodnight to her after I help her with her suitcase, closing the door behind me and flicking on the light to my room. I lie on the bed, knowing that India's in the room directly beside me.

I flick on the television and watch the sports network for a while, but after about an hour, I think of India and what Marina said, about her being so lonely and lying in her bed all alone and feel like talking to her all of a sudden.

*JON: Are you still awake? I can't sleep. I'm always hyped up before a big presentation.*

After a moment, she replies.

*INDIA: I always have trouble sleeping the night before, too.*

*JON: It's late but do you feel like going for a walk?*

There's a pause.

*INDIA: No. I really need to just shut off the light and go to sleep. I'll probably just be tired. If I went for a walk now, I'd really be awake. But thanks anyway.*

*JON: Okay. I think I'll go for a quick run. I need to exhaust myself physically if I'm going to sleep. See you in the morning.*

*INDIA: Good night.*

I put my cell away and do exactly what I said – I go for a run down the street where the hotel is located, needing to burn off some excess energy before I'll be able to sleep. The night before a big meeting is often stressful, even though I'm sure India will do a magnificent job. I need to completely exhaust myself, and my little bout of self-abuse earlier in the day wouldn't be enough.

So I run. I run in the dark, the only sounds accompanying me the distant sound of the freeway and the noise of my breathing and my feet beating the pavement. After about twenty minutes, I stop near a bus shelter and sit on the bench, catching my breath while I adjust my running shoe laces, which have come undone. I check my watch and decide I've done enough for the night, so I run back to the hotel, taking the same route.

I glance up at the hotel and run my eyes up the side, mentally counting off the floors so I can find our floor and our rooms. I figure out which room is mine and which is India's and am surprised to see her curtains open and her figure silhouetted in the window. The drapes have been opened and she appears to be staring out at the city around the hotel.

She *looks* lonely.

My watch reads fifteen past eleven and she can't sleep either.

Why she refused to go on a walk with me, I don't understand. We used to run together back in the day. She said it helped her sleep, so I can't figure out why she wouldn't come with me.

That kiss must have really freaked her out.

That's not a good thing. The last thing I need is for there to be any tension between us. I'll have to clear things up as soon as possible if I want our partnership to flourish.

I return to my room and after sitting in front of my television while my sweat dries, I have another quick shower and go to bed. My last thoughts as I lie in the darkness are not about the presentation in the morning, but of India and what Marina told me about her being lonely.

I'm too busy to be lonely, surrounded all day and most of the evening with my team, working on Pacifica. I'm never alone, and neither is India. In fact, she and I are almost always together, working away side by side in meetings and on various parts of the Defense Department project.

How can India be lonely?

# CHAPTER FIVE

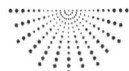

INDIA

THE MORNING GOES SMOOTHLY, from the time I wake up until the presentation at the Pentagon is over and Jon and I are in the car, driving back to the hotel. I was on point, and the general who organized the meeting was polite, interested, and encouraging, asking all the right questions and sounding extremely impressed with Pacifica's new HUD for combat.

Jon's super stoked on the drive back to the hotel, and I can almost feel his happiness while we sit in the back of the limo and watch the Washington scenery go by.

"What now?" he asks, almost twitching with energy. "I feel like celebrating."

"It's only noon," I say, infused with his excitement, but realizing that we can't celebrate. "Our flight leaves in three hours. We should pack up, check out and head to the airport. We can eat in the lounge there. They have great food. Plus champagne."

"Champagne it is." He looks over at me, his eyes softening. "You were great."

I smile, genuinely pleased that it went well. "I think they liked the presentation."

"You were great," he says again, taking my hand and squeezing it. I squeeze back and then, when he holds on a little too long, I gently slip my hand out of his and take out my cell.

It's not that I don't appreciate his show of affection. It's just that after the other night's kiss, it seems like he's getting a bit too touchy-feely with me.

He says nothing, but I can see him glance out the limo's window, his hand remaining on the seat between us. Now I feel like a bitch for taking my hand out of his first, but I don't want him to think we're just going to fall in bed and fuck out of convenience.

"We should party when we get back home."

I glance over. "I didn't sleep well, so I'll be taking the rest of the day off. We have the party at Marina's Saturday night. We can party then."

"That's right," he says and nods, rubbing his square, scruffy jaw. "She had me re-do the questionnaire and wants to set me up with a perfect date."

"You should let her match you up," I say, knowing that Marina thinks Jon is a hard nut to crack. "If she can nail you, she can find a mate for anyone."

"Why would you say that?" he says, his voice sounding all insulted. I can't quite tell if he's being serious or joking.

"You're a confirmed bachelor. No one woman would ever be enough for you."

"What?" He sits up a bit, grinning at me, and now I know he's joking. "Me? No woman good enough for me?"

I laugh at the expression of mock-surprise on his face and

make a joke. "Yes, you. No one has ever broken your heart. We all know that you don't have one."

I wink at him but his face falls and the grin is gone. Of course, then I kick myself mentally because of Dee.

"That's not true," he says softly. "My heart was broken."

I bite my lip, feeling bad now that I've made light of his failed relationship. I heard the story of how Dee broke his heart, sending him a 'Dear Jon' letter while he was deployed, but nothing more. He avoids talking about anything too personal.

"My heart was broken by Mary-Louise Stevens in third grade," he says, his grin returning. "I wanted to kiss her and she said no. Since then, no one's gotten close to my cold black heart because I ripped it out and threw it away."

*Nope.*

"You're a bastard, you know that?" I say and lightly punch his shoulder. He mock-grimaces and rubs his bicep. "Here I thought you were going to confess to me all about your broken heart.

He laughs out loud at that. "Never. Never let them see any weakness."

"Like you have a weakness."

"I have weaknesses. Several."

"What?" I say in disbelief. "You were a soldier. You do Iron Man competitions. You work like a machine. You put in ten- and twelve-hour days six days a week. You demand punctuality and total preparation on the part of your staff and you're even harder on yourself. You skydive. You base jump. You surf and snowboard. You don't smoke and you only drink when you party." I smile because even though I'm trying to give him a hard time, I actually do admire him. "You're just a top performer. I don't see any weaknesses. You even take your vitamins every day." I raise my eyebrows, because I'm always ribbing him about his concern for fitness and nutrition.

"I sound insufferable."

"You sound like a man with no weaknesses."

"Oh, but I assure you, I do. They're just secret."

Now it's his turn to wag his eyebrows. He tries to hide a grin behind his hand.

"Would these weaknesses shock me?" I say, curious now what he considers to be weaknesses.

"You might be surprised."

Now *that* was suggestive. He's just playing with me.

"You're full of it."

"You'll never know either way unless you try," he says, an evil but playful gleam in his eyes. He swipes his tongue over his bottom lip suggestively. It makes my flesh throb in a very annoying way.

I glance away, unable to keep from smiling. "I don't want to know," I reply but of course that's a bald-faced lie. I do want to know. I'm totally curious.

He's grinning and when our eyes meet again, he laughs out loud. "Come on," he says, his voice chiding. "I was just kidding. I'm in a good mood and want to celebrate. That was a good morning."

"It was. I'm happy, too."

We drive the rest of the way to the hotel and each return to our rooms to pack and get ready for checkout. Then, we take the car to the airport and after checking in, we find the Virgin executive lounge and sit at a table, eating the gourmet food and drinking some actual champagne.

"To Pacifica." Jon raises his glass of champagne.

"To Pacifica," I reply and raise my glass, too.

Our flight is routine, if very comfortable and after we land and get our bags, our car takes us to my apartment.

Jon hops out to help me with my bag, and walks me to the front door.

"Well, I'm going home to shower and unpack, then I'm going back to the office to go over some numbers."

I turn to him and frown. "Don't you ever just take a night off?"

"Saturday night. I'm going to Marina's. I guess I'll see you at the office tomorrow?"

I shrug. "I'm taking tomorrow off. I've put in a lot of late nights these past two weeks. I'm exhausted."

I force a smile at him. I know he thinks the week we just put in is child's play compared to the conditions he lived in while deployed to Afghanistan, but I'm truly wiped.

"So, I won't see you until Saturday night at Marina's."

"If you need me, you can text me. Good night," I say, making sure I'm nowhere close to him in case he gets it in his head to kiss me goodnight again. But he's probably realized that was a mistake, and stays his distance.

I enter my house, glad to be back home so I can collapse on the sofa and watch some Netflix.


MARINA TEXTS ME LATER.

MARINA: *How did it go?*

INDIA: *Great. I think we may have clinched the deal.*

MARINA: *Fantastic. Oh, by the way, I've got a match for Jon. She's coming to the party Saturday night.*

INDIA: *Yeah, he told me he re-did the questionnaire. Who's the lucky gal?*

MARINA: *I ran him through the system and came up with this woman who's dying to meet him. Especially when she saw his picture. You have to admit most of us would do Jon, if we were into one-night stands. He looks like a cleaned-up surfer-Ragnar.*

INDIA: *Who is she? I mean, Jon will fuck anything with a pretty face. I'm totally curious. I'd love to read his answers...*

MARINA: *You know I could never reveal his answers.*

53

*INDIA: I'm just kidding.*

I feel a jolt of emotion at the thought Marina might have truly found a perfect match for Jon.

*MARINA: She's perfect for him. She was a swimsuit model and now she works as a beautician at a local shop downtown. She's beautiful.*

A silly stab of jealousy goes through me. I try to tamp it down.

*INDIA: A swimsuit model? She does sound perfect for him. LOL*

*MARINA: I tell you, I got this questionnaire honed. I want you to do it again, now that I've tweaked it. I'll send it right away. Do it now, before you go to bed. I want to see who I come up with this time.*

*INDIA: Send away. I'll do it, but I hope you come up with someone better than Dr. Thomas the Blowhard.*

*MARINA: I will. I'll come up with the perfect match for you.*

*INDIA: Forever optimistic.*

*MARINA: I am. Goodnight!*

I GET an email with a link to the questionnaire and so I open it up, despite being tired. I fill it out and then submit it. I don't see anything different from the one I filled out before, but who knows? I can't remember all the questions.

Then I lie on the sofa, pull a blanket up almost covering my head, and listen to an episode of Seinfeld.

The last thing I remember is Neumann muttering something under his breath.

I SPEND the entire next day lying on the sofa, eating microwave popcorn and catching up on some recorded episodes of Orange Is The New Black.

Jon texts me later in the afternoon and I'm surprised he hasn't texted me sooner with some issue or other. I rarely take a day off and when I do I never get through a full twenty-four-hour period without him texting.

I hear my cell ding at around four thirty. Right on schedule.

*JON: Where are you? I need you. We've got a dozen requests for more info from General Neilson.*

I sigh and chew a fingernail. Jon knows full well that my assistant Caroline can provide the general with any information he needs.

*INDIA: Ask Caroline. She'll do it right away. That's why I have an assistant.*

There's a pause.

*JON: Oh, yeah. Okay.*

An hour and fifteen minutes passes.

*JON: Have you eaten? I haven't had any food since this morning.*

I sigh, smiling to myself. The man eats like a horse when he eats, but then he practically starves himself the rest of the time.

*INDIA: I had a nice bowl of pho delivered from the Vietnamese restaurant down the street. I'm good.*

*JON: Oh, damn. Why didn't you text me? I would have come and joined you. You know I love pho.*

*INDIA: It's my day off. I'm supposed to not have anything to do with the office on my day off.*

*JON: Dream on.*

I laugh because he's right. It never happens. Usually, I end up zipping over to the office to take care of some emergency. I'm surprised that no one called me earlier in the day.

*INDIA: Those were your orders, Mr. CEO. You said that when we take a day off, we should turn off our cells and not accept texts.*

JON: *That was aspirational. It wasn't meant to be achieved.*

INDIA: *I'm trying my best to achieve it.*

JON: *Okay. I'll leave you alone. Do you want me to come by with a beer?*

INDIA: *That wouldn't be leaving me alone.*

JON: *Ha ha. You got me. Good night.*

INDIA: *Sleep tight.*

JON: *:)*

ABOUT AN HOUR LATER, Marina texts me and claims she has a new match for me and is arranging for us to meet at her party.

INDIA: *Isn't that awfully quick? I mean, I just filled out the questionnaire.*

MARINA: *Trust me. This is a sure thing. His name is Evan. He's hot as hell. And he likes your pic and profile.*

INDIA: *I don't remember creating a profile. You have to ask me about these things!*

MARINA: *Hun, you gave me permission to create a profile and match you up with guys, remember? You gave me permission to arrange a first date. You can always decline, but this is important. Take a look at his pic and see what you think. Tell me he isn't right up your alley.*

I open the link to the guy's profile. Evan Moran. He's tall and dark and bearded. He looks really metrosexual, his moustache curled up on the ends. On closer examination, his dark hair is cut short on the sides but long and slicked back in a very trendy man bun.

She's got to be kidding...

INDIA: *A man bun?*

MARINA: *He's got a masters in Political Science and is doing his Ph.D. at Stanford. He's vegan and likes jazz and grunge metal. He drives a Jeep and does Bikram Yoga.*

INDIA: *Vegan? I'm a devoted meat eater. My favorite food is steak.*

MARINA: *He's flexible about dating omnivores.*

INDIA: *And hot yoga? You know I melt at room temperature unless I'm beside a large body of water.*

MARINA: *You're beautiful and sexy. He likes curvy women. He said yes as soon as he saw your pic.*

INDIA: *If you think so...*

I pause for a moment, rethinking the whole business.

INDIA: *Maybe I shouldn't meet him at the party on Saturday.*

MARINA: *Why? It's all arranged, hun.*

INDIA: *Jon will eat him alive.*

MARINA: *Jon will be too busy drooling over the swimsuit model beautician.*

I think back to the night Jon dropped me off.

INDIA: *Jon kissed me the other night. It was weird.*

MARINA: *DANGER WILL ROBINSON! Do NOT hook up with Jon. It will mean the end of your business relationship. I know what I'm talking about.*

INDIA: *I have no plans to hook up with him. He's not into relationships. He's a bonobo and likes to fuck every woman he meets. That's all. It's his natural mode of interaction.*

MARINA: *You two have got to find partners and stop thinking that getting together will solve your problems.*

INDIA: *We're not thinking of getting together. We're friends. Good friends. We're business partners.*

MARINA: *Honestly, you can't get together with Jon, even if it would be easy and logical.*

INDIA: *I know! Believe me, there's no intention on my part to hook up with Jon. It's the last thing I'm thinking about.*

MARINA: *Don't go there. Seriously. Big mistake. Huge mistake.*

INDIA: *Why do you think that?*

*MARINA: Because he'll break your heart. You know I'm right...*

*INDIA: Message received*

*MARINA: Good. You need to meet my match for you. Give him a shot.*

I sigh, wishing I could say no, but I promised her I'd help her out. Besides, I want someone. I need a man.

Badly.

*INDIA: Okay, but if things don't work out on this date, you have to give up and realize that either your app is wrong or there's something wrong with me.*

*MARINA: There's nothing wrong with you that a nice hard man won't fix. ;) Your date is ripped on top of being very urbane. He does say he knows how to please a woman on his profile.*

*INDIA: UGH. Really? That's a plus in your mind?*

*MARINA: At least he's confident.*

*INDIA: All right... But this is the last time. Seriously, Marina.*

*MARINA: I guarantee this will be the last time I match you with someone. K?*

*INDIA: K...*

*MARINA: Later.*

I close my texts after reading them over once more, then put my cell away.

*Evan Moran.*

Man bun? Jon will tear him apart, limb from vegan limb.

What on earth is Marina thinking? The last place I should be meeting another date is at the party where Jon will be, even if he is distracted by Ms. Beautician Bathing Suit Model. He'll still give Mr. Evan Moran a hard time, embarrassing both Evan and me in the process. I can just see Jon's smug face as he finds something to make fun of. I know right away it will be the man bun. Jon had super short hair when he was an Army Ranger. I've seen pics of him when he was on his last deployment.

A man bun would be laughed off the battlefield.

I sigh and lean back on the couch, pulling covers up over my shoulder and trying hard to forget the upcoming party at Marina's.

I have this feeling it's going to be a disaster.

# CHAPTER SIX

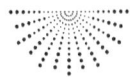

Jon

ON SATURDAY AFTERNOON, after forty-eight hours without India at work, I text her and offer to pick her up and drive her to the party. Her place is on the way to Marina's. I thought it would be easier than if we both took our cars.

She refuses, insisting on taking her own vehicle.

INDIA: *I better not. I may need to make a quick exit tonight.*

JON: *How so?*

INDIA: *Marina's got me matched with some new guy. He's going to be there. If he's as good as her last match, I'll be glad to have my own vehicle so I can escape.*

I frown. Another date so soon? Marina seems desperate to match India up with someone.

JON: *Another guy? She's really trying to push someone onto you.*

There's a pause.

INDIA: *She wants me to have a life, I guess.*

61

*JON: You have a life. A pretty great life, if you sit down and really think about it. You have one of the best educations money can buy. You're a partner in a business that's doing exceptionally well. You live in a great house overlooking the fucking San Francisco Bay, India. Your life is great.*

*INDIA: According to Marina, I'm practically an old maid...*

*JON: HA! As if. You could get any man you wanted if you wanted. Just go to a classy bar where the billionaires hang out and you could pick one up, if that's what you want.*

*INDIA: That isn't what I want. I want something meaningful. Something real.*

I read her text over, imagining what kind of man India deserves. She deserves someone real. Someone rich, successful, handsome, strong. Someone who realizes what a gem she is. Because she *is* a real gem. There aren't many women like India. Probably not very many men who can compete with her in terms of brains and work ethics and looks.

*JON: You'll find someone when the time is right. When you're ready, you'll look up and realize that someone you're with is perfect for you.*

*INDIA: What happened? Has someone mugged you and taken your cell and is texting me crazy stuff? That sounds so romantic and so totally unlike the Jon I know.*

*JON: What do you mean? You think I don't know anything about love?*

*INDIA: You're the king of hookups. The prince of fuck buddies. The duke of a good time, not a long time. I just didn't expect something so romantic coming from you.*

I laugh, even though she means it as an insult.

Then I feel slightly insulted – like I don't know what a good relationship is, don't know what real love is.

I do. I thought I had it.

I'm just not ready to settle down and become a stuffed grey suit.

JON: *You don't want to settle down and get married, do you?*

There's a long pause and I wonder whether she put her cell down or is busy doing something else – or doesn't like my question.

INDIA: *No, but the truth is that I want a man in my bed, Jon. Is that so wrong?*

JON: *You could have that any time you want, India. All you need to do is signal your interest and you could have practically any man you want, seriously. You should already know that. God, you're smoking hot and smart and successful. A man would have to be a total moron not to want to be in your bed.*

She doesn't reply and so I wait, knowing that she's also not promiscuous. She doesn't sleep around, even though she honestly *could* get any man she wanted in her bed.

INDIA: *I want someone who loves me in my bed, not just any man with a dick. I know damn well I could get that any time I want. I don't want that.*

JON: *Well, I can't help you find someone who loves you. But you could sure find someone to spend time in your bed.*

INDIA: *SIGH.*

INDIA: *Gotta go. Later.*

I don't hear back from her for the rest of the afternoon.

Instead, I sit at my desk at the office and fume. My good mood has vanished and I feel a vague sense of anger at the world, which I can't explain.

At six, I decide to leave the office and go home, take a quick shower, and change for Marina's party. I don't really feel like going, but India will be there and if I don't go, she'll never let me hear the end of it.

So, I do exactly that, my mind still on the contracts I've been looking over all day, wondering if they're solid or whether we need to work on them some more before signing.

After my shower, I change into something casual, and then take my car to Marina's house. It's a pretty sweet house on the beach not too far from India's and has all the amenities – an outdoor bar, beach umbrellas and chairs, plus a great patio where the party will take place.

When I arrive, there are already a dozen cars parked in the driveway and on the streets. Marina's parties are notoriously filled with people from the tech industry and from Stanford, including faculty and grad students. The people are smart and geeky and mostly rich or student-poor. The music is good – Marina always hires a DJ who plays a good mix of hits and oldies.

I'm a bit late, so I end up parking down the street and walking the rest of the way to the house. It sits on a rise on the edge of a hill, affording a great view of the bay and beach below. I walk around the side of the house to the back and see a couple dozen people standing around or sitting on beach chairs, drinks in hand. I don't see anyone I know – neither Marina or India – so I go inside. That's when I see them – India and some tall dark-haired guy.

With a man bun.

And a curly moustache.

He's wearing a Hawaiian shirt, shorts and sandals, and is leaning against the wall beside her, smiling as he listens to her talk. The two of them laugh over some private joke and an emotion runs through me that I don't recognize at first.

A man bun?

Marina appears out of nowhere at my elbow, her green eyes bright behind her dark-rimmed glasses, her hair in a ponytail. She looks like the total geek-girl that she is.

"Leave them alone," she whispers. "They're hitting it off so I don't want anything to ruin it."

"Who the hell is he?"

"That's Evan Moran."

"He has a man bun." I grab a beer out of a bucket of ice. "What the hell, Marina? A man bun?"

"He's a PhD student in political science at Stanford."

I shake my head and take a long pull on my beer. "His moustache curls up at the ends like he thinks he's a fucking Musketeer."

India seems to be enjoying their discussion. She doesn't look bored or irritated. Does she like men with man buns? I run a hand through my hair, and take another drink of beer.

"Do you have something harder?" I ask Marina, who's watching India and Evan with delight.

"You know where the bar is. They're hitting it off."

"You already said that."

Then she turns to me. "Don't get drunk. I have someone I want you to meet. She'll be here soon, so stay sober, okay? I don't want you too wild."

"Who is it?" I ask, curious but, at the same time, unable to take my eyes off Evan, who's leaning closer to India. She's not backing away, so that means she actually likes him.

"Her name is Heather, and she's a former bathing suit model. You'll love her."

I frown. Bathing suit model? This is the match Marina's app has picked for me?

"What does she do now?"

Marina smiles up at me. "She's a beautician. She specializes in color. You know, the new trend in rainbow hair color. She works miracles, or so her client testimonials say."

"And you think I'd be interested in a beautician?"

Marina laughs. "I think you'll be interested when you see her. She's tall and hot. Any man would be glad to be matched with her."

To change subjects, I ask about India's date.

"Who's this man-bun musketeer you matched India with?"

"He's a vegan," Marian says, like that's something great.

"Vegan? India loves meat."

"He's omnivore-tolerant.

"What's his dissertation topic?" I ask, although I really don't give a shit.

"I think it's the political economy of capitalist imperialism or something."

"Ha!" I shake my head. "India's a capitalist. Another totally wrong pick for her, Marina. I think you better give up on the matchmaking app if this is what it comes up with."

"Opposites attract," she replies, smiling widely. "A little friction gets the blood pumping. Speaking of getting blood pumping, he does Bikram yoga. That's hot yoga, in case you didn't know. It gets people all sweaty."

"India runs. She doesn't do yoga."

"She always wanted to start. Can't you see him helping her with her poses?" Marina says, wagging her eyebrows in a most disgusting way. "She'll get a great workout with him."

That almost makes me crazy. I can't help but imagine Man Bun bending India over a desk at the university and taking her from behind, with pictures of Lenin on the wall behind them.

Just when I'm going to lambaste Marina over her choice for India, her face lights up and she points to the entry.

"Oh, look who's here. Heather!"

Marina goes over to the front door where a tall bleached-blonde woman stands, looking lost. I swear she looks like Daryl Hannah from *Splash!* with hair that is practically down to her waist and all crimped. She's wearing something tight and short and flowery, exposing legs that go on and on, and strappy sandals on her feet. Two half-cantaloupe breasts peek out from under a scoop neckline.

She smiles when she sees Marina and waves, then brightens up even more when she sees me. Her eyes move up and down over my body like she wants to eat me.

In truth, all I want to do is make a break for it, because I'm already bored imagining having to talk to her.

Make no mistake, if we were at a bar and I was a little drunk and she was a little interested, I'd be all over her. We'd be in the bathroom and she'd be sucking me off with those plumped-up lips, or we'd go home together and I'd fuck her brains out, but for some reason, I don't feel it tonight. She looks like cake frosting or cotton candy, with the streaks of pink and blue in her hair. Like if you fucked her, you'd need to eat something meaty to get the cloying sweetness out of your mouth.

I paste on a smile when Marina takes Heather's hand and pulls her over in my direction. I take in a deep breath and glance over to where Man Bun and India are busy talking, their heads together. India looks amused and is all smiles, but she glances over in my direction and raises her eyebrows meaningfully.

She thinks he's a jerk and is being nice, for Marina's sake. I'm certain of it. How could she think anything different?

India has often made fun of hipsters when we've seen them wearing their thick beards, their fancy moustaches, their man buns, their lumberjack shirts and prayer beads. She scoffs at all pretense, preferring honesty over artifice. Realism over idealism.

Man Bun is another bust on the old dating-app score sheet.

Marina brings Heather over and introduces us, then leaves the two of us alone. I shake her hand; she's impeccably mani-cured, her nails long and lacquered. Her hair is something else. It looks like she just stepped out of a steam room, all crimped and fluffy. Like unraveled yarn. Rainbow yarn. That's what it looks like to me.

"So nice to meet you," she says in a heavy Valley Girl accent, her words rising at the end. It grates on my nerves. "Marina says you're a perfect match for me." She looks me up and down, her eyes widening like she approves. "She's right in the looks department. Has anyone ever told you that you look like a younger Ragnar? She says you surf, too. I don't surf, but I love the beach. Maybe we could go some time. She says you have a place down south. Maybe you could teach me to surf. I spend all day in a beauty salon, breathing in hair color. I could use the fresh air. Marina said..."

The rest of the next hour is spent with me nodding and offering one-word answers to Heather as she breathlessly opines on everything from the latest blockbuster superhero movie to the election and the price of apartment rentals in the city. I encourage her, not really wanting to talk about myself, and she only seems interested in what kind of car I drive, where my apartment is located, and what kind of investments I have.

She's not bad, as people go. She's not the brightest star in the heavens, but she's not mean or rude. She's just really enthusiastic about everything. And none of it interests me in the least.

I honestly don't care about one word that comes out of her perfectly painted mouth. I can't even muster up the interest in what those lips might do when around my cock. Instead, I glance at India while Heather's talking about hair color and how intricate it is. I see that Man Bun is leaning in close to her and now he's pulling on a strand of her hair. She looks all coy, like she's eating this up.

She likes him?

What the *hell*?

I turn back to Heather, who's telling me about semi-permanent and permanent dyes and how colors have to be developed, and a bunch of other stuff I should be paying attention to if I want to seduce her.

But I don't.

At that moment, I don't want her. Her melon breasts are far

too perfect. I suspect that if she jumped up and down, they wouldn't move an inch. They're so obviously false and as a result, totally unappealing to me. Other men may like falsies. There's no accounting for taste. Only the very best augmentations are appealing. I've seen and felt a number in my time. I prefer a real breast, even if it isn't large.

Heather takes a break from telling me about the market for beauticians, and begins to ask me questions.

"Marina tells me you own a satellite company. Do you do communications satellites? Like AT&T?"

"No," I reply, wondering if there's anything upstairs in that bubble head of hers. "Military."

"Oh," she says, her eyes wide. "Like spy satellites?"

I smile to myself. "Something like that."

"Cool," she says. "Marina says you're a Ranger."

"Former Ranger," I say with a nod and mumble something about my time in the Army and my work as a Ranger. She seems even more appreciative as I regale her with a story about my last deployment, how we survived an IED and were held down in an ambush by a group of ISIS insurgents.

She rubs my arm appreciatively, really laying on the admiration. She moves closer to me, and although I could easily take her home with me tonight because she's clearly into it, and into me, I want to escape and go home, have a shower, and watch the news before hitting the rack for some solid shuteye.

"Excuse me," I say, and make an excuse about using the men's room. In reality, I want to make a quick escape. I glance around but can't find India – she's gone somewhere and I hope to hell it isn't home with Man Bun, because I would think a whole lot less of her if so. The main floor bathroom is taken, so I take the stairs to the second floor. It's in use as well so I wait in the hallway.

When the door opens, it's India. She's surprised to see me and stops short.

"Oh, it's you."

"Yep," I reply. "Feast your eyes on me."

She laughs lightly, her eyes crinkling in that way that I love. "You're a sight for sore eyes, that's for sure."

"No man bun to be found," I quip, grinning. "Not that there's anything wrong with that."

She laughs out loud at that and holds her hand over her mouth. "I'm sorry," she says, barely able to talk. "He actually invited me back to his place for a full-body coconut oil massage and hot rock experience."

"No way," I reply, amazed at the man's tin ear. "You turned him down?"

She play-punches my shoulder, grinning like a crazy person. "I said thanks for the offer but I couldn't be out too late because I had to go into the office early in the morning. In other words, I lied."

"I was almost bored to tears by my date, Heather. She was telling me the intricacies of hair dye."

"I don't get it. It's like Marina's app is totally broken."

"You said it. She better go back to the drawing board on that one."

We stand there for a moment, and stop laughing when someone walks by. I glance down into her eyes and see a gleam in them. I know she's relieved she can talk to me and escape Man Bun. I lean in closer and somehow, we kiss.

As I kiss her, I wonder how Man Bun could ever imagine that India was the type to be into that airy-fairy stuff. More likely she'd want an ice-cold beer, a thick juicy steak, and a baseball game to watch for relaxation.

It's then I realize I'm kissing her for real now.

And she's kissing me back.

It's not just a friendly peck or even a sympathy kiss like the other night. It's a *kiss* kiss.

I feel her tongue against mine and it sends a shock of lust through my body right to my dick.

*I'm kissing India and she's kissing me back...*

What the fuck am I? A teenage boy?

All of a sudden we pull apart, and I feel like a total idiot. Here I am, kissing her again after the very awkward kiss the other night. I kick myself mentally.

We cannot go there.

"We can't do this, Jon," she says, her voice a little breathless like she's as surprised and aroused as I am.

"I know," I say, a surge of something rushing through my body. I know we can't do this, but my body and mind say *fuck it.*

I want her. I think of Man Bun wanting to rub coconut oil all over her body. Right now, that sounds exactly like what I want to be doing with India.

"Marina will kill me if she knows I kissed you instead of Man Bun, even if it was a mistake."

"I know. And me kissing you instead of Mermaid Lady."

"That's right," India says, her eyes widening. "She *does* look like that actress in *Splash!,* doesn't she? I always envied her all that blonde hair."

I shake my head. "She has nothing on you."

I say it in complete truth, meaning every word. I say it solemnly because it's true and India should know it. At that moment, I want to lean closer to her and kiss her again, but I hold back.

India sighs audibly. I know she's thinking the same thing as I am.

We can't do this.

It would be so easy, but it would fuck things up completely.

"Do you want to blow this popsicle stand? I'll give you a ride home."

She shakes her head. "Thanks, but I brought my car."

71

I nod and take in a deep breath. "I think I'll take the back exit so I don't have to see Marina."

"You're really going to skip out?"

"Yeah. I guess I'll see you at work Monday."

She smiles softly, and I can almost imagine I see regret in them. "Okay. See you then."

I turn and walk away, taking the stairs to the main floor. I get to the landing and see Mermaid standing talking to Marina. I cringe and hope I can escape Marina's wrath unscathed. I hope neither of them see me. My plan is to take the back door and leave without saying anything, even though it's rude.

All I want is to hop in my car and drive off into the night, try to put the kiss out of my mind before it's time to go to bed, but from the way my body feels, a deep ache in my balls and a slight thickening of my dick, I won't get to sleep without yet another bout of masturbation to images of India lying on my bed, her body slick with coconut oil, her eyes closed in pleasure as I lick it off her hard little clit.

Marina's got to either fix that app or go into another line of work.

# CHAPTER SEVEN

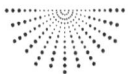

## INDIA

I GO BACK down the stairs after Jon, grinning to myself when he turns around and goes back up because Marina and Mermaid Girl are standing blocking the doorway. He can't escape and so he goes back upstairs, probably planning on waiting until they're somewhere else so he can escape.

Of course, I'm hoping for the same, but I'm also out of luck because before I can get to the back door through the kitchen, I'm corralled by Evan.

"There you are," he says, all pleased to find me. "I thought you might have skipped out on me."

"Why would you think that?" I say, a little bit too emphatically, my laugh nervous, my pulse still up a bit from Jon's kiss.

"I looked around but you were gone. I asked Marina and she thought you might have left without telling anyone. She said you do that sometimes."

"She shouldn't be telling stories," I say, shrugging. "I was just upstairs using the ladies'."

"Want another drink?" he asks, pointing to the kitchen.

"Sure," I say, sighing. "I'll take a Corona."

"Oh, don't have a beer. I make a mean mojito."

I don't want a mojito. I want a Corona. But I acquiesce.

"That sounds great," I reply, forcing a smile, resigned to my fate of putting up with Man Bun for another hour or so before I can ethically escape. I glance around and see Jon trying to slip past a small group of people from Marina's grad class. He tries to do what I'm planning, but then Marina calls out and he stops walking, his body stiff. He turns to face Marina, and his smile is so fake, I'm surprised anyone is fooled.

Marina drags Mermaid Girl over and pushes the two of them together. She says something and then leaves them alone.

Poor Jon. Like me, he's trapped by his own unwelcome date. Now that they're alone, she stands really close, and they're almost eye-to-eye. He's smiling back at her and she runs her hand over his chest suggestively.

I know he doesn't think much of her, but she seems really interested in him and I wonder if he'll go home with her, like he has dozens of women when we've been at parties like this. He thinks she's a flake but she's got a good body, and that's always been good enough for him.

She stands even closer, and he leans forward, his head tilted to one side. She leans in and whispers something in his ear and he smiles and raises his eyebrows. I just know she's asking him back to her place – or inviting herself to his.

God, what ovaries.

At that moment, there's this part of me that wishes I was more of a slut so I could go home with Jon and it wouldn't matter. I wish we could be friends with benefits and still maintain a successful partnership. It's not like I haven't imagined Jon in bed

74

before – I have. I just know that the first time after we fucked that he took someone home besides me, my heart would break.

I'd resent him, and then how would we work together?

Jon opens the door and the two of them leave, Jon closing the door behind him without even a glance in my direction.

Before I can do anything, Marina comes over to stand beside me. She's grinning from ear to ear.

"Guess who just left with his new MATCHED date?"

"I saw," I say, trying to hide my displeasure. "It's not all that hard to get Jon to leave with a beautiful woman. He does it every weekend. I wouldn't credit MATCHED for that. In fact, he told me he thinks she's a bit of a flake."

"Jon likes flakes. He always picks them out of a crowd of women. He just doesn't want to admit it."

I turn and look in her eyes. "You think so?"

"I know so. Jon thinks he wants to have a meaningful relationship, but he isn't ready for a real commitment. He wants a regular fuck buddy with no strings attached. Heather wants a hot guy to bang whenever she has a night off. They're made for each other."

She's smiling so wide it makes me feel depressed because, well, I am underwhelmed with Man Bun.

On paper, he should tick all my boxes. Smart. Educated. Ambitious. Sensual. Cultured. Tall. Dark. Handsome even if he has a man bun and curly moustache.

Many women would be happy to have his attention.

"Oh, here comes Evan," Marina says, wagging her eyebrows. "He's a hunk, isn't he? Admit it – you think he's hot and smart."

I watch Evan approach, two glasses of what looks like storm drain water in his hands.

"Man bun," I say, disheartened.

"What?" Marina turns to me, frowning. "You don't like his hair? It's very fashionable."

"He's a hipster," I say under my breath.

A pretentious hipster.

"Exactly," she whispers. "He's cool. And very sensual. Now enjoy."

Then she leaves me, passing Evan on his way from the kitchen. "Hey, Evan. How are things going?" she asks as they stop briefly in the middle of the room, her voice loud enough that I can hear.

"Good," he says and raises his eyebrows to her. "Very good."

Then he turns to me, a smile on his face, and holds up the glasses. "Cheers."

I force yet another smile. "Cheers."

I take the swamp water and drink half of it down, squinting at the taste, needing at least some of the alcohol to help me tolerate the rest of the night.

AN HOUR LATER, after Evan has recounted the bartending course he took so he could work at the campus pub, he moves on to how he loves really great bourbon and talks about taking a sommelier course, which is a course on how to drink wine.

"What's your favorite wine?" he asks, leaning closer.

"I like beer."

"Oh, so do I. There's this great craft beer company that has its microbrewery down close to the campus. I go there all the time. Steam, it's called. Have you tried it?"

"I like Corona."

"Imported beer is good," he says, and I can see his mind working on how to be nice with such an uncultured person as myself.

I hide my yawn behind my hand. "Gee, Evan, it's been really great meeting you, but I really have to get home so I can get up at the crack of dawn and go to work."

I shrug helplessly and smile.

"Oh, that's too bad. Are you sure I can't give you a ride? You've been drinking."

"So have you."

"But I'm a lot bigger and stronger than you," he says, standing a bit taller. "I can take it. I wouldn't want to see you get pulled over for a breathalyzer."

"I'm fine," I reply. "I know my limit. It's been an hour so I'm good."

Besides, there's the rest of the glass of mojito left because I don't drink weed water, even if it does taste like mint rum.

"Will I see you again?" he asks, his voice hopeful. "Give me your cell number." He takes out his smartphone. "I'll call you."

I comply, although I don't really care if I ever see him again. I'll just block his number.

He leans over to kiss me but I turn my head so that he ends up kissing my cheek, his hand on my arm.

"See you!" I say and pull away, making a beeline for the front door.

Before I can leave, Marina grabs me and pulls me to the side. "Where do you think you're going? It's only been two hours."

"Jon left after only an hour."

"Yeah, but he's getting some. And he doesn't need any. It's you I'm concerned about. You're the one who needs it."

"I don't need it," I say, although that's a bald-faced lie. "I want it, but I want it with someone I'm attracted to."

"You're not attracted to Evan?"

I shake my head and try to edge my way past Marina to the door. "Nope. Lady parts not responding. Sorry!"

"Oh, that's too bad." She frowns and examines me, her hands on her hips. "You and I are going to have to go over that questionnaire again. Maybe you're not answering truthfully?"

"Yeah, okay, we'll do it. Next week. Gotta go," I say when I see Evan approaching. "Bye!" I say and wave at Marina and Evan.

I leave and close the front door behind me, relieved that I've escaped having to say anything more to either of them.

I get in my car and drive off, glad to finally be free of the party, Evan, and Marina with her judging eyes.

I arrive home without being stopped by the police and go inside my place, locking the door and arming the alarm system. Then I plop onto my sofa and turn on the television, scanning the channels to see what I can find to watch. I should try to go to bed so I can get up and ride my bike before going to work, but I'm wide awake.

I find nothing to watch, so I switch on my Apple TV and watch Netflix instead, selecting the next episode of *OITNB* and pulling the crocheted afghan throw blanket around my shoulders.

I don't even know when I fall asleep.

WHEN I WAKE up on the sofa, I wipe my eyes and notice I've drooled all over the throw pillow. My back aches and I really should have brushed my teeth before falling asleep but the alcohol made me so tired, I didn't bother before I started to watch television.

Sunday is my decompression day, when I do nothing. I'm not even meeting the girls for brunch this weekend, and so I have all day to think about what happened with Jon and that kiss – two kisses. I don't know what happened but whatever it was, it wasn't good.

I spend all day on the sofa, watching Netflix and eating every carb I can find in my cupboards, ordering in when I run out of food and all I have left is pickles and green olives.

I go to bed Sunday night feeling disgusted with myself for wasting an entire day, but I didn't want to face Marina and I didn't want to go into work to hear all about Jon's date with Mermaid Girl and see his self-satisfied grin.

Monday morning, my cell alarm goes off and I wake, the early morning light streaming in from the picture windows overlooking the Bay.

I check my cell. It's seven a.m., and I'm late, having slept through my first alarm at six thirty. I get up and go through my routine, then go outside and get on my bike for a half-hour ride along the road that runs along the highway. The exercise will blow off all my fatigue, and clear my head so I can go to work refreshed.

When I get back from my ride, I shove down some yogurt and eat a banana, then I have a shower and get dressed for work. Within an hour, I'm on my way to Pacifica's offices, ready to face another day of reviewing specs on the new satellite.

I CLIMB the stairs to the third-floor offices and open the door to find Jon in his office, his laptop open and his cell to his ear. He's busy talking to someone, but glances up and waves at me as I pass by.

I wave back and think he looks a big haggard, and I wonder if he hasn't spent another late night with Mermaid Girl. Then I kick myself mentally. He doesn't do second dates.

In my office, I try to focus on work, but I can't help but imagine Jon and Mermaid Girl going at it. Would she be a squealer? I can't imagine she doesn't make a lot of noise. She seems like the enthusiastic type.

After about fifteen minutes, Jon pops his head in the door, a cup of coffee in his hand.

"Have you had your coffee? I picked this up for you on my way."

"Oh, no, I haven't yet, " I say, and he comes in and hands me the cup. "Thanks."

I take a sip. He must have heated it up in the microwave

79

because it's steaming hot. I glance at him. "How long have you been here?"

"An hour. I had a call to Australia I had to be in early for. Why don't you come to my office? We can look at a few numbers."

"Sure," I say and follow him out of my office and across the hall to his. He sits down in the chair behind his desk, watching me, a strange expression on his face. I take the chair across from him.

"So how did you and Man Bun make out Saturday night?" he asks, opening a file on his desk.

"We didn't," I say plainly.

"You didn't go home with him?"

"Nope."

He seems to relax a bit, leaning back farther in his chair. "I knew he wasn't your type."

"He wasn't," I reply, "although he ticked all my boxes, apparently. At least, according to Marina's app."

"I think it's a bust."

"Why?" I say, peering at him, curious. "You seemed to be happy with Mermaid Girl."

He shrugs. "She's pretty. A man is always happy with a pretty woman."

"How did your night go? I saw that you left together."

He grins at me. "I'll never tell."

I laugh, but there's a part of me that's annoyed at him. Will he ever be serious about a woman?

"Too bad for you and Man Bun."

"Yeah, another failed attempt at having a real life," I say with an exaggerated sigh.

"You have a real life," he says, frowning. "A pretty damn good life, if you ask me."

"But no nooky," I say, and drink down some of my coffee.

"You could have it any time you wanted. You could have had it Saturday night, by the way Man Bun responded to you."

I shrug and pick up this tiny stuffed elephant he got as a gift after making a donation to some wildlife rescue agency. "It's different for women. We're choosier."

He snorts at that. "Not my experience. Pretty much any woman I offer it to takes me up on the offer."

"Yeah, but that's because you have bimbo radar. You can pick them out of a crowd, so your sample is biased towards the women who will fuck any hot man who makes it available."

"You think I'm hot?" he says with a huge grin.

I throw the elephant at him in response and he ducks, laughing at me like he enjoys tormenting me.

"Seriously, India," he says, holding his folded hands in front of his chin, taking on a very thoughtful expression. "You could be having wild sex any night of the week you want. You just have to ask."

"Yeah, right," I say and stare off into the distance. There have been so few men I would even consider for a hookup. "I have standards."

"What do you mean?"

"Exactly what I said. I have standards. I know I could pick up any man I meet at a bar or party, but that's not what I want."

"You don't want just any man."

"No," I say, thinking about my perfect man. "I want someone smart and ambitious and funny and affectionate," I say and then I look at him. He's listening intently. "And loyal."

"Ahh, you mean monogamous."

"Yes, monogamous. I don't want to share."

He shrugs. "You have to be pretty damn good to entice a man to be exclusive."

"I am," I say, grinning at him.

He nods. "I bet you are."

There's a moment between us, and it's like we're staring each other down. Like he's waiting for me to say something in particular. Like, 'Do you want me to prove it?'

But I don't.

"Well, if you ever change your mind and want something hot and satisfying but with no long-term commitment, I'm your man." He grins at me and then turns to his computer, opening some program and typing, the smile lingering on his face.

"Ha!" I respond, but damn, the very thought of us being fuck buddies sends a jolt right to my clit.

I've thought of that already – many times. But up until now, I've never said it nor has he. Now, it's out there. It's hanging in the air between us.

"That would probably destroy our business relationship."

"It might. It might make it better."

I frown. "How could it make our business relationship better?" I could squirm in my chair right now because of the uncomfortable swollen feeling in my core.

He speaks, and his voice is a bit breathless. He's feeling the same thing I am and it's only eight in the morning. "We wouldn't have to resort to other people to be satisfied sexually."

*Damn...* I'm always a bit aroused first thing in the morning and having that thought in my head – well, it makes me even more aroused now.

I stand, because I should leave now, and go back to my office before I say something stupid.

He stands as well. "We haven't finished talking."

"I think we have," I say, raising my eyebrows.

I turn but he gets to me before I reach the door. He actually puts his arm out and blocks my way.

"Think about it," he says and yes, his voice is definitely husky. "I know I think about it a lot more often than I should. If we became lovers, it would simplify things."

I look in his eyes, and they're half-lidded, and I think I can detect desire in them. Or is it my own desire for him that I perceive?

"It would complicate things," I reply, equally breathless. Oh, God, what is happening?

He leans closer and I'm waiting for him to kiss me. Before he can, I hold up my finger and press it against his lips.

"I don't like sloppy seconds."

He stops. "We didn't fuck. I took her home and said goodnight."

"You didn't fuck her?" I say, a strange sense of relief flooding through me. "Why?"

"Because I wanted you."

# CHAPTER EIGHT

JON

I kiss her. My lips press against hers, and they're warm and soft. I can tell that she's surprised at first, but then I become demanding, my need for her outweighing my sense and she finally responds. My lips part and hers do as well, and when I feel her tongue against mine, that does it. My whole body tenses, a rush of blood to my dick.

She kisses me back, and so I pull her into my arms. Hers slip around my neck and we're devouring each other.

Nothing is holding either of us back.

I run my hand over her body, up and down her back, grabbing her butt in one hand, a breast in the other. I squeeze her nipple through the fabric of her shirt and bra and she moans while I kiss her neck.

"I want you," I say, my voice hoarse. "I need you."

"We can't," she replies even as she's kissing me back. "We shouldn't."

"We can." I stop kissing her neck and look in her eyes. "Tell me you don't want me and I'll stop right now. I'll never touch you again."

I stare into her eyes, and I can sense her indecision. She's torn between her body and her mind.

I know I have her body. It's her mind I have to convince.

"I do want you, but if we fuck now, here, at the office, what will happen tomorrow when it's business as usual?" She looks at me, her brow furrowed. "What will happen when we're at a party or the bar and you pick up some babe and take her home instead of me? My heart will break and I'll hate you. I'm not a fuckbuddy."

"I know you aren't," I say, filled with exasperation. "Do you really think I'd treat you that way?"

"I don't know." She glances away. "I've never known you to have an actual girlfriend."

I try not to show my frustration, but it's hard. "I've never had you." I don't say anything else; I just wait for her to say yes or no.

My body is ready, my dick hard and swollen. If she could only shut off her damn mind...

"Fuck it," she says, looking up into my eyes.

"My thought exactly." I kiss her once more – a blistering kiss this time, slipping my hand under her shirt, under her bra so I can tweak her nipple directly between my finger and thumb.

She groans and I can feel her shudder against me. When I slide my hand around and try to unhook her bra, my fingers get tangled, so I stop kissing her and pull her shirt up and over her head after she unlatches the back of her bra.

"You need to wear one of those bras with the catch at the front," I say. My dick throbs when I finally see her topless. Her breasts are magnificent, soft and round and full, her nipples dark, hard nubs that I can't wait to take between my lips and suck. "Better yet, no bra so I have direct access at all times."

I stop and just stare at her, reaching up slowly to cup one breast, squeezing it gently. "Beautiful." I bend down and take one nipple in my mouth and suck, sending a bolt of lust right to my dick when I feel the nub against my tongue. I can't wait to run my tongue against her hard clit when she's finally naked.

I move from one nipple to the other and back, and when I look up at her, she's closed her eyes, enjoying the sensation.

"Hey, what's up?" Grant, one of our tech guys, pops his head in the door, which of course, we left open, thinking we were alone.

"*Fuck.*" I rise from India's breast, covering her with my body.

"Crap," she mutters, and covers her breasts while I pull my shirt out and down to hide my very large erection, which is obviously and painfully pressing against the zipper of my jeans.

"No, don't answer that," Grant says, a sheepish grin on his face. "I'll leave you two alone." He closes the door behind him, and India's face is red and hot.

India grabs her bra from the floor and fumbles with it, trying to put it on at top speed while I pull her t-shirt over her head.

*Great.* One of our staff knows we were getting it on at the office on a Monday morning.

India stands there, her eyes closed. She's breathing rapidly, and I can tell she's upset.

I can't stop myself. I laugh out loud.

India's eyes fly open and she glares at me. I try not to smile too broadly but I can't help it.

Then, India can't help but laugh in response either and soon, we're both laughing our heads off. We stand together, my hands on her shoulders, my forehead pressed against hers and we just laugh.

"Jesus *Christ*," I manage, my eyes wet from laughing so hard. "One fucking kiss and we're found out."

India wipes her own eyes. "Well, it was more than just a kiss. I'd say you definitely got to second base."

I smile and pull her closer, and she slides her arms around my neck.

"More than second, if you think of it. I mean, I was sucking your nipples," I say and run my fingers over her breast, over her nipple, which is still hard underneath her bra. "That has to count at least for half-way between second and third."

We stand in each other's arms and enjoy the moment.

"So, are we going to do this?" she asks.

I run a finger down her throat to her breast. "Do what?"

She narrows her eyes, because she knows that I know exactly what she means.

"Do whatever this is." She points between us.

"What is this?"

"No," she says, shaking her head. "I want you to answer."

I grin. "What do you want it to be?"

"I want it to be real."

"Oh, it's real," I say and press my hips against her so that she can feel my erection, which hasn't calmed down just yet.

She groans when she feels it. I want her to imagine how it would feel inside of her.

"I don't want to share you," she says, and I know that's the real issue. That's what's holding her back.

"I'm not into threesomes," I reply, jokingly because I would definitely be with India.

She pulls back and forces me to look in her eyes. "I mean it. I want you to mean it, too. If you can't be exclusive, I don't want to start anything."

"It's already started, India. In case you didn't realize that sucking a woman's nipples usually means you're intimate."

"You're in the heat of the moment. You're vulnerable to my womanly charms."

"I am," I say with a chuckle. "Very vulnerable. But I've been vulnerable to your womanly charms since I met you. It was you who resisted me."

She pulls out of my arms and puts some distance between us. "We should hold off and think about this. Think about what it will mean to our business relationship. To our futures. I don't want to fuck things up."

"I want to fuck you," I say and move back closer to her, pulling her hard against my body. "Tell me you don't want to just finish things right now, with me bending you over there on the desk like I've imagined."

She closes her eyes. "You imagined that?"

I don't reply. Instead I pull her against me harder.

Yeah, I imagined it. I imagined taking her in my office so many times, or her office – or the staff lounge – hell, anywhere. My body wants it. Her body wants it. I don't understand why she's so damn afraid of just doing what we both want and need.

"We need to seriously think about this before anything else happens, Jon." She pulls away again.

"Okay," I say, disappointment and frustration in my voice. "If you want us to think about it, we will. How long do I have to think about it?"

"How long do you think we need?"

"India," I say with a sigh. "I've been thinking about it for years."

"And yet you've never acted on it."

I nod. "Because I know you. I know you don't want something simple and easy. You want something difficult."

"So, what's changed?"

I shake my head and glance away, running my hand through my hair. "I don't know," I reply and turn back to her. "All I know is that I want you now. If not now, when?"

"A week."

"A week?"

A fucking week?

"It's barely any time."

"I thought maybe a day or two. Seven fucking days?" I turn back and look in her eyes. "How will I get through seven days and seven nights?"

"You'll figure it out. I need time away from you to know if I can handle it. If I can trust you."

"You don't think you can trust me?"

"Jon," she says softly. "You're a manwhore."

"All right, a week," I reply, not wanting to argue with her on that particular point. "But I don't know whether I'll be able to last."

She smiles coyly. "I'm sure you can take matters into your own hands."

I laugh out loud at that. "Oh, believe me, I can. I already do. In fact, in the last few days, I've been busier than usual, imagining you."

She closes her eyes, and I wonder what she's thinking about my admission that I've been beating off to fantasies of us together.

"Well, at least you'll keep busy," she says with a smile.

"What about you?" I fold my arms. "How will you get through the week?"

"I'll manage," she says lightly, trying hard to hide a smile but failing. "I'm very handy."

"Oh, *God*." My body responds to the image of India getting herself off. "Now I won't be able to not imagine you with your hands on yourself." I look back at her, wanting her right now, not certain I can wait that long. "Couldn't we just say until Friday night?"

"No," she says firmly. "We should take an entire week. Not spend any time with each other except at work. No going to the bar. No going out for brunch or supper. Really think about whether we want what we already have to be put in jeopardy over something as animal as lust."

"I'm an animal and I lust, India. There's nothing wrong with it."

"There isn't, unless it ruins things and we stop being partners," she replies. "You have to decide how much our partnership means to you. Whether breaking that wall is worth the effort and whether being lovers is worth the risk."

I say nothing and just look at her, my eyes moving over her body from her head to her toes and back again, but I'm sure she's more than worth the effort and risk.

"I already know, but if you really want to wait a week, I'll comply. But," I say and go closer to her, one hand at her waist, pulling her against my body once more. I stroke her cheek with the back of my fingers. "I'm not a patient man. Three days should be good enough"

I wait for her response.

"Seven days." Her eyes widen in expectation.

"Okay," I say quietly, because I can tell she's not going to give an inch on this. "But it's not necessary on my part. I know what I want. Don't you?"

She shakes her head. Then, she smiles. "I know what I want, but it may not be good for me – for us."

"Sometimes, you have to just take a risk."

"Easy to say," she replies, her voice soft.

"Easy to do," I say, leaning closer, my lips just an inch from hers. "There's something my instructor told me when I was learning to skydive."

"What's that?"

"Just jump."

"My father always said don't jump out of a perfectly serviceable airplane."

"You don't know how good it can be until you try." We stare each other down. "It'll be torture waiting an entire week."

"You'll survive," she says. "We really have to think this through and be sure."

I don't know if I'll survive. The idea of us being together...

"I already have thought this through, India, but you go ahead and take a week." I run a hand over her hair. "I don't need a week." I slide my fingers beneath her hair, then I bend down and kiss her.

Our kiss is deep and passionate. For the first time, I feel like I'm finally going to get exactly what I've wanted all these years.

We've always played around, joking about the two of us, but it's no longer a joke.

WE ADJUST our clothes and India leaves my office, returning to her own across the hall from mine. I go to the door and glance out to find Grant standing at the photocopier in the alcove by the supply room. He glances up and sees me, so I decide to go and have a word with him about what he saw.

"Honestly, I had no idea you guys were... um..." he says and shrugs helplessly. "In the office so early." He's got a shit-eating grin on his face and I know we'll never live this down. It'll spread through the staff at the head office and then it'll fan out to the other satellite offices in DC and New York.

Crap... I know India won't like that.

Just then, India walks over to where we stand. She still looks a little flustered.

I smile at Grant, my hand on Grant's shoulder.

"You know, Grant, what you saw in there goes nowhere. I'm not telling and India's not telling, so if anyone so much as says a word about it to me or India, or either of us hear about it from anyone, I'll know it was you who spilled. You can consider your job over at that point. Do you understand?"

Grant glances between India and me, his eyes wide. "Ah, of course, sure," he says, and his voice wavers. "I'd never gossip about you two, but you have to know everyone already believes you two are a couple."

I frown. "What?"

"Oh, yeah. All the staff think you two are in love and secretly carrying on an affair, but don't want us to know. It's common knowledge."

"It's not true," India says, and then glances at me. "We aren't having an affair."

"Not yet," I say and pat Grant on the back. "We're thinking about it."

Grant holds his hands up. "Look, it doesn't matter to me. I think you two belong together. But if you don't want me to say anything about this morning, I'll keep it zipped."

"Don't say anything, please," India says, her voice pleading.

"At least, not yet," I say, eyeing her. "We'll be the ones who confirm it."

"If it's confirmed," she says.

I frown. "I *hope* it is," I say emphatically.

She says nothing in reply. I thought she wanted me as much as I wanted her. The kiss and the way she said *fuck it* earlier seemed to suggest that.

Now, I'm not so certain.

I know I want her. That much is undeniable, considering the way my body reacts to her and how often I think of her. I thought she was just as eager based on how she responded to me.

If Grant hadn't interrupted us I'd probably be in the throes of an orgasm right this moment, deep inside India.

Which sounds pretty damn good.

"No problem," Grant says. "I hope you two get together. Seriously, everyone expects to hear that you're getting married, so it would be a real let-down to find out you guys weren't even dating."

"We'll let you – and everyone else – know when the time is right."

"Sounds good," Grant says and then points to the hallway containing the offices. "If you don't mind, I'll go and get some work done."

"Later," I say and we watch Grant walk down the hallway, popping into his office.

"Phew," India says and wipes her brow dramatically. "That was close."

"It was really bad timing," I reply, my hands on my hips. I can't help but frown, upset that we were interrupted and that now, India has time to rethink things.

"It was good luck. We have to be sure," she says and comes closer, touching my face. "We have a beautiful relationship now. If things don't work out, and most relationships don't, it will be hard when we break up."

"You see, you're already thinking the worst."

"I'm being a realist."

"You're being a pessimist," I reply. "I always think that whatever is meant to happen will happen and it'll be for the best."

She shakes her head and steps back. "It won't be for the best if my heart gets broken when you find someone better to fuck."

"I'm not interested in you just because you're going to be a fantastic fuck, India."

She stands there and stares at me. "It's all so easy for you to just start this with no hesitation? You're not the least bit worried about us becoming involved?"

I move closer and slip my arm around her waist, pulling her close. She tries to resist, but I'm bigger and stronger. Despite her resistance, she finally gives in and lets me embrace her.

"I've wanted you for years," I say, my voice low and throaty.

She doesn't say anything but her eyes are soft.

I lean down and try to kiss her, but she leans back, one finger over my lips.

"One week, Jon. Those are my terms. After that, if we decide to go forward, I'm all yours when we, you know. Do it."

"When we *do it*?" I say, grinning.

"You know what I mean," she replies, unable to keep a smile off her lips.

"I do, and I look forward to when we *do it*. Which I expect will be a lot. If I had my way, I'd take you into my office right now, close the door and strip you naked, then eat and fuck you till you screamed my name."

She closes her eyes at that and I'm glad that at least I can elicit a response in her. She won't kiss me, so I finally release her and she turns away like she has to leave, and quickly, or she'll change her mind.

As for me, my pulse is racing once more from the feel of her body in my arms and at the thought of us finally – *finally* – fucking. I walk down the hallway to my office, wishing I could just take her hand and pull her with me, strip off her clothes, and do exactly what I've imagined for years. Eating and fucking India.

One day, she *will* let me take her into my office and I *will* do exactly that, just the way I want.

I SPEND the rest of the morning recovering from my encounter with India and Grant's discovery of us on the verge of truly getting it on. It's hard to focus on work, but I try, reading over the latest quarterly reports from our competitor so we can keep one step ahead of them. They have new tech in development that might be better than our latest, so we have to keep up on things.

I look at the design specs of our latest drone and think about how it might have helped India's brother when he was deployed in Iraq. This is what keeps me busy and dedicated to Pacifica – the desire to develop technology that improves things for soldiers in war zones.

When my watch says noon, I decide to acknowledge the grumbling in my stomach and grab my jacket, deciding to go down the street to get some food.

I see India leave her office.

"Hey," I call out. She keeps going, like she wants to pretend she didn't hear me. She gets to the front entry before I catch up. "Where are you going?"

"Home," she says, turning after she gets to the front door, a sheepish expression on her face. "I'm taking the rest of the day off."

"You were going to leave without saying anything?"

"I usually do," she says. "Nothing's changed."

"Everything's changed, India," I reply, frowning. "I'm waiting for your answer."

"I'm waiting for yours as well," she says, her voice low. She glances down the hallway to Grant's office a few doors away. "In case you didn't remember that this is a two-way thing."

"I already gave you my answer. I'm being patient with you, letting you take some time to say yes."

She takes her hand off the doorknob and gives me a stare. "You're obviously not taking this very seriously, if that's the case. This is serious. We can't fuck this up."

"We won't. We'll do what's right."

She shakes her head and sighs audibly. "You're so sure about this?"

I step closer. "I've never been more sure of anything."

I bend down and kiss her and she lets me this time, offering no resistance.

Then Grant comes out into the hallway. When he sees us, he

turns right back around and goes back into his office, a grin on his face.

"Crap," India says and pulls away from me. "I'll talk to you tomorrow."

"Okay," I say and watch her leave.

Then I turn leave to get my lunch, wondering how I'll make it through the week.

# CHAPTER NINE

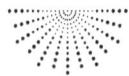

INDIA

I ARRIVE BACK HOME and flop down on the sofa, my channel changer in hand, and stare blankly at the television. I flip between channels, but nothing catches my interest. My mind is still going over my almost-sexual encounter with Jon.

What the hell have I done?

My cell dings and I check to see who's texting me.

It's Marina, of course. The very last person I want to talk to, considering.

Oh, God... What do I tell her about what happened? She'll absolutely kill me if she finds out that Jon and I almost got the dirty on.

MARINA: *What's up, sug? Where are you? Why did you bail on Evan Saturday night? You didn't like him?*

INDIA: *He really wasn't my type.*

MARINA: *What do you mean? He's a perfect match for you, according to MATCHED. 100% match was the score.*

99

*INDIA: Are you sure you used the right questionnaire for me? He and I did not click at all. In fact, I couldn't wait to escape. He reminds me of my father, and not in a good way. I don't want my father. I want a hunky sexy man in my bed. Someone who knows what he wants and takes it. Confident. Alpha. Not Mr. Metrosexual Man Bun.*

*MARINA: Oh, you! You're just as bad as Jon. He skipped out on his date as well. What am I going to do with you two? I'll have to look down the list and see who's next best. I'll set up a date this Thursday. How's that sound? Do you prefer a dinner date or some other kind of event?*

*INDIA: Maybe we should lay off the date this week. Jon and I have a lot on our plates. We have another meeting at the Pentagon to prepare for.*

*MARINA: You got a second meeting? That's great!*

*INDIA: Yeah, so maybe we should focus on that instead of our love lives.*

*MARINA: Okay, but I have some good candidates for you. Let me look through them and get back to you. When you get back from Washington, we can do another meet and greet. Maybe this coming Saturday?*

*INDIA: Okay, if you insist...*

Of course, I have no interest in another one of Marina's matches. Zero for two is not a good track record. Her match for Jon wasn't much better.

*MARINA: When are you and Jon going to DC?*

*INDIA: Wednesday. We'll be back on Friday.*

*MARINA: Okay. Saturday night, you'll both have a new date. I'll pick someone out for each of you, and maybe this match will work out better.*

*INDIA: If you think so.*

*MARINA: I know so. I've been working on the questionnaire*

*and I think it's working even better now. Give it a chance. You'll see. I have an instinct for this.*

INDIA: *Uh huh...*

MARINA: *Don't you uh huh me, sug. I got this.*

INDIA: *Later.*

MARINA:

I shut off my brain and turned back to the latest episode of *OITNB*, trying to lose my own troubles by focusing on the troubles of the girls in jail.

Their problems make mine look like successes.

THE NEXT DAY I spend an awkward morning at the office, avoiding Jon as much as I can, ducking into my office when I see him coming down the hall, hiding in the bathroom when he's out by the water cooler talking to staff. But I can't avoid him during our weekly meeting to set the agenda for the week. We always do the meeting together, sharing the duties.

I go into his office a half hour before the meeting to make sure we have the agenda down.

"Hey," I say and plop down on the chair across from his desk.

"Hey," he replies. "How are you? Recovered from yesterday?"

"I'm fine." I quickly change the subject. "What's on the agenda for this week, besides our trip to DC?"

We discuss the big project and the various tasks we have to get done this month, and who will be lead on each one. I draw up an agenda on my laptop while we speak, print it off quickly, and we discuss it. After a final revision, I leave his office, glad he didn't say anything else about what happened on Sunday.

I pass the staff room and see Grant there, sitting on a sofa, talking to a couple of our staff. He sees me and stops talking, then nods to me. I hope he isn't gossiping about Jon and me getting undressed in his office or I won't be able to face the rest of the staff.

I spend the rest of the day hiding from Jon. I try my best to avoid doing what we would usually do together – coffee, lunch, more coffee, an after-work drink at the local watering hole, maybe a late supper after another couple of hours of work.

In other words, things are not back to normal between us. In fact, they have never been so estranged.

We're scheduled to fly to Washington on separate flights because I cancelled my seat and quickly arranged a meeting with staff that prevented me from travelling with Jon. When Liz tells Jon that we're taking separate flights, I see a muscle in his jaw pulse.

He turns to me, his eyes narrowed. "I thought we could use the time to talk about the meeting, but I guess not."

"You can always text me."

"Yeah, right."

He grabs my arm and pulls me down the hall and into the stockroom, closing the door behind him.

"You're not going to avoid me completely for the rest of the week."

"I'm going to do exactly that," I reply. "I need to keep my distance. No more sneaking in kisses and gropes to influence my decision."

"India," he says, exasperated. "We have to work together this week. We need to talk."

"We'll talk about business. If you need to ask about something, just arrange a meeting."

He lets go of my arm and I leave the stockroom, noting the barely-suppressed grin on Liz's face as I pass her.

"What are you smiling about?" I ask, stopping directly in front of her.

"Nothing," she says. "You two are so cute."

"What?" I lean forward. "What do you mean by that?"

"You know," she says, a coy smile on her face. "Sneaking into the stockroom like that for – well, whatever."

"Have you been talking to Grant?"

"No," she says and frowns. "It's just that we all know you two are in love."

"We aren't in love," I say, more forcefully than I intend. "We're partners. Business partners. Nothing else."

Liz shrugs. "Sorry. We all thought..."

"You all thought wrong."

I turn on my heel and march to my office. When I get to my door, I turn and see Jon come out of the stock room with a couple of packs of paper in his arms. He's pretending that he needed some photocopier paper and that's why he went into the stock room.

Yeah, right.

It's not like Jon loads paper in the photocopier on a regular basis.

"I can do that," Liz says and steps around her desk, taking the paper out of Jon's arms.

"Thanks," Jon says and comes down the hallway. He shrugs helplessly and smiles at me.

I enter my office and close the door behind me. Once alone, I lean against it and close my eyes.

One stupid kiss and look where we are now – the entire office thinks we're in love and hiding in the stockroom so we can get it on.

I sit behind my desk, open my laptop, and try to finish work on my new project.

Plus, I have to get some work done before I have my fake meeting with a few staff tomorrow morning about something I could have put off until after the trip. I just didn't want to spend the entire day with Jon, waiting at the airport, on the plane together, on whatever layover we might have, then waiting for luggage, taking a taxi together to the hotel, and then dinner at the hotel or whatever.

Later that afternoon, Jon pops his head in my office.

"I'm going home early. I guess I'll see you Thursday morning before the meeting. Should we meet for coffee? Go over the presentation?"

"Sounds good," I reply without looking at him. "I'll text you once I arrive."

"Okay."

I nod and glance at him, feeling like I have to make eye contact at least once before he leaves. He has this expression in his eyes that is somewhere between amused and angry.

I hear him sigh heavily like he's resigned to my efforts to put a distance between us.

The door closes behind him and I relax, leaning back in my chair.

I close my eyes for a few moments, relieved that he's gone and out of my hair for at least twenty hours. Maybe now I can focus on work instead of imagining what it would be like if the two of us were lovers on top of being business partners.

AFTER MY TOTAL-WASTE-OF-TIME meeting with my staff, I grab my luggage and bag and take a taxi to the airport, checking in and sitting in the lounge to wait for my flight.

Of course, I get a text from Jon.

JON: *I'm in the airport in Atlanta waiting for my flight to Washington. You really should have come with me. I have a beautiful first-class seat and you would have had one too if you weren't so damn stubborn.*

I can't help but smile at his obvious frustration and attempt to make me regret my decision.

*INDIA: You always told me that my stubbornness is why I'm successful. I refuse to compromise. I want the best and am willing to work – or wait – to get it. That's true. I want the best, Jon. In all parts of my life.*

*JON: You've made that perfectly clear. Let me know when you have your answer. I can wait.*

I can tell that he's frustrated. If he had his way, we'd be going at it in the airport bathroom right now. That thought makes me squirm a bit and I feel a little breathless at the thought. Knowing him, he'd wear me out.

I can't help but think I want him to wear me out.

I want to feel well-used, my body aching from him and for him.

MY TRIP GOES AS PLANNED, with only a short delay when I get to Atlanta due to some storms in the region. I arrive in DC and gather my luggage, take a taxi to the hotel we always stay at, and I check in. It's late. I put my suitcase on the stand, turn on the television, take out my laptop, and crash on the bed.

In fact, I'm exhausted. The room is dark except for the television and my laptop. I fall asleep with the channel tuned to CNN and my laptop playing the latest Casey Neistat vlog.

A knock at my door wakes me up and I check my cell. It's after midnight.

Crap. That has to be Jon.

I check my cell and see that he's sent me seven texts that I haven't seen. The sound of the television and the videos must have drowned out the sound of my cell dinging when each text arrived. I scroll through his texts quickly. He sent me a text earlier asking if he can come by and talk.

Yeah, right.

Talk. People don't talk at this late at night.

They fuck.

The next text is from a few minutes later.

*JON: Are you in your room? I think we should talk. I have a bottle of wine.*

Fifteen minutes later:

*JON: It's really good wine. Nice body. I promise I won't touch you. I just want to talk. No nookie. I promise.*

Another fifteen minutes:

*JON: Are you purposely ignoring me? Come on, India. We're almost best friends. I need my ABFF.*

An hour later:

*JON: You haven't answered my text. Are you okay?*

Another fifteen minutes later:

*JON: Please respond so I know you're alive and not abducted by some serial killer who stalks expensive hotels.*

Another text comes, almost two hours after the first.

*JON: This wine is almost gone. Actually, it's completely gone. I hope you know that I blame you.*

Finally, a text from five minutes earlier.

*JON: I'll be right there.*

I get up and check the peephole and sure enough, there's Jon, leaning against the wall, his arm outstretched, holding himself up. He glances up, then presses his face to the peephole and all I can see is his blue eye.

"Jon," I say, frustrated. "Go back to your room and go to sleep. We have an important meeting tomorrow."

"I'm drunk."

He laughs, grinning like an idiot.

"Shh," I say, afraid he'll wake up other hotel guests. "Keep your voice down."

"I will if you let me in," he says and holds up a bottle of wine. "I have some more wine left. It's really good."

"Go back to your room and drink some water, take an aspirin. General Newton won't appreciate it if you're hungover."

"General Newton can go fuck himself," Jon says. "Let me in or I'll start serenading you with a love song."

Oh, God.

"Jon, stop this. Go back to your room. "

Then he starts singing, a horrible drunk warble.

*I can't liiiiiiiive...*

Oh, my *God*, he's singing 'Without You' by Harry Nilsson. He is so drunk. I cover my eyes and try not to laugh because as funny as he is, he's making a scene.

I open the door and he stumbles in, mid-sentence.

*"Can't liiiiiive anymooooore..."*

I have to catch him when he falls into the room.

"Oh, so sorry," he says, a half-grin on his face, his arm around my shoulder. "Not very good on my feet for some reason."

"Half a bottle of wine?" I say, checking the bottle he hands me. "Is that all you've had?"

"Well, there was another bottle..."

"Jon!" I stare open-mouthed at him. "That's way too much."

"It was over several hours, so..." He flops on the bed. "I think I need to lie down for a while."

Then he passes out.

He actually passes out. Within about five minutes, he's snoring.

I'm afraid that he'll puke and drown in his own vomit, so I roll him over on his side. He doesn't fight me. Instead, he pulls up his knees and licks his lips before falling back into unconsciousness.

I sit beside him and listen to him breathe.

He figured out a way to sleep in my room, in my bed, with me. I have to hand it to him – he figured out probably the only way I'd let him do it.

Usually, I'd go into the bedroom and get into my pajamas, brush my teeth and then crawl under the covers and go to sleep. With Jon lying on the bed, drunk, I don't. He's young enough to recover quickly from too much wine and sneak under the covers with me.

If he did, and if he got his hands on me, I don't know if I could resist him.

So, instead of my usual routine, I go the bathroom and brush my teeth, and then I take a pillow over to the sofa, grab an extra blanket from the closet, and fall asleep to the sounds of Jon's intermittent snores and the talking heads on CNN.

.

"OH, DAMN," I hear Jon say when he wakes in the morning. I crack an eyelid and see that he's sitting up at the side of the bed, rubbing his eyes. He glances in my direction and our eyes meet. "Sorry. What a jerk."

"My thoughts exactly," I say, but can't stop a smile.

"It's not funny," he says, rubbing the heel of his palms against his temples. "I have a raging headache."

"Serves you right. Harry Nilsson? At 12:38 a.m.?"

He shakes his head. "I seem to recall singing a verse or two. I thought you loved the seventies."

"I loved Harry Nilsson's version. Yours left little to be desired." I sit up and stretch. The clock radio beside the bed reads six forty-three. We have a meeting in two hours and fifteen minutes at the Pentagon.

"I better go back to my room and shower." He stands up and gives me a smile. "Sorry about last night."

"It's okay. It'll be one of those stories I get to tell the rest of my life whenever I want to embarrass you."

He points to the door. "My room's just down the hallway. Can you bring me some fresh coffee, black, in about fifteen minutes?"

I nod. "I have to have a shower first, but I'll get us some coffee from the café downstairs. You should take some aspirin and drink some water."

He nods and walks to the door. "See you in fifteen."

I get up after he's left, smiling at the memory of him singing, and have a quick shower. I brush my teeth and get dressed for the meeting, choosing a silk blouse and pencil skirt. Then, I take my laptop and bag and go down to the cafeteria and get us some coffee, two bottles of orange juice, plus a couple of Danishes. That will have to do for our breakfast.

I take the elevator back up, wondering how Jon will be when I arrive. Contrite? Apologetic?

I go to his room and find that the door is held open by the deadbolt.

"Jon?" I say as I open the door and enter the hotel room. "I've got coffee and Danishes."

The room is empty, but the door to the bathroom is closed and I can hear water running.

He's still in the bathroom.

I start to say, "I'll just leave the coffee and come back later," but the door opens and there's Jon, half naked with just a wisp of a towel around his waist, tucked in low on his hips so that I can see his amazing washboard abs over a very ample bulge. His chest is magnificent – broad, his pecs well-developed, his biceps bulging, an amazing tribal tattoo on his arm and chest.

God, he's gorgeous. A surge of desire flows through my body at the sight of him, standing in the bathroom doorway, his hair wet and falling into his eyes in that sexy way...

"Stay," he says. "I won't be long."

I go into the room and put the food and coffee cups down on the desk. While he finishes whatever he's doing in the bathroom, I sit on the bed and turn up the volume on the television. It's tuned to CNBC and two talking heads are discussing the stock market's latest heights. A stock ticker runs along the bottom of the screen.

Jon comes out of the bathroom and opens the closet door, removing his suit and shirt from hangers. Then, he proceeds to slip on his shirt.

"Are you going to get dressed in front of me?"

He fastens his cuffs. "Nothing's stopping you from looking away if you want."

I glance away, staring out the window, through the curtains at the city beyond. I clench my fists, angered that he's being so damn provocative.

"Are you trying to turn me on by getting dressed in front of me?"

"Is it working?"

I laugh out loud. "No," I say, although the prospect of seeing Jon completely naked is very tempting.

"Then no harm, no foul."

He finishes dressing while I watch out the window, unable to stop smiling at his audacity. Was he really hoping that seeing him get dressed would turn me on so much that I'd jump his bones for a quickie before our meeting?

Men are such strange creatures.

"You're thinking like a man," I say, still grinning. "That might work in reverse, but not with a woman."

"Damn," he says, his voice amused. "Can't blame a guy for trying."

He goes to the desk and picks up one of the bottles of orange juice and hands it to me. "Here. A peace offering."

I take it from him and force a smile. I've been so discombobulated by his antics that I forgot to drink one. Oh, he's enjoying this. He's enjoying my discomfort.

Then, while I watch, he grabs a Danish and eats it with gusto. He turns to me. "It's really good. Do you want one?"

I nod, because I need some sugar if I'm going to make it through this next two hours.

Jon sits on the bed beside me, and together we eat our breakfasts and watch the news in silence for a few moments. When I'm done, I wipe my hands on the napkin he hands me and take another sip of my coffee.

"Should we go over the presentation?"

He nods. When I stand up, he grabs my hand and stops me.

"I'm sorry I was such an idiot last night." He squeezes my hand. "I can't resist you." Then he opens my palm, kissing it, his lips pressed against my skin. "I don't want to ruin things between us. I just got a bit carried away."

He looks up into my eyes, and I can't help but feel my heart squeeze a bit at his expression. So serious.

"It's okay." I smile at him and try to pull my hand out of his, but he doesn't let me. Instead, he kisses it again.

Then he pulls me close so that I'm standing between his thighs and my face is almost level with his.

"Jon," I whisper, because I can tell where this is leading.

"*India*," he says, his voice soft. He pulls me against him and looks in my eyes. "I want you to know that I care very deeply about you. And not just as a business partner. As a person. As a woman."

I can't help but rest my hands on his shoulders.

I don't know what to say. I don't want to say, "I know," which feels like the right thing to say, because I don't know.

"A week, Jon. A full week."

"I've had more than enough time to know what I want," he says softly. "I want you."

Then he pulls my head down and kisses me and I'm so overwhelmed with emotions and desire that I let him. I feel such emotion in that moment that I almost gasp for breath from the strength of it. Our arms go around each other more tightly. When the kiss ends, he buries his face in my neck, kissing the skin beneath my ear, and despite everything, I close my eyes and just let it happen.

Then he's kissing my throat and the swell above my breasts, his hands pulling my body closer.

"We don't have much time," I say, my mind going to mundane things like what time our meeting is and whether I can do this, even though my body is wet and swollen already at the touch of his lips on my skin.

"I won't need it," he murmurs against my breast. He bites my nipple through the fabric and I groan, closing my eyes.

I know I won't need it either.

Am I going to let this happen?

He squeezes one of my buttocks, then unbuttons my blouse and I realize I am. I'm going to let him do this.

I'm going to let him fuck me – finally.

The thought of it makes my core throb almost painfully, because I need him to fill me up, to pound me hard and make me orgasm the way I've imagined for years. The next thing I know, my blouse is off, and I'm unlatching my bra and he's once again sucking my nipples like he can't get enough of me. He buries his face between them, squeezing and sucking until I'm squirming in need.

He stands up and turns me around, pointing to my skirt. "Take it off."

I comply, and while he removes his shirt and slacks, I'm unzipping the back of my skirt, letting it fall to the ground, leaving only my thong on. He's wearing a pair of black Joe Boxer boxer-briefs, his erection outlined clearly through the fabric.

My thong is skimpy see-through lace, flesh-colored, showing my very neatly trimmed pussy. When he pushes me back onto the bed, I almost laugh but then he drops his briefs and I get a look at what has been rumored, by those women of his who have talked about him, to be very thick and long.

They weren't exaggerating. It's both.

Knowing it will soon be inside of me makes my breath catch in my throat. I want to be impaled on him, and I don't care what position. Him on top. Me on top. From behind. Reverse cowgirl. It doesn't matter. All I want is to feel him in me.

He pushes me farther up on the bed and when I reach down to remove my thong, he stops me with his hands.

"No," he says firmly. "Let me."

He licks me over the thin fabric, pressing his tongue exactly over my clit, which is throbbing in delight. Then, he strips them off me and throws them onto the floor. He spreads my thighs, his head hovering over my pussy, his eyes taking me in, roving over my body from my face down to my clit, which he's exposed with his fingers, spreading me wide.

"Nice and wet," he murmurs and bends down, covering me with his mouth, his tongue finding my clit and stroking firmly.

"Oh, God," I groan, and close my eyes. It feels so good and I know I'll orgasm quickly if he keeps that up.

He does keep it up, licking me firmly, then swirling his tongue over my entire slit, tonguing the entrance to my body, then slipping a finger inside me.

"So wet," he says again. "So ready."

He slips another finger inside me, then resumes licking and sucking my clit. Before I can warn him, I'm over the edge, the pleasure like fire through my veins, down my thighs and up into my chest.

"Oh, God, I'm coming," I say, and feel the first spasms of my flesh around his fingers, the pleasure so exquisite I'm panting from it. He doesn't stop through my orgasm, just keeps licking me and sucking me, his fingers stroking inside of me. My pleasure goes on and on until it's too much and I have to stop him, pushing away his head.

"No, stop, please – it's too much..."

He finally stops, his fingers still inside me, his mouth poised over my pussy.

"That was fast," he says, grinning up at me like he's won. "You were ready."

I lie back, my eyes closed, not wanting to see the victory on his face and in his eyes. Yeah, I was fast. I haven't been eaten or fucked for a very long time. Having Jon eat me until I come is like the biggest turn-on I could imagine, and has populated my masturbatory fantasies for months.

Hell, a year...

"Don't relax just yet," he says and leans up, his fingers still deep inside of me, and kisses me. I can taste my saltiness on his tongue. He thumbs my clit, which is still swollen, pulsing occasionally in the aftermath of my orgasm. "I want another one of those, this time with my cock inside you."

"You're in charge," I say, my eyes closed, my arms thrown up over my head.

"I am," he says and I can hear the pleasure in his voice. He begins to suck my nipples once more. I'm not sure I can come again, but my core still feels achy and he may be able to work me up again if I just relax. I try to turn my mind off, turn off my awareness of the time and the reality of what's happening, and focus on how good it feels to have his mouth on me, sucking my nipple, biting it gently while his fingers continue to move inside me, his thumb pressing beside my clit, stroking all around it, avoiding direct contact.

He's damn good at this.

He finally pulls his fingers out of my body and it's then I realize we don't have a condom.

"A condom," I say, my eyes flying open.

He rises, reaching over to his bag on the bed, and unzips a compartment. He searches inside it and removes a two-pack of condoms, ripping one open and then unrolling it over his erection.

Then he kneels between my thighs, and begins to stroke my pussy with the head of his cock. I'm so wet from his mouth and my own orgasm that it feels amazing, and I squirm beneath him.

"Squeeze your breasts for me," he says in a throaty voice. "Pinch your own nipples."

I do what he asks and watch him watching me, his eyes moving from my breasts to my pussy where he strokes his cock over my clit.

"I'm going to fuck you now," he says in a low husky voice. "I'm going to make you come again."

I don't say anything because I know he's right, and he will.

# CHAPTER TEN

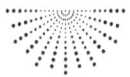

## JON

I HOLD off for as long as I can from entering India's body, wanting to build her up far enough so that she'll come again. She's still wet and ready. I want to hear her cry out when she comes on my cock.

That will be sweet victory.

I want to come while her body spasms around me. Timing it just right will take skill, but I'm determined to succeed. I enter her just enough to stretch her out while my thumb does slow circles around her hard, swollen clit. In and out, circle and stroke.

"Tell me when you're close," I say, watching her body for signs of her impending orgasm. She's breathing fast and shallow; her nipples are swollen and her eyes are half-lidded. She is magnificent – beautiful and hot and my cock is so hard now, I know that a couple minutes of fast thrusting will push me over because she's so tight, despite how wet she is.

She hasn't been fucked for a while. The thought that I am her first in a long time makes me even harder. I want to claim her as my own. I want to possess her cries of pleasure, see her eyes roll up in her head from how intense it is.

I slide deeper inside her, thumbing her clit, one hand squeezing her breast. Now, I'm completely inside of her and she moans beneath me. She likes how thick I am and I know that once I start to thrust, it won't take long. The skin on her chest is mottled, and it's rising up to her neck.

She's so close.

I begin to thrust, slowly, deliberately, pulling out each time to stroke my cock over her slit, her clit, before pushing inside again. I repeat this over and over, until I'm very close and I have to breathe deeply to prevent my own orgasm.

"Tell me when you're ready," I say, thrusting several times before I pull out and stroke her entire slit with my cock. "Tell me to fuck you hard," I say, wanting to see her let go.

I thrust harder, longer, and pull out again, push inside again.

"Oh, God," she says, "fuck me harder."

I do, filling her up, thrusting deep and hard, until my balls slap against her ass, her thighs lifted up and spread wide. I keep my thumb on her clit while I pound her and then I see it – see her lose control. Her eyes roll up and I thrust faster, turning myself over to my own orgasm, certain of hers. Her cunt spasms around my cock as I pound her, and then my orgasm begins, the pleasure almost blinding me, my balls tightening, my cock pulsing with spasm after spasm as I ejaculate.

"Oh, fuck..."

I ram myself deep inside of her, the pleasure peaking as I come, waves of pleasure washing over my body from my balls to my thighs to my head.

I finish and lean over her, my arms on either side of her shoulders, my face beside hers. Both of us are breathing hard, lost in the sensations.

It was so fucking good...

*So* fucking good.

My cock spasms and I feel her cunt convulse around me. I rise and rest on my hands, watching her as she lies beneath me. Her nipples are hard buds but her body is otherwise slack, her thighs spread wide, my cock still buried inside her.

She's so beautiful.

She's mine now.

This is happening. *Finally.*

When she opens her eyes, there's a moment of recognition on her part that we've done this. We're into it now. No more delaying. No more excuses.

"Jon," she says, and I know what she's going to say, but I stop her, my finger to her lips.

"No, don't say a word."

She looks in my eyes and I know she wants to protest or say 'we can't do this' or whatever she thinks has to be said. It doesn't have to be said. I already know all her excuses and reasons why we can't be a couple.

It's all bullshit.

This – this great fuck – this *fantastic* fuck – just means that we should be together.

And we will be. We are.

"You're mine," I say.

"But –"

I bend down and kiss into silence what I know will be her meek protests. I kiss her deeply, emotions welling up inside of me. Possession. Ownership. Lust.

We kiss like we both mean it and when I pull back, she's silent, not protesting, and I think that maybe she realizes that this is happening and there's no stopping it now.

I'm going to indulge myself in her body until she's so satiated from my mouth and my cock that she's almost drunk on it.

*After* our meeting at the Pentagon.

Then I come back to the present and look at the clock radio beside my bed.

Damn. We have exactly forty-five minutes to get dressed, go over the presentation, and drive to the Pentagon.

It'll be close.

"We better get ready," I say, kissing her breast, biting gently on her nipple. "As much as I'd like to make you come again, we have a contract to negotiate."

"We do," she says, smiling softly up at me.

My cock is still semi-erect and I could come again if we had time, but we don't.

"I don't want to pull out of you," I murmur against her neck, kissing her throat. "But I have to."

"You do," she replies and when I lean up, she's smiling, her eyes closed. She runs her hands through her hair and I know she's basking in the delicious after-effects of her two orgasms. "I don't know if my brain will work after what you did to me."

I laugh, and suck on her nipple once more, running my tongue around the hard areola. She squirms beneath me.

"Don't," she says in protest. "How will I be able to focus if I'm still aroused?"

"You'll have to deal," I say, grinning widely. "Maybe I better do the presentation today."

She opens her eyes. "Do you want to?"

"No," I say, and kiss her on the lips. "I want to watch you give it and remember how your face looks while you're coming on my cock."

"Probably ugly," she says with a laugh. "My eyes all screwed up, my jaw slack like I'm brain dead."

"Hardly," I say, and roll her over on top of me and smack her butt. "You could never be ugly. A woman in the throes of an orgasm is a thing of beauty."

"Oh, yeah?" She makes this wacky face that looks nothing like her during an orgasm and I can't help but laugh.

"I'm sure I look handsome and dashing when I'm coming."

"Oh, you do. You look like a raging bull."

I laugh again and then I stop and just look at her. "There's nothing else to compare. Seriously," I say, enjoying the way her hair falls over us. I imagine it draping over my body later as she sucks my cock. Which she is definitely going to do later, after our meeting. I'll reserve the room for another night so we can spend the entire night eating, fucking, and sucking ourselves into oblivion. "I could watch you coming forever."

She smiles and leans down to kiss me once more.

We kiss, and it's so much more meaningful than any kiss I've had in a long time.

Maybe forever.

ONCE WE'RE DRESSED and have tidied ourselves up, we do a quick run-through of the presentation and then haul our computers and files into a waiting Uber to take us to the Pentagon. I think the driver doesn't really believe us when we ask him to take us there, but he does anyway. I think about how we must look to him – two fashionable millennials. Me with hair a bit too long and a bit too much scruff on my jaw, India far too beautiful for some stuffy military facility.

But we're the dynamic duo. Brains and beauty. Ambition and lust all mixed up into a hot beautiful mess.

THE PRESENTATION GOES SMOOTHLY – as usual – and if India's orgasms scrambled her brain, it doesn't show.

In the hallway as we're walking out of the facility, escorted by a civilian employee who's there to make sure we get out safely, I lean over to her.

"Obviously, those two orgasms weren't enough to throw you off your game," I whisper. "That's good to know."

She gives me a horrified look, like the walls might have ears and learn that we're fucking and not award us the contract. I laugh at the expression on her face.

"Jon," she whispers back. "Don't talk like that in here."

"Why not? Don't you want to give the eavesdroppers working in those small dark rooms somewhere in the bowels of the Pentagon something spicy for a change?"

I wag my eyebrows at her, amused by her expression.

"You're incorrigible."

"I am," I say. "You already knew that."

She tries to hold back a smile but fails. "I did."

We bump shoulders together as we walk down the long hallway behind our escort. We say goodbye and haul our stuff into the trunk of a vehicle waiting to take us back to the hotel.

"I'm ready for more to eat," I say, eyeing her suggestively. "That little tidbit I ate this morning wasn't nearly enough."

"Jon," she says, her eyes wide.

"Feel like a nice thick sausage?"

"Jon!"

She punches me in the arm and I mock-wince. I slip my arm around her shoulder.

"This is going to be so much fun."

"It's not supposed to be fun," she says, and frowns at me.

"What do you mean? Of course, it's supposed to be fun. Otherwise, why do it?"

"No, I mean, it's not a joke."

"What makes you think I'm joking?" Then I lean closer, my mouth at her ear. "I really do want to know if you'd like a nice, hot, thick, juicy sausage, because I have one for you," I whisper, so the driver doesn't hear me. I want to spare India any embarrassment.

Or at least, too much embarrassment.

*Some* embarrassment has to be expected.

We drive the rest of the way to the hotel without further comment, because I want her to think about sucking my cock the way I've been imagining her doing for years. On her knees at my feet, my hand guiding her.

But that's for later. It's now been five hours since we ate and I'm hungry. I need some protein if I'm going to keep her busy all night long the way I plan.

While we're driving, she gets a text. I look out the window while she reads it and then she covers her mouth with a hand.

"Oh, God," she whispers.

I glance over. "What's the matter?"

"My mom," she says. "She fell while painting the house. She's in the hospital."

She dials her cell and looks at me, her eyes wide, waiting for the call to connect.

"Dad?" she says, her voice panicked. "How is she?"

There's a long pause while she listens to what he's saying.

"When? How long?"

She listens more and I'm frustrated, because I want to hear what's happening. India's parents are flakes, but they're lovable flakes.

"I'll catch the first flight out," she says, and I can hear the fear in her voice. "See you as soon as I can get there."

Then she hangs up and looks into my eyes. "She's in surgery. She had some kind of head injury and was moved right from the ER to the OR." She leans forward and asks the driver to redirect. "Drive me to the airport. I have to go back. I'll take whatever flight I can get out as soon as possible."

"Your luggage –"

"You can send it to me. I want to go right there."

"Okay," I say and pull her closer, hoping that Joanne survives whatever's happened to her. India is nothing like her flaky parents, politically, but she's her mother's daughter. Smart. Funny. Loving.

I know how devastating it would be if anything happened to her.

WE ARRIVE at the airport and India goes up to Virgin Atlantic counter, trying to get on the first flight out, but it won't be for an hour. There's a three-hour layover in Charlotte, North Carolina. She won't arrive back in San Francisco until nine p.m. local time.

"We may have enough time to drive to the hotel and get the bags."

She glances at me, her eyes wide. "I'll stay here. You go, okay? I don't want to leave in case I miss the flight because of traffic."

"Okay," I say. "I don't want to miss saying goodbye. Just in case."

She nods and we embrace, hugging each other tightly. Her eyes are wet, and she's really upset.

"Maybe I should stay," I say, concerned that she'll be alone, panicking about her mother. "I can call the hotel and get them to send our suitcases and they'll get back tomorrow. I don't want to leave you alone."

She forces a brave smile. "I'll be fine. You go and try to get everything. If you miss the flight, it won't be such a big deal, but I can't miss it."

I agree, and kiss her once more, squeezing her tightly, then I flag down a taxi and we drive off in mid-day traffic to the hotel.

· · ·

I END up missing the plane. I call India from the taxi when we're caught in traffic and there's no way I'll get back.

"Hey," she says when she answers. "Let me guess: you're not able to make it back."

"I'm so sorry," I say. "I wish I was with you and you didn't have to go on your own but there was an accident and we're being redirected."

"I wish you were with me, too," she responds. "I'm glad I didn't go back to the hotel with you. Catch the next plane out and come and see me at the hospital when you get in. I expect I'll be staying there all night depending on how she does."

"I will. Text me when you get in. I'll be thinking of you. Give your mom a hug and kiss from me. And your dad."

"I will."

While we're stalled in bumper-to-bumper traffic, I sit and re-read her texts. All of them from the last couple of days.

I wish I was sitting beside her on the plane right now, holding her hand as we take off.

I sit and stare out the window as the streets of Washington pass slowly by.

I GET TO THE AIRPORT, swap my ticket for one leaving in a couple of hours, and spend the rest of my time sitting in Virgin's first class lounge, reading a copy of the *Wall Street Journal* and watching CNBC on the television screen.

JON: *Any news about your mom?*

INDIA: *Nothing, but she has to have surgery to relieve the pressure.*

JON: *How are you holding up?*

INDIA: *I'm holding up. I think all my adrenaline ran out and now I feel like a rag doll. But I won't be able to sleep. I'll probably watch a movie or something to keep busy.*

*JON: Text me when you can. I'll drive to the hospital as soon as I get in.*

I try to keep my mind occupied, and not think about India's mom, hoping that things are going well for her and they're able to prevent any lasting damage. India won't get to SF until after nine and then she'll probably go right to the hospital.

I try to keep occupied on the flight, glad that I upgraded to the first-class section, able to at least stretch my legs out and enjoy some decent food. I think of India cramped in economy, sitting beside people who have no sympathy for her. I hope she's able to distract herself as much as possible during the trip. She'll probably watch the inflight movie, but knowing her, she'll chew her fingernails down to the quick as she worries about her mom.

MUCH, much later, after we land in LAX for our one-hour stop, I get a text from India.

*INDIA: Just called my dad. She's out of surgery but they're keeping her sedated. The doctor thinks that she has a pretty good chance of a full recovery, so it's just a matter of waiting to see how she does when they take her out of sedation.*

*JON: That's good news, at least. How's your dad holding up?*

*INDIA: He's really upset. He blames himself – he wanted to hire a painter but my mom insisted they could save money if she got up on the ladder and did it herself. He's afraid of heights and tried to stop her but she's very stubborn.*

*JON: Sounds like someone else I know...*

There's a silence, and I feel bad for teasing her at a time like this, but I was teased mercilessly when I was growing up by my father and older brothers.

*JON: I've always admired that in your mom – her independence. She's a trooper.*

*INDIA: She is. She's a top scholar in her field.*

*JON: I know. You got your brains from your mom and dad. And your dad says you got your beauty from him.*

*INDIA: I know. He's kidding, of course.*

I think of India's dad. He looks like Jeff Daniels in *Dumb and Dumber.*

*JON: He's great.*

*INDIA: I know. Oh, God, I don't know what he'd do if anything happened to her. She's such a rock.*

*JON: She is.*

*INDIA: Gibraltar. He's lucky to have had her all these years. He admits that all the time. Says that without her, he would have likely smoked and drank himself into an early grave.*

*JON: They're really happy together.*

*INDIA: They are. \*sigh\**

*JON: Keep strong. Your dad will need you.*

*INDIA: I wish you were with me.*

*JON: I will be soon.*

I GET BACK on my flight and spend the next hour thinking of India and how our lives have become so entwined.

I don't know what changed, except seeing the two idiots that Marina had the audacity to match India with – two guys so totally wrong for her that I realized how right she was for me. And then meeting Heather and realizing that was not the kind of woman I wanted to become involved with, except for a quick fuck. An alternative to masturbation. Tits and ass and pussy and that was it.

India is so much more.

# CHAPTER ELEVEN

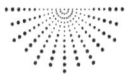

## INDIA

THE HOSPITAL IS quiet when I arrive. My mom is in surgical ICU and is on a ventilator. She looks so frail lying there on the bed, wires and tubes attached to her, the *beep beep* of the monitors making my heart race out of anxiety. I hate hospitals and I hate being in ICU, although I realize it's the best place for her given her injury.

My dad is a basket case, sitting by her bed, holding onto her hand. His face is pale, his eyes red from tears. He just sits there watching her, stroking her hand, talking to her.

He reminds her about their first date, and talks about how they took a holiday together to Alaska, driving up in an old van and watching the Northern Lights together while they camped. Seeing icebergs and being afraid of grizzly bears and polar bears, neither of which they saw.

He talks about their wedding, and how they went to

Nicaragua and got married on the beach, good Neo-Marxists who were upset about the Reagan administration's attempts to overthrow the government. How they both got *la turista* and had the runs the entire time they spent in the posh hotel.

He seems like he's trying to coax her into coming back and not dying by telling her how great their lives are together.

They do have a great relationship – one I could only be so lucky to have for myself. They are two peas in a pod. They not only share the same values and goals, they love each other with passion and affection even after thirty years. They want to spend the rest of their days together, growing old together, enjoying their retirement together.

He tells her all this, his eyes filled with tears, and it only makes me cry all the harder to see him so afraid.

"Fight," he whispers to her before he takes a break so I can go in and sit with her for a while. "Don't leave me."

He kisses her tenderly on the cheek and strokes her brow, her head wrapped in bandages. Her eyes are shut, blackened from the fall. I am so afraid that she's going to die and I'll never be able to talk to her again.

Dad leaves the room, wiping his eyes, and gives me a big hug on the way out.

"I need to get something to eat," he says. That's when Jon arrives, his eyes expectant. I go out to him, and he pulls me into his arms and we hug. I'm so glad to see him, so glad he was able to get out on the next flight and is here with me now.

"Dad, you know Jon," I say to my father, who's busy mopping his eyes with a tissue.

"Of course, I know Jon. Good heavens." The two men shake hands and Jon takes my dad's hand in both of his, squeezing, and I think it's such a nice gesture on Jon's part. I've never seen him be affectionate to another man. I guess he sees my dad and wishes his own were still alive.

My dad leaves to get something from the cafeteria vending machines and I fill Jon in on how my mom is doing.

"I'm going to sit with her for a while," I say and point to the family room, with a kitchen and sofas for family members with loved ones in the ICU. "I'll probably stay all night with dad."

"I'll stay with you," Jon says.

I smile at him. "That's okay. You don't have to stay."

"I do," he says and shakes his head, pulling me closer. "I want to stay with you."

"Remember that we have a staff meeting tomorrow to go over the contracts. One of us has to do it. You should go home and get some sleep, because I won't be in."

Jon realizes I'm right and nods. "I'll stay for a while at least," he says. "When you take a break we can sit together and talk."

"There's really no reason," I say, because I know Jon is an early riser, getting up really early for a run before going to work. "We can text. I'm with my dad. It's best that you go now and be ready for the meeting tomorrow."

He looks so reluctant, but I really don't think it's appropriate for him to be here other than to bring me my stuff. It's not like my parents know that there's anything going on between us, and frankly, at this moment, my relationship with Jon is not my first priority. It's nice he wants to be here to support me, but this is a close family matter.

"Go," I say and squeeze his hand. "I'll talk to you in the morning."

"Okay," he finally says, resigned. He slips his hand behind my head and bends down to give me a kiss. I kiss him back and he squeezes me once more and then leaves.

I turn and begin my vigil by my mother's bedside, taking her hand in mine.

. . .

I KNOW she can't hear me, but I talk to her anyway, telling her all about what happened between Jon and me, leaving out the more graphic details (although I'm sure she'd be pleased to hear them) and telling her that I'm going to give Jon a chance so that I can either be with him or cross him off my list. I wish she was better and could offer some motherly advice, but that will come – hopefully as soon as she's better and back home.

My father returns about fifteen minutes later. He holds up a bottle of my favorite iced green tea and I'm glad that he thought to bring some for me. I turn back to my mom and tell her I'll be back later. I kiss her cheek and squeeze her hand and then leave.

"Here, sweets," my dad says, handing me the bottle of green tea. "I'll sit with her for a while. You can go home whenever you want, but I'm staying."

"I'll stay, too."

He goes back in beside her, taking the chair I vacated and I return to the family lounge and take out my laptop and message Marina.

*INDIA: I'm here. Mom is still sedated, but they should start withdrawing the drugs tomorrow once they do another scan to see if the swelling's gone done.*

*MARINA: Oh, poor you! You must be so scared. Take it easy and let me know when she comes out of it and how she is. How are you holding up?*

*INDIA: I'm fine. Jon brought my stuff from the airport. I won't be going in to work tomorrow.*

*MARINA: Oh, that's good. He doesn't need you tomorrow or probably for a few days. That man works you too damn hard. Take a few days off. If you're up to it, you can come to my party on Saturday and meet my latest conquest for you.*

Damn. I forgot about Marina and her damn dating app match. I don't want her to know what happened between Jon and me in Washington. She'll kill me.

132

*INDIA: I don't really think I'll be up to meeting some new man, Marina. My mom is seriously injured.*

*MARINA: Of course not. It's entirely up to you. Play it by ear, of course. I think you'll really like this guy, though. According to MATCHED, he ticks all your boxes. Things like your mother's fall make it all too clear how short life is and how things can change in an instant. Don't put off things that are important because there may not be a tomorrow.*

*INDIA: Of course you're right. But at the moment, meeting someone new is the last thing on my mind.*

*MARINA: As I say, play it by ear. We can always reschedule the date.*

*INDIA: Okay. Deal. If I don't feel up to the party, I'll cancel.*

Marina says goodnight and I sit and read my Facebook feed, losing myself for a while in the mindlessness of social media while I wait to spell off my father at my mother's side.

I SPEND another couple of shifts with my mom before I finally crash on the sofa when they turn the lights off. My dad has a recliner in the ICU room with my mom, so he sleeps at her side. I wake frequently as the doctors and nurses move around the hallways, visiting with patients and checking their stats.

When the sun rises, the bright light peering in from beneath the blinds at the family room window, I sit up and stretch. My neck is sore from the hard arm of the sofa I slept on, but at least I got some sleep.

I go to the washroom and am thankful that Jon brought my suitcase so I can brush my teeth and change my underwear. After I've freshened up, I slip in to my mom's room. My dad must be in the bathroom or maybe down at the cafeteria.

A nurse comes in while I'm there and checks on my mother. She smiles at me.

"She had a good night," she says with a smile. "They'll probably reduce her sedation today to see how she does."

"Thanks," I say, glad that the nurses are so good and attentive – not only to my mom's needs, but also her family's needs.

When my father returns, he has two cups of coffee in his hand and he looks like he's brushed his hair.

"I bought a toothbrush down at the gift shop and washed my face. I feel like a new man with the caffeine. Here," he says and hands me one. "I got you one. One Splenda, right?"

"Thanks. I need some," I say and take the cup. "You can sit with her for a while. I'll go and get some breakfast."

I trade places with my dad and leave him, taking my laptop and cup of coffee and head to the cafeteria.

GRADUALLY, over the course of the day, my mom's stats improve.

Jon texts me to let me know that the staff meeting went well and that if I want him to come by, he'll be here in fifteen, but I put him off again.

INDIA: *Maybe you better not. I need some distance from you so I can think things through.*

JON: *I don't like the sound of that. There's nothing to think through, India. You were all ready to give this a try before your mom's accident. What changed?*

INDIA: *Right now, I can't even think about it and what it means that we've decided to give this thing a try. Just give me some time, okay? We were supposed to take a week.*

JON: *We didn't need a week. Don't change your mind.*

INDIA: *I won't. I want this, but let's take it slow. Wait at least until my mother's better for God's sake.*

JON: *Whatever you want. You let me know.*

Then I feel bad. I don't want to hurt Jon, but right now, I can't be trying to deal with my mother *and* him.

*INDIA: Just give me a few days, okay? When I know my mom's in the clear, I'll be happy to take up where we left off. Believe me.*

*JON: Like I say, you're in the driver's seat until I take over.*

*INDIA: You are so bad...*

*JON: You love it. Confess.*

*INDIA: I'll need much more experience before I know that for sure. Hours and hours more of experience...*

*JON: :)*

*JON: Call or text me at any time of day or night if you need me, or if you just feel like talking, okay?*

*INDIA: Okay. Thanks. I appreciate it. But please, do not let anyone know we're giving this a try. I don't want it to be public just yet.*

*JON: Why? Everyone already thinks we're fucking.*

*INDIA: I don't want it to get in the way of our business relationship, so I think it's best to keep it quiet until we're both sure.*

*JON: I'm sure so I guess that means you're not. Okay. I can handle that. My lips are sealed.*

*INDIA: Thanks for understanding. Talk later.*

Jon doesn't reply. I know he's upset that I want to keep things quiet for now about our decision to try it as a couple, but I just feel strange if everyone is looking at us, wondering.

I want to fly under everyone's radar.

Most of all, Marina's.

The very last thing I need is Marina on my case, reminding me why Jon is the worst possible match for me.

No one needs that kind of shit.


THE DAY WEARS ON, with my dad and I taking shifts beside my mom or spending time in the family room watching television.

Finally, they scoot my dad out of the room while they bring

my mom off the drugs keeping her sedated and she wakes up. Their tests show she's still in there and can move all her limbs. There's no permanent damage, so they withdraw her breathing tube and she's breathing on her own.

She sleeps because of the injury and the drugs, so we don't get to talk to her, but we know she's better.

Dad is so relived, he cries and I hold him in my arms, patting him on the back.

He loves her so much.

"You go home now," he says to me, stroking my hair when he recovers a bit. "The doctor says she's over the worst of it, and now she just needs to heal. They'll move her to the neurology ward soon."

"Okay," I say and I'm honestly glad to get home so I can crash on my own bed. I need a shower badly and am sick of the cafeteria food. "When she wakes up, tell her I love her and I'll be up to see her later. Call me if anything changes."

"I will."

Then I go to my apartment and sleep for eight hours straight.

Jon shows up at my door early in the morning, his SUV pulling into my driveway while I'm standing at the kitchen sink, washing a few dishes.

Damn. I just woke up and haven't had a shower. I'm still wearing a little silky nightgown and have no underwear on.

I rub my eyes and stand at the door, not letting him in because I don't want to get into anything. He's wearing his shorts and a t-shirt and has been out for a run.

He holds up two cups of coffee.

"I come bearing gifts."

"I'm not presentable right now." I hold the door almost closed.

He peers at me, his eyebrows raising.

"You look very presentable to me." He hands me a cup of coffee. "You're not going to invite me in? I drove all the way out here just to bring you this."

"I'll come in to work later this afternoon, after I've visited my mom. I'll see you then."

I try to close the door but he puts his foot in between the door and the jamb.

"You're really not going to invite me in? Do you think I'm going to ravish you or something?"

I smile at his cheeky grin, unable to resist. "Yes."

"Damn," he says, smiling more widely now. "Busted."

He laughs and then nods at me. "Okay. I'll see you this afternoon. This is me getting the big hint."

"See you later," I say and then stick my head out of the door when he turns to leave. "And thanks for understanding."

"Oh, I don't understand," he says, walking backwards. "But I'm willing to cooperate anyway."

Then he turns back and hops in his vehicle. He drives off, giving me one last smile before he disappears onto the street.

I feel like a real bitch, and I really do appreciate his thoughtfulness in bringing me my favorite coffee, which I have every morning before work, but I need my distance now.

When my mom is fine and I can stop worrying about her, I'll let myself fall.

Not until then.

In the meantime, I'll have to work on Marina, convince her that becoming involved with Jon is not a terrible idea.

That's going to be a real challenge.


I VISIT my mom at the hospital and spell my dad for a couple of hours while he goes home and showers. Then I head back to work for the first time since I left with Jon for our meeting at the Pentagon.

My staff welcome me back and offer their words of comfort for my mother's health and recovery, and I finally make it back into my office after about fifteen minutes of it. I'm just getting settled back behind my desk and opening my laptop when Jon comes in.

He plops down on the chair across from me, a thermos of coffee in his hand.

"How's your mom?"

"Better," I say and describe how she's improving and will be moved to the neurology ward later in the day. "I'll probably go up after six and spend a few hours up there, so no working late for me tonight, I'm afraid."

Jon nods. "Take whatever time you need. We're managing without you – barely."

He smiles. I realize he means that as a compliment and wants me to know that I'm an indispensable part of the executive team. My staff can hold up my end for a few days.

"Thanks." I turn back to my laptop and the reports I have to review. "Maybe we should meet in an hour and go over what I've missed. Right now, I need to check my email and go over a few things."

He nods. "Okay," he says, and leaves me, closing the door behind him.

I sigh and turn my attention, such as it is, towards my email. I've read some of them from my external access, but haven't really answered any. Now I have work to do, and it's a welcome relief from worries about my mother.

AFTER ABOUT AN HOUR OF WORK, I get a fresh cup of coffee

from the staff room. Liza, one of our employees, comes up to me and offers her personal well-wishes for my mother.

"Jon told us all about it, how he wished he could have come back with you on the plane but he missed it. That must have been so nerve-wracking for you, not to have him with you. You must have been beside yourself."

"I was, but I was glad to get home as fast as possible."

"I think it's so sweet that you two are finally getting together."

I frown. "Who told you *that*?"

She shrugs. "I thought it was common knowledge. I hope you're not mad at me for mentioning it."

"Did Jon say something?"

She shakes her head. "No, but he really didn't have to. We already know."

"What do you think you know?"

"I'm sorry." She blanches, and now I think she's worried that I'll get mad at her for talking about something personal. "I didn't realize you didn't want people to know..."

"You all assumed that we were a couple?"

She nods and stirs her coffee. "Yeah. We all assumed you were together but wanted to keep it quiet at work. Then Grant said—" She bites her lip and I realize that Grant has spilled the beans and demanded they all keep it secret.

"Grant told you we're together."

She steps away. "Don't tell Jon I told you or he'll get in so much trouble. He said Jon would fire him if he knew."

"Don't worry," I say with a sigh. "I won't say anything to Jon. But please, don't make a big deal about this. We're not together, okay? The business is the most important thing and we don't want to risk that."

She nods and leaves the coffee room. I stand there and fume a bit.

I return to my office and pass Jon's office. His door is open and he's busy on the phone. When he sees me, he smiles and waves.

I nod and close the damn door.

I don't want to give him any ideas.

# CHAPTER TWELVE

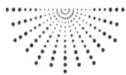

## JON

THE NEXT COUPLE OF DAYS, I let India keep her distance.

She has a lot on her mind, with her mom recovering in the hospital and the specs she has to review on the new satellite. She'll come to me when she's ready and when she needs me.

In contrast, I want her right now.

I want to take her home to my place at night and fuck her brains out. I think it would be good for her during this time of stress. God knows how great sex distracts me from any stress I'm feeling.

But India has her own way of dealing with things. I have to give her room and accept her for what she is.

I listen to the mix playlist she gave me after we first met, filled with songs her parents like – an odd assortment of music from the seventies that I would never have heard if I didn't know her. My father was into country music, and I listened to metal most of my life.

One song plays on the playlist by Cat Stevens, "How Can I Tell You." It seems like a metaphor for our relationship.

I'm not an overly sentimental type, but that song just gets me in my gut and I can't get it out of my head. For the rest of the day, it plays over in my mind, even – especially – when I'm trying to sleep.

I want India in my bed. I want to fuck her brains out. It's only a matter of time before she comes around and asks me.

FRIDAY COMES AND SO FAR, India has not given in to her desires and asked me to fuck her brains out.

She does, however, come into my office Friday afternoon.

"I'm going to Marina's party tomorrow."

"That's good," I say, hoping it's a sign that she's feeling better about her mother and things in general. "Maybe you can come by to my place after. I miss you."

She doesn't say anything. "Marina thinks you're coming as well."

I nod. "Oh, yeah. I did say I'd come. She wanted to match me with someone else, though," I say with a frown. "I'll have to tell her no."

"She wants to match me with someone new as well," India says, her voice soft. "I was thinking we should play along with her. Humor her."

I glance at her, focusing on her eyes. "What? You really want to meet her match for you? You want me to meet her match for me?"

India shrugs. "I don't really want to, but I promised I would before this happened between us. Since we're keeping it quiet—"

"At your insistence, not mine."

"At my insistence, maybe it would be good to just play along. Neither of us have to actually go on a date. We could both go to the party, meet our respective matches, make Marina temporarily happy, and then say goodnight to them. No harm, no foul."

I sigh. "India, I don't want to meet Marina's match for me. And I don't want you to meet yours. I want *you.*"

"I want you," she says softly. "But this is for her app and—"

I interrupt her. "Be honest. You just don't want her to think we're together."

"This is for her app," she repeats, "and *both* of us promised to help out. I want MATCHED to succeed for Marina's sake."

"This is ridiculous. We should just admit the truth – that we want to be together – and to hell with Marina," I say, looking deep in her eyes. "I want you. I can't stop thinking about you. I don't want to go to Marina's party and meet her match for me. I want us to go together and then I want to take you home and fuck your brains out."

She smiles, her cheeks flushing in that way that I love.

"I want that too, but I have to work on Marina and she's already arranged the date. Don't worry," she says and squeezes my hands. "I'm not interested in her matches for me. They've been total busts. I want you."

I lean down and kiss her, and she doesn't pull away so there's that at least. Her kiss feels like it's passionate. She even leans into it willingly so I think I can believe that she truly does want me and doesn't want to meet whatever stuffed shirt academic Marina's matched for her.

The door opens and Janice, my admin, sticks her head in the door.

"Oops – sorry, you guys."

She quickly pops back out and I shake my head and press my forehead against India's.

"The cat is really out of the bag now, I guess."

"It really is," she says. "Liza as much as said so. She said she thought it was so sweet that we were finally making it public. I didn't know we had. Grant must have said something and sworn her to secrecy."

I tense at that. "Dammit," I say, my fists clenching. "I warned him what would happen if he told anyone."

"They all suspect it, Jon," India says and squeezes my shoulder. "They all suspected it for years, apparently. Don't blame Grant. I know you said you'd fire him, but I think that would be wrong."

I shake my head. "Loose lips sink ships. He should have kept his lips zipped and let us decide when to confirm the rumors."

"He should have, but he's still a good employee. It's our fault for even considering getting it on at work, even on a Sunday. We shouldn't be kissing at all unless we're fine with the staff knowing."

"No, we shouldn't," I say, because she's right. Still, I don't want to stop showing her how I feel, so I lean in and kiss her once more. She slips her arms around my neck and kisses me back and that gives me some heart that maybe, just maybe, she's coming around to letting this really happen between us.

I want her to be happy about it, and not feel like we have to hide it.

Dammit Marina – quit messing with India's head.

"You have to tell Marina."

She bites her lip guiltily. "I know. Just this weekend – let's let her match us up. We can look across the room and make meaningful eye contact at each other when we meet our latest match."

"You're not worried that I'll like my date a little too much?" I ask, taking a lock of her hair in my fingers and playing with it. I glance in her eyes, trying to look coy. "Because, I'm worried that you'll like *your* date a little too much..."

"Jon," she says and punches me playfully on the arm. "She's been totally wrong so far. I think the questionnaire is a bust, so I'm not worried in the least. I promise you that you and I will go back to your apartment and spend the night together, laughing at her matches and doing whatever you want, okay? Just indulge me."

I exhale, resigned that I'll have to go through with it. "Okay, but we do whatever I want to do, right?"

"I promise," she replies, her voice a bit breathy, like the idea arouses her. It immediately arouses me, a jolt to my dick at the thought of having my way with her. "You can count on it."

"Good," I say, and kiss her once more, this time more passionately. "You can count on it being really pleasurable."

Then, I gesture to the door. "Shall we? I believe we have a conference call with the General."

"Lead the way."

I grab my laptop and India grabs hers and together, we take the hallway to the conference room where my admin is busy setting up the conference phone and screen so we can videoconference about the contract.

INDIA LEAVES the office early to go to the hospital and visit her mom, and I go out with the rest of the staff for a beer after work. It's a bit of a tradition to go out together every second Friday to a local pub that has great appetizers and cheap beer. I buy everyone the first round of draft beer and the first tray of appetizers, and we bond over alcohol and snacks.

Out of the blue, Janine, a married mother of five and one of our admin personnel, blurts out a question about India and me.

"So, are you two a thing now?" she asks, her eyebrows raised.

Kal, beside her, gives her an elbow. "Janine..."

I take a sip of my beer and then carefully put the glass down, trying to form my words carefully.

"I know you've all thought India and I have been having a secret affair all these years, but honestly, we haven't. It's only

145

been recently – very recently – that we have finally decided to give it a try. India wants things to remain private, so I hope you all can give us that privacy. We won't make a big deal of it and hope you won't either."

"See, I told you," Janine says and elbows Kal back. "I knew it. I've always said you two should get together if you weren't already. You're both so cute. You belong together."

"Thanks for the endorsement, but seriously, don't say anything to India. She'll kill me for confirming it, but I don't like to lie to you guys."

"We all knew you were either in love and together, or in denial. At least now we know we're not all crazy."

I lean back and laugh. "I can't get over how comfortable you guys all feel asking me outright about it. I'm your freaking boss. You should show proper deference and all," I say, only half-jokingly.

"We've been talking behind your backs for three years," Janine says, grinning.

"So I hear," I reply. "Now, you can still talk behind our backs but at least it'll be something real instead of just your filthy fantasies."

"Or your filthy fantasies," Janine quips and gives me a wink.

"I hope so." I take another drink of my beer.

I check out earlier than usual, citing a late night, and everyone goes "Uh-huh" and gives me the eye.

"Serious," I say, holding my hands out in supplication. "India's at the hospital and won't be coming back to my place tonight, so calm yourselves. And remember, nothing about this to India until I give you the a-okay. It'll be when she feels comfortable, okay?"

I make a point of looking them all in the eye. To a person – with the exception of Janine, who is recalcitrant – they nod.

"Janine?"

"Oh, all right," she says and waves her hand. "I'll zip my lips, but don't make me wait too long."

"I hope it won't be too long, but that's up to India."

We say goodnight and I leave, enjoying the friendly and casual relationship I have with my staff. It's only possible because they are truly professional in the office and I know I can reply on them to do the work and do it right.

I return to my apartment and take off my clothes, then pace around like a caged lion, feeling like I want India here right now so I can calm down and get some sleep after a good fuck. I want her in my bed. I want to wake up with her beside me.

I'll be sleeping alone at least until Saturday.

It's going to be a long night.


THE NEXT DAY GOES FAST, and it's almost eight when I finally leave work and go home for a quick shower.

*MARINA: Are you coming tonight? I have your next match coming by at around nine to meet you. I think she's right up your alley.*

*JON: Yes, I said I would. I'll be there. Just remember my terms – if I don't want to go on a date with her, no harm, no foul. I'll meet her and give her a chance to wow me but after that, it's entirely up to me.*

*MARINA: And her, of course. She may not like you when she meets you, but we won't know that until you two meet. See you at nine.*

*JON: I'll be there.*

I dress in something a little classier and check myself out in the mirror. I look presentable. I know India likes this suit and the shirt-tie combination, since she picked it out for me once when we were in New York for a conference and my suitcase had been lost in transit. The suit is black, and the shirt white, the tie a deep blue. India says it plays off the color of my eyes. The way she looked at me when I put it on in the store said all I needed to know. It passed muster.

I take my SUV and drive to Marina's place, parking on the street for a quick escape if I want to make one, and walk into her house. The sky is dark, and the interior of her house is lit up with a warm yellow light. Music wafts to me as I walk up the path to her door. I enter, checking the place out to see who's there. I see a few of Pacifica's staff, and a bunch of people I don't know. After saying hello to my staff and giving them the reminder not to talk about India and me, I'm accosted by a smiling Marina who has a pretty blonde woman in tow. That's apparently my date.

In any other circumstances, I'd be licking my lips when I see her and realize she's there for me, but now? Now, I feel deflated.

Yeah, she's attractive. Tall, built, a real blonde, perfect teeth, and perfect breasts underneath a silky dress.

"Jon," Marina says, her voice carrying across the room. "There you are!"

She pulls my date across the room and stands her in front of my like she's a specimen rather than a person.

"Here she is," Marina says, her eyebrows wagging in this ridiculous way. "MATCHED's latest match for you. Jon, this is Cindy. Cindy, this is Jon. You already read his profile. You two are almost a perfect match. Please – enjoy each other! I have to go and take care of business."

She smiles at the two of us, and then leaves, and it's then I see India walk in from the patio. She looks fantastic, dressed in this amazing black dress with thin straps that shows all her curves in a sexy but not too trashy way. Her dress is to her knee, and she's wearing my favorite strappy sandals that play off her shapely calves.

God, she's a sight for sore eyes.

I smile at her, forgetting Cindy for a moment, and she sees

me, but she's not smiling back. Behind her is a tall dark bearded guy wearing a very fashionable suit. He takes her arm and leans in to say something to her over the sound of the music, which is a touch too loud.

I hate him.

Instantly, I want to go over there and plow him one in his handsome face. Yeah, I can recognize a handsome man when I see one. I'm secure in my sexuality. This guy is definitely debonair, in a Clark Gable kind of way. Dark eyes, neatly trimmed beard, taller than India by a foot at least, well-dressed, hair slicked back and a bit longer.

He whispers in her ear and the two of them laugh, and India glances surreptitiously in my direction.

She thinks he's funny.

She likes men with a sense of humor.

My fists clench without me thinking and so I take in a deep breath and try to talk myself down a few notches.

She's doing this for Marina's sake, as I am. So, I turn to Cindy, or whoever she is, and try to make polite conversation.

"So, Cindy, tell me about you. What do you do for a living?"

I watch her as she talks about herself, trying to focus, but all the time, my mind is thinking of India and her date and whether she thinks he's a better match for her than I am.

I know Marina thinks so.

Cindy is in banking, working as a teller at a local branch in downtown SF. She took a securities course and would like to be an investment advisor at her bank eventually. She's well-spoken and attractive, and if I didn't want India, I'd be happy to give Cindy a roll in the hay. I might even consider a second round, if she was particularly adventurous in the hay-rolling department.

But all I can think of is whether India likes her match.

They're laughing together at something he says. He seems like a real joker. He's leaning in closer to India, their eyes locked

149

together, and I feel like I have to go over and interrupt, fill him in that India is not his.

Of course, I can't do that because she's technically not mine either.

If she was, we wouldn't be at this party pretending to be interested in Marina's dates for us.

"What about you?" Cindy asks, and I have to pull myself back into the moment.

"I'm the CEO of a tech firm."

"I know that," she says. "Marina showed me your bio. Tell me more about you – personally. I already know the C.V."

I frown, and try to make conversation but I can't help but glance quickly at India and see that she's alone while Mr. Tall, Dark, and Loathsome goes to get her a drink at the bar, which is set up in the corner of the room.

"Can you excuse me for a moment?" I say to Cindy, who nods and says sure.

I make my way over to where India is standing and she frowns when she sees me coming.

"Hey," I say and lean in closer. I want to kiss her – kiss her in front of everyone and let them know she's mine – but of course, I don't.

I can't.

"Jon," she says, her voice miffed. "You should be with your date."

"I wanted to say hi. Can't a guy say hi to his business partner?"

Her brow is furrowed. "I know what you're doing. Go and play nice with your date."

I exhale heavily. "This is ridiculous, India. We should be together, not with other people. I don't like putting on a charade like this. You should just tell Marina her app needs to be fixed and get it over with."

"I can't and you know it. After tonight, we'll come clean, but tonight, just go along with it, okay?"

She gives me this pleading look that I can't resist and so I nod.

"Okay, but I expect fun and games when we get back to my place. Fun and games."

"You'll get them, now go," she says and pushes me lightly on the arm. I see that Mr. Loathsome is on his way back, carrying two drinks. He sees me and raises his eyebrows as if he doesn't like the fact that his date is talking intimately with another man.

Tough luck, buddy. She's fucking well mine.

"Hello," Mr. Loathsome says, handing a drink to India. "You're the business partner, right? Jon Thorson?"

"That's right," I say, certain that he put emphasis on business, like he wants to accentuate that I am not a romantic partner, but maybe that's me being slightly paranoid. I wouldn't put it past myself, the way I'm feeling, seeing India with a really handsome man.

"Who are you and what do you do for a living?"

"Jon, you have a date to talk to," India says and gives me the evil eye.

Mr. Loathsome smiles. "John McMaster. I'm a portfolio manager and angel investor. When I'm not doing that, I surf, snowboard, and base jump."

"Ahh," I say, hating him even more. "That's something we share in common."

"You base jump?" he asks, like he's the only rich alpha in the world who likes the adrenaline rush.

"I do. Spent time in Argentina and Chile. Also skydive when I can get a chance."

Mr. Loathsome nods, sizing me up. I think he realizes I feel possessive towards India and is now going to bring out the big guns. "I love to jump."

"I jumped with the $75^{th}$ Ranger Regiment."

He nods even more meaningfully at that, realizing now that I'm a veteran as well as being a very rich business owner. "I was with the $507^{th}$, Bravo Company during my service," he replies.

"Jon, your date is waiting for you," India says, her eyes wide, her voice frustrated.

"Oh, yeah," I say, feeling guilty for being such a terrible date, but needing to check out this guy before I can relax.

Now, I can't relax.

He's like me, except dark-haired and -eyed. Former military. Investments. Adrenaline junkie.

"See you later," I say and point at India.

Then I return to Cindy and feel like I've scored a point, but it feels hollow. Even though I hate his guts, I realize that India should be with someone like Mr. Loathsome. He's smart, successful, good looking. He probably looks at India and sees an amazing catch – someone he could use both as arm candy and maybe even a wife he could show off to all his banker buddies. He probably is one of those guys who's ready to settle down and wants to find his wife. I imagine India in a wedding dress, walking down the aisle with him and it makes my gut knot.

I talk to Cindy about her job and her aspirations. She's definitely hot, and most men would be happy to have her as a lover. She's not the dip that Marina matched me with the last time, but she's about as interesting as yesterday's newspaper. I've been there and done that with a number of women just like Cindy. They're looking for a rich husband so they can work less and spend more time at the spa.

I don't want to be someone's conquest.

I can practically see the dollar signs in her eyes when I tell her about Pacifica and our current round of contract negotiations with the US military.

India isn't like that. She's on my level. She's as ambitious as me. She wants to run her own show and make a real contribution in life. She wants to make a difference and build something that will last.

She is my equal.

When I glance over at Mr. Loathsome, I see someone else like me and it unnerves me. I can't help but think that he would be so much easier for her than I would be.

I'm standing there, half-listening to Cindy, the other half of my brain thinking of India and Mr. Loathsome, when Marina comes up to us.

"How are things?" she asks, her eyebrows wagging in that disgusting manner.

"Great," Cindy says, meaningfully.

Marina turns to me expectantly. I realize she wants me to wax poetic about the great time I'm having with her match for me.

"Oh, fantastic," I say, only a little too emphatically. "Of course." I give her a big smile but at that moment, the only thing I want to do is get another drink and down it as quickly as possible. "Excuse me," I say and point to the bar. "I'm going to get another drink. How about yours? Do you need a refill?"

Cindy shakes her head. "No, thanks. I'm good."

I turn to Marina, who apparently isn't going to leave. "You?"

"I'm fine as well."

I turn to the bar and exhale, my only wish that I can escape as soon as possible. First, I have to make sure that India will be following me home, because that was our deal and I intend to collect on my end.

I'm searching through the bar fridge for another beer when Marina walks over and stands beside me.

"Things are going really well tonight, I think," she says, her eyes bright.

"Oh, yeah?" I find my beer, open it, and drink down a third of it. "How so?"

"I think India really likes John. He's right up her alley. He's a veteran."

"He didn't see any action," I say. "He wasn't deployed to a war zone."

"Whatever," Marina says. "He's rich, professional, alpha, and he's incredibly hot in the looks department. What's not to love?"

"Yeah," I say, silently fuming. "What's not to love?"

"I think she may have finally found someone who can give her what she needs."

What India needs is my cock deep inside her. That's what she needs.

*Damn, woman.* It's like Marina's deliberately rubbing my nose in the fact that India has met her perfect man. She's so unaware of the fact that India and I have been fucking behind the scenes, lusting after each other, but are reluctant to dive in head first because of our business relationship.

How can a matchmaker be so blind?

# CHAPTER THIRTEEN

## INDIA

I STAND and look John over, thinking about Jon and how these two are so alike, and yet so different.

Even the name is the same, for God's sake. It's like Marina found the one man who is as close to Jon as possible just to goad me. She knows that Jon and I have been hovering around each other for several years without acting on our feelings. She totally disapproves. So she finds a Jon-clone, except with dark hair and eyes.

And far too smooth. John has all the lines down. He's extremely attentive. He's looking into my eyes purposely, watching my mouth as I talk, nodding, focused on me. I can feel his attempt to win me over. He feels so damn secure in himself, how attractive and rich and in control he is.

Usually, I'd be a bit weak-kneed at meeting someone like him. He does tick all my boxes. I like ambitious men. I like men who have a military background because it speaks to their courage –

like my brother. I like men who know how to seduce me. You gotta respect that, right?

But then I glance over at Jon and see him standing with that beautiful blonde with the great body and I think how usually, he'd be going home with her, would fuck her senseless, and then probably never see her again.

*That's* what's keeping me from saying a full yes to Jon.

My heart starts to beat faster and at that moment, I have to leave.

"Excuse me," I say, interrupting John while he's discussing his investment business. "I'll be right back."

I leave the main living room and try to find the bathroom, because I'm feeling overwhelmed right now and need to take a few deep breaths.

I go upstairs and when I get to the door, someone grabs my arm, stopping me.

It's Jon.

"I've had enough of this bullshit," he says, pulling me close. "More than enough."

Then he kisses me, his hand slipping behind my head and pulling me up to his mouth. He devours me, his kiss so intense I'm breathless by the time it's done. He pulls away, his eyes burning into mine. "Let's leave."

"You want to leave now? We've only been here for half an hour."

"That's more than enough time to know."

I look at him. He's angry. He hates being forced to do the dating thing.

He just wants to take me home and fuck me the way he said he would.

It turns me on completely.

"But Marina..."

"Who do you want to please? Yourself or Marina?"

"She's my best friend."

"What am I?"

I don't know what to say. "I don't know what you are."

"I'm a man who wants you."

"That's not enough."

"Do you want me?" he asks, his hands spread out.

"Yes," I say, "but—"

"Then you got me. Let's go."

He takes my hand and pulls me to him, his arms around me, trapping me in his embrace. He kisses me and I can feel his frustration in his kiss, in the way his arms hold me tightly.

I do want him.

He wants me.

Why can't that be good enough, for God's sake?

"Fuck it," I say when he breaks the kiss. "Let's get the hell out of here before Mr. Tall, Dark, and Handsome comes looking for me."

Jon looks pleased, but he stops, and there's this look in his eyes. Teasing. "You think he's handsome?"

"It's obvious."

"More handsome than me?" he says, a grin starting. He presses me against the wall, his fingers digging into my ribs, tickling me. I squeal, then cover my mouth to stifle my laugh.

When he stops, we stand together, our faces inches away. He has his arms spread on either side of me, his body pressed possessively against mine.

"Well? Is he?"

"No," I say because it's true. Jon is not only more handsome, he's actually beautiful, in a masculine way. His face is all perfect lines and angles, his eyes large and blue with thick lashes. His dark blond hair falls in his eyes in that sexy way that I've always secretly admired. His lips are full and soft. There's just enough scruff to remind you that he's all man. He's ripped, tall, and he has that easy smile and twinkle in his eye that suggests so much.

I want him more than anything.

"So, what are you waiting for? I'm yours."

"As what?" I can't not ask the question.

"As your lover. Isn't that good enough?"

I don't say anything for a moment. "Exclusive?"

He sighs heavily. "India, why do you need me to say yes to that? Don't you believe me when I say I want only you? I don't want Heather or Cindy or anyone Marina wants to match me with."

He pulls me against him again. "Right now, I want *you*. I can't promise it will be forever. Don't ask me to."

I nod, because even I know neither of us can make such a promise.

"I'm going to say goodbye to John," I say, pulling away from Jon. "I owe him that much. He was nice enough to come tonight to meet me. It would be totally rude of me to leave without saying goodbye."

Jon steps back and shakes his head slowly. He runs his hand through his hair and I know he's angry at me for not just slipping out with him. I go to the stairs, but before I go down, I turn and meet his eyes.

"You should say goodbye to your date, too. It's the adult thing to do, Jon."

He doesn't say anything, just rubs his jaw thoughtfully.

"Okay," he says and waves me on. "I'll be a grownup if I have to. You go ahead. I'll come down in a moment."

I nod and take the stairs back to the living room where Marina is standing with both John and Cindy.

"There you are," Marina says, and glances at John and Cindy. "We thought you'd left."

"Why would you think that?"

"You've been upstairs," she says and raises her eyebrows, "for about fifteen minutes. What were you doing up there?"

Jon comes down the stairs and then Marina sees him. He stops in the middle of the staircase when he sees the four of us standing together. I can sense the hesitancy in him. He doesn't want to have to face this, but he visibly steels himself and comes over, a smile pasted on his face.

"There you are," he says and puts his hand on Cindy's arm. "Care to have a little chat?"

She looks at Marina and then at me and John. Marina pushes her. "Go." Marina smiles widely and then looks back at me. "I'll leave you two alone."

She scoots off, smiling like she's happy with her accomplishments. Little does she know...

"I'm sorry," I say when I turn to John. He bends down, smiling at me, his dark eyes amused. "I didn't mean to abandon you for so long."

"No harm done. Cindy and I had a nice chat. In fact, that's what I wanted to talk to you about. She and I have decided to leave together. She's telling Jon right now, actually."

My mouth is wide open at that.

*What?*

"Oh," I say, struggling for the right words. "That's great. Can I ask why?"

He smiles. "We actually met before you arrived and got to talking. We... well, we have a lot in common and since things didn't seem like they were working out with either of you, we decided to leave and go get some coffee."

"Really?" I glance over at Jon, who appears amused by whatever it is that Cindy is telling him. He rubs his jaw. Then he glances over at me, a half-grin on his lips.

I turn back to John who adjusts his tie. "I hope you don't mind."

"No," I reply, completely flummoxed but relieved as well. "No, I think it's great that you two met and hit it off, considering that things didn't work out for us. All's well that ends well, right?"

"My thoughts exactly. So, if you don't mind, Cindy and I are leaving."

"Nice to meet you, anyway," I say with a laugh. "Have a nice evening."

He smiles and turns away. I can feel his relief at leaving me and going to retrieve Cindy from Jon.

Marina comes right over, her expression concerned. "What's going on? Where's John going?"

I turn and watch as Jon and John shake hands like a couple of gentlemen.

"I guess John and Cindy matched themselves together. You really need to work on your app..."

"You're kidding," Marina says, her mouth wide open. "What on Earth? They weren't a match at all." She turns to me, taking hold of my arm. "I'm so sorry, sug. You must be crushed."

"Oh, I'm terribly crushed," I say, barely able to hold back a grin.

"You're joking?"

I laugh out loud at that. "John's handsome, but he didn't do it for me. I'm actually going to go now. Maybe I'll stop by the hospital and see my mom before she goes to bed."

"Oh, sure, I understand," she says and gives me a quick hug. "Give her my love, okay?"

"I will." I hug her back and then pull away.

"You sure you're okay about this?" she asks, squinting at me. "Not too depressed about it not working out with John? He was a really good match for you."

I shake my head, my relief that I wasn't the cause of the problem making me almost giddy.

"Not at all,'" I say with a laugh. "It is what it is. I'm just sorry that MATCHED seems to have such a bad track record. Aren't you worried?"

"Nah," she says and waves her hand dismissively. "It's fine. Not every match is going to work out."

"It's zero for three for me and zero for two for Jon."

She shrugs like it's nothing. If I were her, I'd be going back to the old drawing board to fix it, but she seems oblivious. "It's a sample of two. That's not nearly enough to learn anything statistically valid."

"If you say so." I smile and point to the door. "I'm going. I guess I'll ask Jon if he can give me a ride to the hospital."

"Okay, sug. You let me know how your mom is."

She waves at me and turns to the living room. I turn and walk over to where Jon stands with his hands in his pockets, a smile on his face.

"You ready to go?"

I nod and walk to the door. Jon follows. I turn when I get to it. "Can you drive me to the hospital? I want to visit my mom."

He frowns. "I thought you were coming home with me."

"I will," I say softly, "but I want to stop in and see my mom first."

"You want me to come in with you? I won't intrude."

"No, it's fine. I can get an Uber to your place after. You go home."

"India..." He glares at me. "You're not trying to escape me, are you?"

I shake my head. "Of course not," I say.

"You're changing your mind," Jon says. "I can see it in your face." He glances away, his hands on his hips and I can see a muscle tense in his jaw. He looks down at the floor.

"Okay, whatever, India. You go to see your mom. I'll drop you off. I'll go to my place and if you show up, great. If not, well, I guess I'll just deal."

"Jon, don't be like that. I just want to see my mom..."

He looks at me without speaking and then turns to the door, opening it and walking out ahead of me. I can tell he's angry.

We get to his SUV and he holds the door open for me. I get inside and try to catch his eye, but he won't look at me.

We drive in silence, and there's an awful iciness that fills the space between us. I want to reach out to him, but at the same time, I want him to agree to be exclusive, and all that it entails.

He drops me off and I go inside the hospital to see my mom, walking through the maze of hallways and then taking the elevator to get to her room. They've taken her off the ICU unit and put her on the neurology ward, so instead of the bustle of the ICU, she's in a much quieter ward. At that time of night, there are only a few visitors, mostly family. I slip into her room after checking in at the nursing station.

She's alone and sleeping, her head turned to the window, which overlooks another wing of the hospital, rows and rows of windows. I feel so bad for her, being alone, and all at once I get this feeling that I've been spending far too much time working and far too little time living.

"Mom?" I say quietly, taking her hand and squeezing it. I don't want her to stay asleep because I want her to know I was here.

She turns her head and blinks, then she finally sees me and smiles. "Sweetie," she whispers. "You're here."

"I am," I say and lean down to kiss her cheek.

"It's Saturday night. Aren't you supposed to be at a party meeting a date?"

I smile and can't help but feel tears in my eyes because she remembers. I've been so afraid that she'd never recover her mind or memory but she seems totally fine.

"It was a bust," I say, pulling up a chair and sitting beside her.

"Another flop?"

"Yes," I say and sigh dramatically. "I guess I'm destined to be an old maid."

"Ha!" She belly-laughs, and I laugh with her. "You're a beauty. If you'd just slow down for a minute or two, one of the men chasing you will catch you."

"Oh, mom, that's such 1970s thinking. Today, both men and women chase each other. Didn't you know?"

She smiles and her eyes close. "I know. I was just kidding. What about Jon? Are you two ever going to just admit what you feel for each other and get together?"

I frown, shocked that she'd say that. "What do you mean?"

She cracks one eye open. "You know exactly what I mean. That boy is in love with you. You're in love with him. The two of you are just stubborn."

I don't say anything for a moment.

"I'm surprised you've been thinking that. You've never said anything."

"I tried but you never wanted to hear it," she says simply. "Plus, sometimes we can only learn something the hard way, and we only hear when we're ready to hear."

"Jon wants us to get together for real, but I'm afraid he can't make a commitment."

"Then don't be with him. Find someone else. Tell him that."

"I want him, but not the way he wants us to be."

"Tell him," she says, squeezing my hand. "Give him the alternative. He has you or someone else does. You want someone exclusive. If he can't give that, move on."

"I don't want things to go sour with us. We've already been... intimate."

"Oh," she says and glances away. "That complicates things." After a moment, she looks back at me. "What do you want? What do you *really* want?"

"I want him to be exclusive. He wants us to just live for the moment together and see where things go."

"No commitment, in other words."

"Nope," I say. "That's what's holding me back. We know each other better than anyone else, so I don't think we need to wait and see."

"There you have it. Tell him that. If he wants you, he'll be willing to make the commitment."

"If he says no, I feel like I'll have to leave Pacifica."

"Why?" she says, frowning. "You built that company just as much as he has. You should just buckle down and work hard, be friendly but not expect anything if he won't be exclusive."

I frown and don't know what to say.

"I'm afraid if I make a decision, it'll be the wrong one. If I just let things go on as they are, at least Jon and I are still friends and we still have Pacifica..."

"You have to decide what you want more – Pacifica or Jon."

"Both."

She shakes her head. "Sometimes, you have to choose. You can try it Jon's way and see how things go, or you can force the issue and see if he decides you're important enough to give exclusivity a try."

"That's it, isn't it? I have to bend or Jon does."

"Life is a big compromise. You have to decide what battles you want to fight and on which hill you want to die."

I make a face of mock surprise. "Mom, that's such a militant thing to say. Battles, fight, dying..."

"Love and war," she says and her voice is now tired. "The two go together. It's always a power struggle when two people get together at some level. You have to decide to stay and fight, or give up and leave."

We sit for a moment while this sinks into my brain. She smiles at me. "Tell me about your date. Why didn't he work out?"

"He was everything I should like – tall, dark, and handsome, smart, successful. Attentive. But Jon is..."

"You're in love with Jon, India. Give it a try. See what happens. The worst is a broken heart and leaving Pacifica with your shares and a lot of experience under your belt. You'll be a success no matter what you try next and eventually, you'll find a man who's right for you."

We talk for a few more minutes about her health and how my father is handling being on his own. Then, I stand and lean over, kissing her forehead.

"I'll go and let you sleep," I say softly. "You look tired."

"Thanks for coming."

Then I leave, with a promise to come by tomorrow, and make my way out of the hospital, intending to call an Uber to get me home. There, waiting by the curb, is Jon.

I go to the car and open the passenger door.

"You waited," I say when I get inside.

"I'm not a fool," he says and waits until I get my seatbelt fastened. "I knew you might get cold feet and go home instead of coming to my place."

"Jon," I say, frustrated that he's right. "You should give me the space to make my own decisions."

"I want you in my bed."

We drive off and he says nothing else.

I watch the roads, wondering whether he's taking me to his place or mine. I finally see familiar scenery and I realize he's dropping me off at my place.

We pull up to my house overlooking the ocean and he stops, not looking at me. It's my move. If I get out, he'll drive off without saying anything and we'll be where we were before any of this happened, except we'll have the sex between us. Maybe we can get back to that place when things were good.

I think I'd rather be there than where we are now.

I open the door. He doesn't say anything and neither do I.

He drives off and I watch him leave, my heart racing.

We're both so damn stubborn.

I key in the numbers to my keypad door lock and miss the first time, cursing my fingers, which are shaking. I finally get it right after a second try and go inside the cool dark interior. The only light comes from over the stove and so I go into my living room and plop down on my sofa. Outside my window is the view of the San Francisco Bay. I can see lights from a ship out in the harbor and it makes me so sad to be alone, looking at that beautiful view.

I don't want to be alone.

In truth, I want Jon with me. But if he can't at least say he wants to be exclusive and won't pick up some woman he meets while he's away on a trip or when he's out and I'm not with him, I can't be with him.

That's my bottom line.

My pride intact, I turn on the flat screen and lie on the sofa but my eyes are filled with tears and the screen is too blurry to watch.

# CHAPTER FOURTEEN

JON

I DRIVE like a maniac down the road from India's place by the Bay. If she could only just relax and let things happen between us, exploring what we can be together rather than trying to force a shape on our relationship, we'd be in bed right now, fucking our brains out.

I *only* want India. I don't want any other woman. I won't be with any other woman. I want India and only India.

Why isn't that good enough for her?

She wants me to say the words – *Yes, I'll be exclusive with you* – like it's a clause in a contract.

I don't want any other women. I won't be with any other women. I want her and only her.

What's the difference?

I pull over and take out my cell.

JON: *I only want you. I don't want any other women. I won't be with any other women. When that's good enough for you, I'll be waiting.*

Then, I turn off my cell and put it away. I'm not going to check it obsessively and see what she's written in response. If my statement isn't good enough, it isn't good enough, but that's how I feel.

The ball is in her court now.

I turn up the volume on a satellite radio station. It's one of India's favorite stations, Seventies Gold, and the song playing is "Baby Come Back," by Player.

Damn.

I turn to another station, Classic Rock. "I'm Not In Love" by 10cc.

Jesus.

I turn to a metal channel. Metallica, "Nothing Else Matters."

*FUCK!*

I turn off the radio completely and drive to my place in silence.

I PROWL MY APARTMENT, stalking it like a lion in a cage, wanting to escape and run free.

So, I go for a run, the way I do whenever I feel too much mental energy and need to sleep. After slipping on my shorts and sweatshirt and my runners, I take off along the streets bordering the waterfront. The night is pleasant, so I run without any effort. After about twenty minutes, I sit along a pier and watch the ships. I watch the sky, and see several planes flying high, bound for the Pacific Rim. I listen to the waves lapping along the base of the pier.

I want India.

Everything was going along so fine between us.

What the fuck happened?

I get back up and run home. I'll take a shower after I've sat in front of the television and cooled off.

Dammit.

I should be with her now.

She's so damn afraid that I'll break her heart – she'd rather be alone than take a chance.

I get up and have a shower, scrubbing myself hard with a rough loofah, determined not to give in to my usual carnal needs in the shower because I know it would be to fantasies of India in the shower with me – on her knees, sucking my cock, or me pounding her while she leans against the shower wall, her arms around my neck, her thighs thrown around my waist, my cock buried deep inside of her.

I won't give in.

Instead, I scrub my skin almost raw and then get out of the shower, wrap my towel around my waist, and brush my teeth like I mean it – too hard probably, but I'm angry and frustrated.

Angry feels better than sad.

Then, the buzzer announces someone at the front entrance.

I leave the bathroom and check the video feed.

*India...*

I buzz her in and open the door, standing in the hallway, still dripping wet with only a towel around my waist.

I push my hair out of my eyes and watch as she comes up the stairs.

She doesn't say anything but I feel her eyes move over my body, from my feet to my groin, briefly, then to my face.

I expect her to stop and be hesitant. For all I know, she was coming by to talk, but instead, she comes right up to me and puts her hand behind my head, pulling me down for a kiss.

That does it.

I kiss her back, pulling her against my body, and I know she's made her decision.

She's decided to be with me and see what happens rather than making me say the words.

In a sense, I've won, but she's won as well, because obviously, this is what she really wants.

She wants us together.

*Period.*

I don't waste any time and I don't hesitate. I pull her into my apartment and we're already taking off her clothes even before I get the door shut. I pull her dress off over her head, and see that she's done what I said – she went and bought one of those front-closure bras so I can more easily remove it, and I do. I figure out how it works on the fly and unlatch it so her glorious breasts – breasts I've fantasized over like a teenage boy – break free. While I imagined her on her knees before me, now I pull her over to the sofa and sit on the arm, pressing my face between her breasts like I can't get enough of them.

And I can't. I nuzzle them and squeeze them and nip at both nipples, one after the other, before taking one into my mouth and sucking until it hardens into a tight bud against my tongue. I move to the other and do the same, sucking and licking her breasts and nipples until she writhes against me, moaning.

"I want to suck your clit," I say, looking up into her eyes. Her face flushes with desire at that and I know I've struck gold. She loves it when I tell her what I want to do to her. She likes dirty talk. "Then," I add, narrowing my eyes. "I'm going to lick your slit and fuck you with my tongue until you come all over it."

"You can do anything you want to me," she says in a breathy voice.

"Oh, I can and I will," I reply. Then I slide her panties off, down over her curvaceous hips to the floor and she steps out of them. Now, she's gloriously naked except for her heels. When she bends down to take one off, I stop her.

"No, keep them on. I like the way you look in them. Like sex on legs."

She smiles, and complies with my demand. I stand and kiss her, then turn her around so that she leans against the back of the sofa and I kneel before her once more and lift her thigh and rest it on my shoulder. Her pussy is right in my face and I spread her so that I can see her slit and her clit, her lips open for me. I lick slowly, starting as low as I can until I feel her hard clit against my tongue. She groans in response and so I keep licking her, circling her clit with my tongue, not touching it directly just yet. I'll make her beg.

She tries to press her pussy against my mouth in her need, but I deny her. "Not yet," I say and slip a finger and then two inside of her warm wetness, her silky flesh hot and ready for me. I reach up and feel that ridge of flesh and stroke while I lick her, each time avoiding direct contact on her clit. I know that will drive her wild.

"Oh, God," she moans, her eyes closed and her body tense.

"What do you want?" I ask, wanting to force her to say the words. "Tell me and I'll do it."

"Lick me," she murmurs.

I do, licking her but still avoiding her clit. I run the tip of my tongue on either side of the bud, denying her contact and she moans once more, moving her hips wantonly. My dick is hard and straining against the towel and I can't wait to plunge it into her deeply when I make her come again, but this time, I want her coming on my tongue. So, I build her up as long as I can, before, finally, I push her back onto the sofa, and spread her thighs wide. I suck her clit hard, tonguing it, pressing against it, and I can tell she's close.

"Tell me when you're going to come," I say and keep up the motions inside her with my fingers stroking her G-spot, my tongue finally stroking her clit. Then she tenses.

Before she can say it, I know she's ready and so I pull my fingers out of her body and ram my tongue inside her, my thumb on her clit and that does it. She spasms, her cunt tightening around my tongue, throbbing as she climaxes.

"Oh, God, oh God, oh, God," she cries, exhaling deeply while I thrust my tongue in and out.

"Stop, stop," she pleads when it becomes too much, pushing my head away. I do, slowing my motions until she's lying beneath me, her body quivering from pleasure overload.

I rise and lean over her, kissing her, and she's almost drunk on her orgasm, her eyes half-lidded.

Good.

Just the way I like her. Wet and ready for me.

"Now I'm going to fuck you and make you come again," I say, catching her eye.

"You think I'm going to say no?" she replies, a cheeky expression on her face.

"Not for a moment," I reply and kiss her again. "But first, I want you on your knees."

She smiles and I help her up, turn her around and now it's her turn to pleasure me. She doesn't disappoint. She slides deliberately slowly down, her hands stroking over my shoulders and chest and while she's kneeling, she removes my towel and my cock springs loose, so that it's directly in front of her face.

It throbs, and precum leaks out of the tip.

Smiling up at me, she takes my shaft in her hand and then carefully and very deliberately, she licks the head, licks my fluid off the tip so that I can see it on her tongue. That makes me even harder, if possible, as she tastes me.

"Oh, fuck," I groan while she takes the head in her mouth and runs her tongue around the crown, sucking while she pulls off with a delicious pop. "Suck me," I demand, thrusting my hips forward.

She takes me in her mouth and then in deeper, as deep as she can until she gags just a bit, before pulling off. She strokes me while she sucks the head and she's good. She's *very* good. I'd like to fuck her mouth like this and come with her lips around me, but I want to watch her come on my cock like she did before.

When I feel close to my own climax, I stop her, panting with lust.

"I want to fuck you until you come," I say, and now I take her to my bed, pulling her behind me. She's still wearing her heels and looks delicious as I push her back onto the mattress. She climbs up higher and I position her so her hips are on the edge. I play with her for a while, squeezing her breast, sucking her nipples, then I run my tongue down her belly to her mound, flicking her clit after I've spread her thighs wide.

"You're so nice and wet for me," I say, stroking her slit with one finger, slipping it inside her. "I'm going to fuck you hard."

Before I do, I lick her to build her up again, and stroke her with my fingers deep inside. I suck her clit and it doesn't take long before she's squirming again beneath me.

I pull away and lean over to the bedside table, removing a condom. I rip the foil packet with my teeth and unroll it over the head of my cock. Then I use my cock to tease her pussy, sliding it over her wetness, pushing inside just an inch before pulling out and stroking her clit with the head.

When she's breathing hard and her eyes close, I know she's close so I push inside all the way and she groans in response.

I stand with my cock buried inside of her and just enjoy the sight of her lying beneath me, her thighs spread wide, her heels in the air, her breasts flushed and her nipples hard.

God, I love the way she looks like right now...

My thumb on her clit, I start to thrust, slow at first and then faster, circling her clit with my thumb to keep up the stimulation.

"Tell me when you're going to come," I say.

She nods, but she's lost in her world of pleasure, her mouth open.

I pump harder, and reposition her to get maximum friction, and then she starts to pant.

"I'm there," she says in a strangled voice. "I'm coming..."

I watch her body as she comes, her belly tensing, her nipples hardening into tiny buds, her eyes half-lidded.

"Oh, God," she cries out and I feel her body squeezing rhythmically around my cock as she comes.

I pump harder, faster, and then I'm there as well and I plunge in deep with each spasm as I ejaculate, almost blinded with pleasure as I do.

Finally, I collapse against her, my face beside hers and we're both panting, catching our breath.

"Oh, fuck, that was good."

I remain with my arms on either side of her shoulders and watch her for a moment while my cock slowly deflates. I kiss her when she finally opens her eyes and meets mine.

"You decided not to fight it anymore?"

She nods. "I want you. I'll take what I can get."

"You got all of me," I say. "Every inch." I flex my cock, and she smiles in response, giggling just a bit the way I love.

"They're considerable inches," she replies.

"I'm no slouch in the inches department," I say and kiss her neck, unable to stop smiling.

Finally, I grab hold of the condom and pull out of her completely, then remove the condom, tie it off and throw it into the trash can beside the bed.

I lie back on top of her and we kiss. Just a tender kiss, to reconnect with her after pulling away.

"So, was it as good as it looked?"

She smiles, her eyes closed. "You need to ask?"

"No, but I like to hear you say it. It's motivational."

She opens her eyes. "It was better than it looked. You can do that anytime and anywhere you want."

I smile. "Is that a promise?"

She smiles back at me and closes her eyes once more, running her fingers through her long hair. "Anytime and anywhere. I'm serious. I'm your sex slave if you keep doing that."

"I'll make you live up to that promise," I say. "I happen to like the idea of you being my sex slave. I'll fuck you in the executive bathroom at work. I'll fuck you in the back of my SUV in the parking lot. I'll have you sit on my face in my office and make you come on my tongue in the middle of the day."

"You can do whatever you want with my body, if you make me come like that."

"I will," I say. "No questions asked, though. No hesitation."

She opens her eyes and then there's a moment of something – if not hesitation, at least intrigue. "What will happen if I hesitate?"

I shrug and lick her nipple. "Maybe I'll deny you an orgasm but still take mine."

"That wouldn't be very nice."

"It would teach you a lesson, though. No hesitation."

She smiles. "I won't. I like the idea of you telling me what to do and when to do it."

"You get off on a bit of dominance and submission?"

"A bit, yes."

I nod, but don't say anything. I enjoy taking control and while I know we're complete equals outside the bedroom, in terms of sex, I'll be the one to decide when and where and how.

Suits me perfectly.

Some women just want to give up control during sex so they can do things they never imagined doing before. They want and need the license to feel pleasure in ways they think might be too dirty or risqué.

I'm the kind of man who likes to take them there.

India in particular.

The thought of having India under my control sexually makes me semi-hard again, a pleasant throb in my dick.

"Looks like I'm going to have to fuck you again," I say, and press my now-thickening erection against her belly.

So I do.

"I don't know if I can come again," she says in meek protest.

"Okay," I say. "Let me use your body. I want to."

"Please do. How do you want me?" she asks, pleased to be ordered around.

"On your hands and knees."

She complies, and I rub her buttocks before sliding on another condom, then I fuck her from behind like I promised. But that's not enough for me. I want her to come again too.

After a considerable number of position changes, sucking her nipples and clit again, and after fucking her in every possible position, she cries out with pleasure once more and I'm right there behind her, grunting like an animal when I come, my pleasure so intense that I can barely see.

She's mine.

Her body is mine. Her cunt is mine. Her pussy is mine. If she thought she could go back to the way we were before I kissed her that night after her bad date with Pencil Neck she was wrong.

We can't ever go back.

After we've both recovered sufficiently, I remove my condom, and this time, I lie back on top of her and I'm exhausted. I really have no more strength after my run and fucking her twice.

"I should get up," she says. "I need to pee."

"You're staying the night," I say and it's not a request. It's an order.

"Maybe I better not," she replies. "I'm going to see my mom tomorrow morning for breakfast early."

"Nope," I say and hold her down when she squirms. "You said I could be in control and fuck you when and where I want, and I want to fuck you first thing in the morning. You have to stay."

"Jon," she says, but she's smiling and I know she doesn't really want to leave.

"India," I say back. "You promised me anytime and anywhere. I want to eat you until you come at least once in the morning, and then I want to fuck you until you come again. How does that sound?"

She closes her eyes. "It sounds wonderful, but now, I have to pee."

Finally, I let her up and she goes to the bathroom. When she returns, we embrace and lie in the darkness.

With thoughts of her coming under my tongue, I fall asleep, my arms around her body.

# CHAPTER FIFTEEN

## INDIA

Jon comes through on his promise.

The next morning, he wakes me up with roving hands that slide up and down my body, squeezing my breasts and pressing his morning erection against my butt. I smile to myself and turn over, and he has this gleam in his eyes that promises so much...

He really is very good at this. I guess all that practice does make perfect.

I stiff-arm him when he tries to kiss me. "You have to let me brush my teeth first."

"All right," he says with a laugh. "Women..."

I escape his arms and grab my bag. I've thought ahead and have squirreled away a fresh pair of undies and a toothbrush in it so I can avoid the dreaded morning breath, and be able to go straight to the hospital when I want to.

Jon follows me into the bathroom and brushes his teeth as well. The two of us stand side by side and brush our teeth and it

179

amuses me that we're both naked. He's definitely interested, his cock – his very ample cock – stiffening while he stands beside me. His eyes move over my body and I know he's already planning how he'll take me and make me come several times before I can leave.

That's fine with me.

I finish brushing and then rinse, before standing in wait while he finishes. He rinses and spits, then grabs me, and I can't help but giggle when he nuzzles his face into the crook of my neck.

"Hey," he says, in mock protest. "No laughing. Only moans and groans of pleasure from now on."

"I like laughing." I wrap my arms around his neck and sigh when he starts to lick my neck, his tongue moving in small circles, making me think of where else I want that tongue to be.

He pulls me into the shower – a two-person version with amazing shower heads on the ceiling and walls. After the water starts, we stand beneath its soft warm stream and get wet, then he starts to lather me up, his hands soapy. "Let me do you first, then you can do me."

"Okay," I say and close my eyes when he begins to wash me, his soap-slick hands moving over my body, my shoulders, my breasts, and then down between my thighs and buttocks. His fingers linger between my thighs, stroking me, working me up and then he takes the shower head off the wall and rinses me off.

When he's done washing me, I wash him, following the same pattern, spending time on his nice thick erection and balls. He leans against the wall with me between his outspread arms, his eyes on mine as I stroke him.

"That's enough," he says, his voice thick and throaty with lust. I rinse him off and then we stand together in the shower stall, the warm water pouring down over his back. He kneels and lifts one of my thighs over his shoulder and does what he promised, making me come the first time with his mouth. When

I'm finished, he shuts off the water, slips on a condom he removes from a drawer in the vanity and fucks me while we're still in the shower. By the time we're both finished, panting from the force of our orgasms, my fingers and toes are all wrinkled.

We dry each other off and it's tender and wordless.

Then, when we're both dry, Jon pulls me into his arms and kisses me, and his kiss is equally tender rather than needy, the way it was before we fucked.

"I could get used to this," he says, his mouth against my neck. "Like every day and night."

"My skin would stay permanently pruney."

He laughs and pulls me more tightly against his body and we rock together, enjoying the warmth of our bodies pressed together.

"Time to go back to the real world," I say and kiss him briefly before pulling out of his arms. "I want to go and see my mom."

"Okay," he says. "I'll let you go, but you have to know that when you step foot into my apartment, you're mine. You do what I say when I say it. You take your clothes off when I tell you and you spread those delicious thighs when I tell you."

"Your wish is my command," I say playfully. "I hope you'll give me a break now and then to come up for air and for food."

Jon laughs. "I'll cook you dinner tonight so don't worry about going hungry."

"Sounds perfect."

I get dressed and so does Jon, the two of us pulling on clothes and talking about the upcoming business meeting we have with one of our suppliers. We're thinking of ramping up production on one of our drones, so we need more parts and we're sourcing more if our current supplier can't keep up.

When I'm finished dressing, I grab my bag and go to the front door.

Jon stops me, putting his arms around my waist and pulling me against his hips.

"Will you be in at work this afternoon?"

"I have lunch with Marina and a friend from Stanford, but afterward."

"You really should tell Marina about us."

I shake my head. "I don't need the aggravation."

"She'll find out from someone at work."

"I won't invite her to any of our work functions."

"She's going to keep trying to match you with a new date," Jon says, frowning.

"I'll humor her. I said I'd help her with the app and I will. Maybe I'll help her re-design the questionnaire. She really has to think twice about moving forward with it if she failed to match either of us using it."

Jon kisses me. "It's up to you. I think you should tell her and tell her to accept it or shut the fuck up, but that's just me."

"She's my best friend, Jon."

"I thought I was your best friend," he says with a big fake pout that's only half-joking.

"You're my best *male* friend and my lover," I say. "A woman needs a best girlfriend to survive. I need Marina. She keeps me sane."

Jon nods, but I can tell he doesn't really believe it. I know he thinks she has far too much influence over me, but that's just because Marina doesn't really like Jon and doesn't want us together.

She's going to have to deal.

They're both just going to have to accept that the other person is important to me, and just chill.

I kiss Jon once more and then leave, taking the stairs to the front entrance and out into the clear, bright morning.

I breathe in deeply, enjoying the morning, then take my car to the hospital to see my mom.

She's doing much better when I arrive and had a good night. She's even sitting up in bed, eating her snack of a cup of tea and a muffin. It's good to see her improving enough that she can sit up by herself.

We talk about everything, and then out of the blue, she asks me about Jon.

"You look happy. What's happening between you two? Did you think about what we talked about?" She raises her eyebrows expectantly.

"We decided to give it a try," I say, unable to hide my smile. "But we're keeping it quiet – at least from Marina."

"You should be honest with her. She's only going to cause you trouble if you don't tell her the truth."

"She's busy trying to perfect her matchmaking app. She needs both of us to help her."

My mom frowns. "You're not going to keep letting her set you up with dates, are you? That won't be good for your relationship with Jon."

"I'll advise her to rework her app. I don't want to go on any more of her dates, and I won't, but I can help her with the questionnaire without agreeing to date any of her picks for me. No more blindly going along."

"Honesty is the best policy."

"I know, I know," I say and kiss her cheek. "I will. Eventually. Right now, I don't want a big kerfuffle when Jon and I are just trying things out. Who knows if they'll work between us? I don't want everyone and their dog giving us a hard time. Especially not Marina."

My mom pouts. "She should be happy for you two."

"She doesn't like Jon for some reason," I say with a sigh. "Probably because he doesn't fit neatly into her view of love and romance."

"Does he fit into yours?"

I shrug. "He fits really well into everything else," I say, meaning work. Then we both laugh at the double entendre. "You know what I mean," I say.

I kiss her again and then leave, making my way home so I can do a bit of work before meeting Marina and the girls for brunch.

While I'm there, I get a text from Marina.

*MARINA: I have someone who really wants to meet you, sug. Are you up for a coffee date this week?*

I sigh, realizing that this is going to continue unless I put my foot down.

*INDIA: I think you better work on the questionnaire before I go on any more of your dates for me. Zero for three is not very good track record...*

*MARINA: This guy is perfect. I mean it. Tall, blond, blue eyes like you wouldn't believe. Smart. Rich. Even in the biz – has a startup in Silicon Valley that's doing well.*

It sounds like Jon and I wonder why, if her app is so good, it doesn't match Jon and me together. It's obvious the two of us want to be together. Yet, Marina's app is so bad that it doesn't catch how right we are together.

*INDIA: I don't think so. I will work on the questionnaire if you want me to, though.*

*MARINA: The questionnaire is fine. It's the people who aren't following the rules.*

*INDIA: You don't really mean that, do you? Supposed to be the other way around.*

*MARINA: Sometimes people aren't being honest with the questions. I may need to tweak it a bit to make sure people are consistent with their responses. That might improve its results. You may be right.*

*INDIA: I'll be happy to sit down with you and work on it.*

*MARINA: Sounds good. How about tonight? I want to get it done as quickly as possible. I have a meeting with my coder tomorrow and we could start tweaking it right away. Come over for dinner and you can spend the evening with me, working on it. We can do some tests of it with different customers.*

I think to myself that Jon is expecting me to come over tonight for supper at his place and to spend the evening together.

*INDIA: Okay. What do you want me to bring?*

*MARINA: Just your sweet self.*

*INDIA: Will do. Later.*

I put my cell away. I know Jon will be upset that I'm breaking plans with him to spend time with Marina, but he's the one who suggested that Marina's app needs tweaking...

I text Jon to let him know.

*INDIA: Have to call a rain check on the date tonight. Marina asked me over to work on the questionnaire because she's meeting with her coder tomorrow and wants it ready to go.*

I wait for the response, figuring he'll be upset.

*JON: When I suggested that you encourage Marina to rework the app, I meant so she wouldn't try to match you up with anyone else and cut into my time with you...*

*INDIA: I know, but this is kind of important for her. I'll make it up to you.*

*JON: Okay... Can you come over after you two are done?*

*INDIA: If I'm done early enough. If not, there's always tomorrow night.*

*JON: Okay. Will you be in the office later today, at least?*

*INDIA: Yes. See you then.*

*JON: K.*

.  .  .

185

DAMN. I have these two very demanding friends and colleagues. They don't like each other, and each expect that I'll prioritize them over the other.

It's going to be a long day...

I MEET Marina and Jill for brunch at a local deli and as usual, we go over our weeks and what exciting or extremely boring things happened to us.

Marina tells Jill about her attempts to match me with a few of her Stanford customers. Jill is all excited for me, her eyes bright.

"That's too bad that none of them worked out," Jill says, her voice sympathetic. "I thought you and Jon were going to be a thing."

Marina glances at me quickly and then frowns. "Jon is a manslut. India wants someone stable and dependable. Jon's the last person she should be with."

"I think he's secretly in love with you," Jill says, a sparkle in her eyes. "He's such a dreamy guy with those big biceps and tattoos. Plus, you gotta admire his face. He's gorgeous. Rich. Alpha..."

"Jon's into casual sex and that's it," Marina says, folding her napkin primly. "India isn't. So they most definitely are not a match, even if Jon does want to fuck her. He wants to fuck every woman he finds attractive."

"And most of them want to fuck him back." Jill raises her eyebrows. "Am I right?" She looks between Marina and me. "Don't you ever wonder what he's like in bed?"

Marina practically glares at Jill. "Look, I've been trying to keep India away from Jon's clutches for years. Don't encourage her."

"I think they'd be a perfect match."

"You're such a romantic," Marina says and takes a drink of her coffee.

"Says the woman who designed a dating app," Jill replies with a laugh. "I can't believe they're not together now. They're like two peas in a pod."

"You're completely wrong. Believe me. They are the last two people who should get together. Jon would have to have an epiphany about life and love, or India would have to give up any hope of having a real partner who loves her. Jon is a dedicated manwhore and I doubt anything will change him anytime soon."

Marina glances at me, and I don't say anything. Instead, I push my food around on my plate, wondering if I'm ever going to be able to tell her about us and what will happen when I do.

"You're right. He is that," I say finally, when I realize it would look strange for me not to agree with Marina.

"He'll settle down when he finds the right woman," Jill says. "Don't you want him, India? We've always thought you two would finally just give in and get together. Stop all of us placing our bets and wondering. Especially after Blaine left you like that and you decided to stay instead of go with him. That was such a shocker. I thought you stayed because of Jon."

"I stayed because Blaine didn't want to tell me what I'd be if I moved with him. He thought I should just move and take a chance. Give up my stake in Pacifica for nothing. I couldn't do it."

"We all thought it was Jon you couldn't stand to leave, not Pacifica. I expected you to fall into Jon's arms for comfort. Remember, Marina? You said it wouldn't happen?" She frowns and looks at Marina expectantly.

"I don't remember. It doesn't matter, anyway. Jon wouldn't know how to be a real partner, so India's better off being single rather than being with him."

"Jon will settle down someday," I say, frowning at Marina.

187

"He's just not ready. He's not a bad person. He's really very smart and nice."

"See?" Jill says and elbows Marina. "She's secretly in love with him."

I don't say anything. I'm not going to lie.

Marina answers for me anyway. "She's not in love with him," she says, and squeezes my arm. "They're business partners and friends. India knows she can't throw her heart away on a guy who can't make a commitment."

Jill shrugs. "I'm surprised your app didn't match the two of them together."

Marina opens her mouth to speak, but thinks better of it. Instead, she forces a smile and drinks her coffee.

I don't say anything because I don't want to risk the wrath of Marina, but the truth is that Jon and I have been circling around each other for five years. If her app hasn't matched us, it really needs work.

Jill seems happy, probably because she's said her piece and got in the last word. Which is unusual in a conversation with Marina.

We move on, but I think Jill gets the hint that the subject of me with Jon is verboten.

When we're leaving, I stop by Marina's car while she searches in her bag for her keys.

"You know, Jon isn't a bad person," I say, wanting to defend him. "He's really very decent. He treats his staff well, and he's a very loyal son to his mother, especially after his dad died. He's always been good to me, and he agreed to help you when you wanted to test MATCHED on him, even though he's not the dating type. I don't know why you hate him so much."

"I don't hate him," Marina says and finds her keys. "I'm just realistic about whether he'd be good for you." She comes to me, her hand on my arm. "I was with you after Blaine left. I'm just trying to prevent you from having a broken heart again."

I can't argue with her.

"See you later," I say and we air kiss before she gets into her car.

I leave, my stomach in a knot, and take my car to the office. I plan on putting in a few hours before I head home for an evening visit to see my mom, then to Marina's and finally, to see Jon. When I slip the car into my spot in the parking garage, I turn off the car and sit there for a moment and just cry.

I don't know why I'm crying.

I wipe my eyes and shake myself mentally. Quit overanalyzing. Just enjoy Jon.

I take out my makeup mirror from my bag and check my makeup, which has smeared a bit. I touch it up and apply some powder to my nose to cover up the redness and take in a deep breath.

I have work to do. I can't let myself be a sniveling female worried about some man. I'm a successful businesswoman, CTO with a multimillion-dollar tech company. I'm smart, attractive, and a good person.

I'll give Jon time.

But I'm not waiting forever.


WHEN I GET to the office, I see that Chris, our CFO, is in his office working on a Sunday. He takes care of all the corporate matters for Pacifica and is usually a straight nine to five kind of guy because of family commitments. It's Sunday so he must have something coming up. Today, he's wearing a Hawaiian shirt, a straw hat, and dark-rimmed glasses. It looks like Bing Crosby slipped into the office during the middle of a game of golf.

"What's up, India?"

I sit in the chair across from him.

"If I were to sell all my shares in Pacifica, how much would they be worth?"

He raises his eyebrows, but doesn't say anything. Instead, he turns to a third monitor on his desk and clicks on a keyboard.

"Let's see..." He clicks through a few screens. "Considering what the company is worth, you're looking at about $3.2 million, if you sold them all."

I sit and consider. "What could I do with $3.2 million?"

"You could invest it and live off the interest if you don't mind living off $120,000 a year. That's about one quarter of your income from Pacifica. It would be quite a decline."

I sigh. I knew it. We'd have to expand Pacifica a lot before I could quit, sell my shares, and move away.

It's not like I want to leave my mom, considering, and my friends are here and I like the climate. But I've always wanted to move out East.

"Thanks," I say to Chris. "I was just wondering how much longer I need to stay with Pacifica. I'd like to get into something else – maybe biotech, so I was wondering how much of an investment I would need to make."

"You could invest as a partner in a startup with the seed money you would get, but it wouldn't be a certain thing like Pacifica. With the potential new defense contracts we're looking at down the road, Pacifica is set to take off in the next couple of years. Your shares will likely quadruple at least. Maybe more if you stay."

I nod. "I'm not planning on leaving anytime soon. Just wondering. Don't say anything, okay?"

"Mum's the word."

I leave his office and return to mine. Jon's door is closed so I'm not even sure he's in. I didn't ask when I came in so I go inside my own office and close my door.

While \$3.2 million is a considerable amount of money, it's not enough to live off. I need more if I also want to start a new business. I hadn't planned on leaving Pacifica until my shares are worth at least a hundred million, so I could really do something big.

If things don't work out with Jon, it'll be really hard to stay.

I have to rethink things.

# CHAPTER SIXTEEN

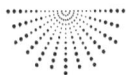

## JON

I GO for a run after India leaves to clear my head and get ready for an afternoon at the office. Although it's Sunday, I usually don't take the day off unless I have out of town travel.

After my run and shower, I get dressed and am a bit late getting in to work.

I check India's office, but she's out with her friends and visiting her mother so I don't expect her in until later in the afternoon. I have a meeting with one of my staff, and after the meeting's over, I go out to the main office and see that Chris's office door is open.

He waves me in.

I go inside and he points at the door. "Close it, will you?"

I do and sit across from him, wondering if there's a problem with the financial side of things.

"What's up?"

He folds his hands and gives me this tired look. "India was in

193

wondering how much her shares would be worth if she cashed them in now."

"What?" I frown and look down at the floor, trying to take in what Chris just said. India's considering selling her shares?

"She asked me not to say anything, but I thought you should know, just in case she's planning to leave. Replacing her would be quite a challenge. There aren't too many CTOs wandering the streets looking for work, especially not with her experience in the aerospace industry. We should do some quiet headhunting just in case."

I sit, unable to respond at first, totally shocked that India would even consider leaving Pacifica.

I could see her telling me to fuck off, but Pacifica? It's her baby as much as mine. Or any of the partners who came together initially to fund and build it.

"Thanks for giving me a heads-up. Don't talk to anyone else until I have some time to feel India out, okay? I don't want us to get ahead of ourselves on this. It may be nothing."

"Sure," he says and gives me a nod. "Like I said, I just thought you should know in case she really does decide to leave."

"No problem." I sit up straighter. "Was there anything else? Anything I should be aware of?"

"Not on my part. Everything's fine."

"Good." I stand and rub my hands together. "I'll leave you to it."

I leave and make my way back to my office. India's door is still closed and I stand outside and debate with myself whether to go inside and confront her or wait.

I don't want her to think I've been gossiping about her behind her back. Which I have been doing, of course.

I decide to wait and bring it up when it's not posed so confrontationally. Maybe tonight after we have dinner together – and I plan on making dinner for her and fucking her brains out –

I'll very deftly talk about Pacifica's market capitalization and how much it's improved, and ask her gently about her talk with Chris.

I try to focus on work and spend some time going over the financial reports that have been sitting on my desk for a couple of days, unread. After about an hour, I look up when India's door opens across the hall from me and she leaves, her bag on her shoulder.

She doesn't look my way or pop her head in to say hello.

She's leaving already?

I sit for a moment and debate whether to follow her.

I hear her speaking with our admin staff, and then nothing.

She's actually leaving without saying anything to me...? That's when I know something's wrong.

I hop up and leave my office, determined to follow her and confront her about that much, even if I hold off talking to her about what Chris told me.

I catch up to her at the stairs and grab hold of her arm, turning her around to face me on the landing.

"Were you going to leave the office without even saying hello?"

"Oh, Jon," she says, like she's surprised. We're alone but she still glances around to check. "You scared me. I'm just going to get a juice." She forces a smile. "I'm feeling a bit under the weather and thought some apple-carrot-kale would be good."

"I'll join you."

Her smile fades.

That's when I know she wasn't planning on coming back.

"I was going to go see my mom after I get the juice."

"You're not coming back to the office?"

She shakes her head. "I've put in a few hours. Besides, I want to cook supper for my dad. He's been eating cafeteria food all week."

I let go of her arm and she starts down the rest of the stairs.

I don't try to stop her. "Come over after you're done supper if you want."

She glances back at me. "I'll see how I feel."

"Open invitation."

"I know," she adds and forces a smile. "If I don't see you tonight, I'll see you at work tomorrow. Same time, same bat channel."

I smile at her Batman reference, but I feel a knot in my gut.

Her leaving and not telling me isn't out of the norm. She would always pop her head in and say hello, but she would often leave without saying goodbye. Not seeing her until tomorrow is totally normal for us – before we fucked.

Now, it feels like she's ignoring me. Deliberately or not.

I don't like the way it feels.

"India," I call out. She stops at the bottom of the stairs and turns around, looking up at me on the landing.

"Yes?"

"Are you all right?"

She nods, but it isn't exactly enthusiastic. "I'm tired. I guess the stress of everything is getting to me. I need to take some time off."

I come down the stairs and stand in front of her, my hand on the door. "You can talk to me about anything, you know."

"I know," she says softly but I can tell from her voice that she doesn't feel that way.

Obviously, she doesn't feel she can talk to me about anything anymore.

"Has this totally fucked our relationship?"

She exhales and looks away, like she can't meet my eyes. "I don't know."

"I don't want this to have fucked things up."

"Me neither."

"You have to tell me how you feel, India."

"I don't know how I feel, Jon, except confused." She meets my eyes finally, and I see the pain in them – in the way her brow is furrowed. It's not anger. It's sadness.

I reach out and cup her cheek, stroke her skin with my fingers. "I only know that I want you," I say, because it's the truth. "Whatever that means and whatever that involves."

She nods, but she doesn't reply with something similar. Instead, she pushes the door open and leaves me standing there in the entrance, the door closing behind her.

Crap.

I watch her walk down the street until she disappears around the corner.

Now what the fuck do I do?

I SIT BACK DOWN behind my desk and glower at my computer screen. On it, a report on third quarter projections sits unread. I try to read it, but end up only re-reading the same sentence over and over.

Then Marina sends me a text.

MARINA: *I have a new match for you. If you want to meet her, she's ready and willing! She'd like to meet at Mulvaney's for a drink if you're interested. I'll send you her profile but she's a massage therapist with an interest in interior decoration and real estate flipping. She's twenty-five and has a certificate in massage therapy from the Brookbridge Institute. You can see that she's gorgeous and blonde, just the way you like them! Tell me this isn't a perfect match! Let me know when you want to meet her.*

I read over the profile Marina sent to my email. The photo depicts a beautiful young woman with long blonde hair and lots of makeup. She's wearing something seductive – a deep-cut sweater that shows off ample cleavage.

Typical of Marina to have matched me with someone who is

everything I would normally prefer in a woman – beautiful, blonde, tall, built, and looking for an uncomplicated relationship for fun and social engagements: *No long-term commitments! I'm too young!*

I want to put her off, but make her think I support her. For India's sake.

*JON: She's lovely, but I'm too busy right now with work to be meeting anyone. Maybe after a few of our upcoming business trips and contract negotiations are finished.*

*MARINA: So you like her? She's perfect, right? I'll tell her you're definitely interested but maybe in a few weeks?*

*JON: I'll let you know if and when I'm available. How's that sound?*

*MARINA: Okay. Don't wait too long. A beautiful woman like her will be snapped up quickly.*

*JON: I'm sure she will be. By the way, I thought your app was for Stanford grads. None of the women you've matched me with are from Stanford.*

*MARINA: Oh, it's for Stanford men, mostly.*

*JON: But you're matching India...*

*MARINA: She's just a test subject to see if I can match Stanford women. There not as plentiful in grad school – only thirty-nine percent – so I'm focusing on the men first. They're pretty easy – a beautiful woman, great figure, smile, and easy-going attitude. Most men are intimidated by a woman as smart and successful as India, so only the most confident and successful guys will do in her case.*

*JON: I think that's sexist, isn't it?*

*MARINA: No, it's realist, Jon. In case you didn't live in the real world. Which you don't. I mean, you're the CEO of a multi-million-dollar tech company. You're handsome and well-educated. You have your pick of the crop as a result. Not all Stanford grads are as successful as you or have the same options as you. You live in a very rarefied atmosphere.*

JON: *Yes, I realize that. I don't need your app to find a date, Marina. I'm only going along to help you out because you're India's friend.*

MARINA: *I know you don't need my help getting laid, Jon. But finding a girlfriend? Maybe, yes. In fact, I think so. Definitely.*

JON: *I don't need help finding a girlfriend, Marina. Given MATCHED's failure to find me anyone even remotely interesting, I think you better go back to the drawing board.*

Oh, crap... Now I've done it.

MARINA: *'Remotely interesting'? Those women were beautiful and sexy and would have been happy to go home with you. That's always been good enough for you before.*

JON: *It's obvious we don't see eye to eye on this. I gotta go and get some work done.*

MARINA: *So, do I strike you off my list of customers?*

JON: *Yes, please do.*

I turn off my cell and slam it down on the desktop.

Goddamn meddling woman.

I spend another couple of hours at work and then plan to leave just after five. Everyone else has left for the day, so I close up and walk down to the parking garage where I keep my vehicle. I get inside and sit there, wondering what the fuck is going on with India.

Is she really thinking of selling her stocks in Pacifica and leaving?

That's it – we fucked and it's screwed with her mind.

She's one of those women who doesn't fuck around. She only has serious relationships – hasn't she told me that for years? Yet, she fucked me.

Now she regrets it. It's not in her to just have casual sex with someone – even someone she really likes. I've always known that.

199

What the fuck was I thinking, breaching that divide between us that kept us professional?

I wanted to have my cake and eat it, too.

India and Pacifica have always gone hand in hand for me. I've always wanted them both – together, preferably. I thought I could have them both.

I hope I wasn't wrong.

I DON'T WANT to go back to my apartment alone, so I call up my old friend Dan from the Army and invite him for a drink. He's only too happy to meet me. We used to surf together, and did some base jumping down in South America one year. He's a wild man and loves the adrenaline rush as much as I do.

We meet at a local bar just down the block from where I live.

He looks just the same as before – tall, heavy-set but ripped, a big fucker with a head of jet black hair and bulging muscles under a white t-shirt and jeans.

We clasp hands and hug briefly before sitting down at the bar and catching up on what we've both been up to.

"I know Pacifica's doing well," Dan says after a long pull on his draft beer. "I saw some report on CNBC that mentioned you guys."

"It is doing well," I say, and tell him about our recent contracts with the Defense Department. As for Dan, he's a consultant in a security company and is thinking of starting his own business.

"So, what about that pretty CTO of yours?" he asks me. "India? Is she still there?"

"She is," I say, remembering how Dan hung around India when he met her a couple of years ago.

"Is she still single?" he asks, his expression unreadable. "She was one pretty little filly."

I laugh at his tone. "You liked her," I say and it's a statement, not a question.

"I did," he says, finally smiling. "What's she doing? Is she married yet?"

"No," I say, then I tell him about us. "In fact, we kind of got together recently, but I'm not sure if things will work out."

"Oh, that's too bad," he says, genuinely sympathetic. "It must be hard to have a relationship with a business partner. Especially when it doesn't work out."

I shrug. "I'm fine with it, but she's uncomfortable. We're trying to figure things out."

"Well, I hope it works out for you."

We talk some more about his life and how he's dating again after the divorce, and is looking for a new woman who could be a mother to his two children, whom he has shared custody of.

"So you're totally domesticated, are you?" I say with a laugh.

"Happily," he replies, holding up his glass of beer. "A man without the love of a good woman is only a shell."

I laugh and take a drink. "Speak for yourself. I'm not a shell."

"Of course you aren't," he says. "But a man can only take so much meaningless pussy before he craves something real."

I don't say anything in response.

After an awkward silence, we move on to future plans and how we both want to do some more surfing when the waves are good. The rest of the hour goes by quickly and then, after we've finished the food, it's time to leave.

We shake hands again and hug, and I walk him to his van, just down the block.

"Don't be a stranger," he says.

We fist bump. "I won't."

I watch him drive off in his van and think how much he's changed since we were in the Army together.

Back then, he was a wild man who picked up every piece of

ass that passed his way and offered. He was an adrenaline junkie who seemed to defy death with every fall and crash and IED. He loved the ladies, he loved his beer, and he loved being a soldier.

Now, he's a security analyst with two kids and an ex-wife, looking for a good woman to move in and take her place.

Is that my future?

I don't want to become the man in the gray flannel suit who is so strapped by debt and busy with responsibilities that I never have any fun.

Is that what India wants?

I can't see her staying at home with kids and a house to clean, giving up business to raise a family. Maybe I don't really know her.

I want her. That's not the issue. I want us to be together. I also want us both to focus on Pacifica and our mutual success.

She was thinking of cashing out and leaving Pacifica.

Fuck...

# CHAPTER SEVENTEEN

## INDIA

MOM IS GETTING BETTER with each day, and is going home tomorrow. The doctors think she'll regain full use of her arms and legs, so that's a relief. She'll have to take it easy for a while and get some rehab but she'll return to a normal life.

"No more climbing ladders," the neurosurgeon says, pointing at her. He smiles at her and she agrees she won't.

When my mom's tray comes for her supper, I check it out and laugh.

"I'm making chicken parmesan for Dad, too."

"Oh, I wish I was home with you two," mom says, staring at her much more assembly-line-looking chicken breast with a half-melted slab of mozzarella on it.

"If I don't kill Dad with my own version, I'll make it for you when you get out."

"You won't kill him," she says with a grin. "Just remember to set the timer. I know you two get distracted and have a tendency to burn stuff, so remember to time it."

"I will." I kiss her and leave, relieved that she's doing so well.

I take my SUV and drive to their place. I turn on my car mix and the next song up is "I Go Crazy" by Paul Davis. It's one of my father's favorites and makes me sad to hear it. Will that be Jon and me?

I pull into the driveway, a knot in my gut that things are so uncertain with Jon. My dad is standing at the door, waiting for me, his apron already on. I swallow my feelings and force a smile.

He and I are not gifted cooks. It was my mom who cooked for us when I was growing up. But we'll try to follow the recipe I printed off the internet. The recipe was apparently fool-proof and so even my dad and I should be able to handle it.

Two hours later, we're sitting at the island in my mom's professional kitchen, smiling at the successful meal we cooked together. I really enjoyed it. My dad and I always shared a love of technology and spent time when I was growing up putting computers together, but we didn't do a lot of talking about life and personal things. That was always my mom's job.

So now, here we are, smiling across the island, a glass of red wine in hand and a demolished dish of chicken parmesan in front of us.

"So, tell me about what's going on with you. Your mom said you and Jon got together but that you're having second thoughts."

"She told you that?"

I didn't think I told her I was having second thoughts. I thought I just said I wasn't sure if Jon was able to make a commitment to the relationship.

"I love Jon," I say to him. "I mean, I love him as a person. I think I could love him as a man, in that way. But I don't know if he can do that back."

"Hun, you two have known each other for how long? Five

years? If you don't know each other by now, you never will. You know him as a person and a man. Do you think he's a good man?"

"He is," I say, imagining him in my mind's eye. "He's a very good person and man. He's a former Army Ranger. He's brave and he's strong and he's ambitious and he's funny. But he plays around and has never had a serious relationship."

"Maybe he's never had you." My father raises his eyebrows like he's made a point in our discussion. It feels like *the* point. "Maybe," he says, and takes my hand, squeezing it, "you have to give him a chance."

"And ruin our business relationship? We have an amazing partnership. We work really well together. We're good together. I don't want to ruin that."

"Then don't. Go all in. It seems to me that you've already more than dipped your toe into this. Go big or go home, I always say."

I smile at him and squeeze his hand back. "How did you get so smart about relationships?"

"I met your mom and she taught me everything I know about love and marriage. You and Steven taught me everything I know about being a father."

I squeeze his hand again. Both of us are silent for a moment, thinking about Steven's death, which has left a hole in my heart that can never be filled. It can only grow scar tissue where the hole still is.

"I hope things work out with you and Jon," my dad says after a moment. "He's a really smart, successful, hard-working, honorable young man."

"You think so?" I say, surprised to hear him talk about Jon that way.

"I do," he says. "If Steven liked him, I know he's a good guy."

That makes me feel better about Jon. I know it's crazy. I'm a grown woman. I should be able to decide on my own who I sleep with and who I love, but I'm afraid of making a mistake. I'm afraid of not having listened to Marina, who has warned me off Jon whenever the subject of me getting together with him has surfaced, which it has on and off over the years.

Dad and I clean up after the meal is over and I kiss him good-bye. He's going back up to the hospital to see my mom once more and I'm going home.

I DRIVE along the streets back to my place, thinking of everything – of my mom's recovery, of my dad's words to me about love and giving Jon a chance, and most of all, about Jon. On my music mix, "If You Leave Me Now" by Chicago comes on. I skip ahead. "Make it With You" by Bread.

I turn off the MP3 player and listen to a local newscast instead.

I don't need the sappy seventies music that I normally love.

I only know I want Jon.

When I get back home, I make a cup of decaf coffee and sit on my patio in the darkness, overlooking the Bay. I love this time of night, just after the sun has set and the horizon is still slightly pink from the setting sun. The stars begin to peek out and I can hear the hum of the freeway in the distance.

I feel so lonely.

My cell pings and I remove it from my bag and check.

JON: *Can we talk?*

I was hoping to spend the evening without thinking about Jon, but I can't escape this.

INDIA: *Talk away.*

JON: *I mean in person. I have more powers when I'm physically present to manipulate events to my liking, which happens to include overpowering your futile resistance to my charms.*

*INDIA: You think your physical presence will sway me more than your words?*

*JON: I've been told I have animal magnetism. I like to use that to my advantage.*

*INDIA: I have an interest in preserving my self-control and personal integrity, and I refuse to be manipulated by charlatans and snake oil salesmen.*

There's a pause for a moment. I'm smiling to myself and I imagine Jon is smiling to himself as well.

*JON: India, we have to talk. We have to work this out.*

*INDIA: I know. Can we meet for breakfast tomorrow and talk?*

*JON: We'll be in public, fully clothed, and surrounded by people. That takes away my advantage. I was planning on coming over wearing a muscle shirt and shorts, with me freshly showered, so you're overwhelmed with lust and can't resist me.*

I laugh out loud at that.

*INDIA: You think a muscle shirt and shorts will work? I got news for you.*

*JON: It's my evil plan.*

*INDIA: The best laid plans...*

There's a pause and I know Jon wants me to either go to him or him to come to me. He wants us to be together tonight. He knows that if he gets alone with me, he can seduce me. It will be all the harder to resist him.

Why do I want to resist him?

*INDIA: Jon, I already know you're great in bed. And out of bed. That's not the issue. You proving just how good you are as a lover isn't going to help me decide.*

*JON: Decide what?*

*INDIA: Whether this thing between us is a good idea or a very very bad idea and should be nipped in the bud.*

*JON: I want to nip your buds.*

*INDIA: JON!!!!*

*JON: Okay, okay. Have it your way. We'll meet for breakfast and talk.*

*INDIA: Sounds good to me. Mulligan's? Around eight?*

*JON: See you then.*

I put my cell down and smile, drinking my coffee and watching the ships in the harbor.

THE NEXT MORNING, I get up and shower, then dress for the day in my typical business suit and heels, my hair pulled back in a neat bun, minimal makeup on. I have a meeting today with some suppliers for a part we need for the drone prototype, so I want to look as professional as possible. When I arrive at Mulligan's, Jon is already there, mug of coffee in one hand and the morning paper in the other. He smiles when he sees me and stands when I get to the table, leaning over to pull out my chair. He kisses me, a friendly kiss. He never would have kissed me before all this happened.

We were just business partners and friends.

I sit, and the waitress comes right over to take my order. I get my usual omelet with bacon and a cup of coffee, then turn back to Jon, who's folded his paper and is waiting, his arms crossed on the table, his expression expectant.

"How are you this morning?"

"In public, fully clothed, surrounded by other people, and unmanipulable." I grin at him.

"You always were," he says, his eyes moving over my face. "No matter what I tried."

"Really?" I say, unable to keep from smiling back at him. "I thought you were just hitting on me the way you do every woman who gets close enough to your orbit."

He smiles and glances down at the table top. When he looks

up again, the humor is gone from his eyes, and I think, *Uh-oh. This is Jon being serious...*

"India, this has been going on between us for five years. For five years, I've tried to indicate that I'm interested in you as more than a business partner, but you've always pushed me away."

"And our business partnership has flourished. Pacifica is very successful."

"It has and it is. But I want you as well." He reaches out to take my hand. "India, I *know* you. I know what you want. I'll give you what I can give. You have to decide if it's enough."

I just sit there and look at him for a moment, hoping to see something in his eyes that tells me I can trust him.

"India, do you really think I'd do this if I wasn't very serious about us?"

"I hope not, but I've seen you with so many women..."

"None of them were you."

"Why can't you say the word?"

He pulls his hand away. "What word? What word haven't I said that doesn't indicate I want you and that I don't want anyone else?"

"You know," I say, frustrated that he won't say it. *Exclusive.*

"Take what I can give you or tell me goodbye."

Our food comes, interrupting this very tense moment between us. I sit and glance down at the food and although my stomach was growling on the way over, now, I feel slightly nauseated. I don't like this tension between us. I don't want the drama.

I realize I do want Jon.

"Okay," I say finally. I look up at Jon. He stops what he's doing, apparently surprised at what I've said.

"Okay what?"

"Okay, I'll take what you can give me."

He reaches across the table and takes my hand. He pulls my

hand to his lips and kisses my knuckles. It's a sweet romantic gesture and it warms my heart a little – well, a lot.

"We only live once, India. Don't let your fears keep you from really living."

"You're so fearless," I say, my eyes stinging at the corners. I bite the inside of my lip, to stop my over-reaction to him. Why am I being like this?

I want Jon.

Why can't I just let myself enjoy him?

I'm determined to let myself enjoy him – for however long I have him.

"India, neither of us can predict the future. All we have is what's here and now. What I want is you being with me at work and here and in my bed. That's something I can trust – how we feel when we're together. How we want to get back together when we're apart."

"I know you're right," I say and pull my hand away. "I'm just afraid of being hurt." I pick up my knife and fork and dig into my bacon and eggs.

"I don't ever intend to hurt you," Jon says and he's still focused on me.

"Someone else said that to me once," I say, my voice low. "He hurt me."

"I'm not him. Hurting you is the last thing I want. I want us to be happy and enjoy each other. What we have is unique. It's special. It's not often a man and a woman start a company together and have a relationship that is more than just business. We've always been friends. Now, we'll be more."

I glance up at him.

"For someone who's so dead set against saying the word, you sure say a lot of them."

He cracks a grin. "You're the one who needs words. I thought they'd make you less afraid."

"I like what I heard."

"Good," he says and grabs his piece of toast, using it to spear his egg yolks. "My job here is done."

We finish our meal and after paying the bill, we walk out to our cars, which are parked close to each other.

Jon leans against my car, and pulls me against his body, his arms around my waist. I have no choice but to slip my arms around his neck. We stand there, like that, and press our foreheads together. He's smiling and so am I.

"I'm happy, India," he says. "Finally happy. Let's just be happy together."

We kiss, the kiss tender and sweet, but then he squeezes me more tightly and the kiss goes on and on. A thrill goes through me that we're doing this.

We're really going to give this a try.

"We have a meeting," Jon says when the kiss ends. "And a busy afternoon, but tonight? I want to cook supper for you at your place and I want to drive you crazy with lust and satisfy your needs. I'm going out of town tomorrow and won't be back until Monday. I want to spend the evening with you."

"You and the boys?" I say, remembering his plans to meet up with his buds from the Army and attend some security conference.

"We've been planning all year. I'm flying to Virginia on Saturday morning early and won't be back until Monday night. Until then, I want you. All of you."

"Okay." I smile, glancing in his eyes, which promise so much. "My mom's coming home today and I want to pop by and see her, but afterwards, that sounds perfect."

"It's a date."

I get in my car and he closes the door for me, then he watches as I drive off. I glance in my rear-view mirror and he waves, one hand in his pocket.

We both take our vehicles to the office, arriving within a few minutes of each other. Luckily, we have a lot of work to do and both of us are busy all day, in meetings and on conference calls. I barely have time to even think of Jon and being with him tonight, except when I go to the washroom and can sit for a moment in the silence.

Jon's coming over to cook for me and then we're going to fuck.

A little throb of anticipation tells me how much I'm looking forward to it.

I CALL it a day around six, and pop my head in to Jon's office. He's got a couple of people in with him and they turn when I open the door.

"I'm taking off now."

"Okay," he says, glancing up from an open file on his desk. "Say hello to your mom for me. Give her my best."

"See you later," I add.

I close the door and wonder if the staff in with Jon will realize that *see you later* was about tonight, or if they thought it was just me being friendly.

Knowing our staff, I suspect they'll think the former.

I DRIVE to my parent's place and see that my mother has settled in to the house. She's lying on the sofa in the living room and my dad is picking something up from a local Indian Restaurant so he doesn't have to cook supper.

I sit beside my mother and tell her what happened between Jon and me and how I decided to just take a chance and be with him, even if he couldn't say that word.

"You're not making him bend the knee?" she says jokingly.

I laugh. "No. I'm going to take him for what he is. We'll live dangerously. Whatever happens is whatever happens. I'll try to be brave."

"Good," she says and squeezes my hand. "He's a good boy. You know that."

"He is."

My dad returns and pops his head in the living room. "Am I interrupting?"

"No," I say and wave him in. "Mom and I were just talking about my decision to give Jon the benefit of the doubt."

"That's great," he says and comes over, squeezing my shoulder and kissing the top of my head. "I like him. You two are really good together. I have supper. Are you staying? There's enough for the three of us."

I stand up and grab my bag. "No, I have to go," I say, and go over to the sofa to kiss my mom goodbye. "Jon's coming over to cook me supper. Can you believe it?"

They both smile, and it makes me laugh to see how happy they are that I have someone.

"I hope his cooking skills are better than mine," my dad says with a grin. "Although I had the leftover chicken parmesan tonight and it was just as good as last night."

"Have fun, sweetheart," my mom says from the sofa.

I say goodbye and leave, but before I can get into the car, I hear my cell ding and check my messages.

Marina.

Damn...

MARINA: *Hey, sug, what's up? Feel like me bringing some popcorn over and we can watch the new episode? I missed it last night.*

I bite my bottom lip. I have to lie.

INDIA: *Sorry. No can do. I have work to do tonight for a big meeting with one of our suppliers next week. Maybe tomorrow?*

I wait for her response.

*MARINA: K. Talk later. Bye*
*INDIA: Bye.*

I put my cell in my bag and drive off, feeling very guilty that I'm lying to her, but I don't need a lecture, especially after it was so hard for me to finally make a real decision. I don't want her doubts to start creeping into my mind.

I had enough of them on my own.

I GET HOME and have a quick shower, wanting to be as fresh as I can because I suspect that once Jon arrives, we won't be doing any cooking until we've fucked at least once. Knowing Jon, it'll probably end with me having two orgasms to his one.

After my shower, I check out my closet and select a sexy black sundress with thin straps and a plunging neckline. It has a single zipper in the back and a built-in bra so Jon won't have to do any fumbling with the catch. I slip on a fresh pair of undies, selecting a lacy black thong. I glance at myself out in the mirror, expecting that Jon will make me stand before him in my heels and thong. I look good.

The doorbell rings and I check my face in the bathroom mirror once before answering it.

There he stands, looking like a million dollars or so, in a fresh white button-down shirt and black chinos. The white shirt highlights his pale blue eyes, and his longish hair is freshly washed. He must have just stepped out of a shower as well, because the ends are still wet.

He leans against the doorjamb, one hand in his pocket, and the other behind his back. He smiles at me in that sexy way, then brings his hand out from behind his back. In it is a bouquet of flowers – white tulips with several large hydrangeas and baby's breath.

"For my lady."

I take them from him and admire the hydrangeas. He knows me so well – purple hydrangeas are my favorite flower.

"Thank you," I say, and stand on my toes to kiss him. "They're beautiful."

He slips his hand around my waist and pulls me against him. I can't slip away and he kisses me again, deeply this time.

When the kiss ends, he doesn't say a word, just pushes me inside and closes the door.

"At least let me put these in water first," I say in protest when he pushes me up against the wall and kisses me again, his hands already squeezing my butt and one breast.

"Be quick," he says, his voice throaty.

I slip away from him, grinning, and he follows me, watching while I find a vase in the bottom cupboard and fill it with water. I break the tiny packet of flower food open and pour it in, and then I carefully cut each stem on an angle and arrange the flowers. I take my time and I can tell Jon's getting impatient, but when I glance over at him, he's smiling, his arms folded like he's trying to be indulgent.

"You like to make me suffer?" he says when I finish arranging the flowers. I take them into the dining room, placing them in the middle of the table. I stand and admire it while he comes up behind me, his arms slipping around my waist, his face in the crook of my neck. He nibbles at my neck for a moment, and I close my eyes and just let myself enjoy it.

No words are spoken. Instead, we stand like that, his arms around me, his mouth on my neck. He pulls down one strap to expose my shoulder and then cups one breast through the fabric, squeezing gently.

When he pulls me into the bedroom, I can't stop smiling, because I was right that we wouldn't be making supper right away.

He pushes me down onto the bed and lies over top of me, his hands on either side of me to support his weight.

"What are you smiling about?" he asks, his eyes narrow.

I run my fingers through his still-damp hair.

"I knew when I put this dress on that it wouldn't stay on for very long."

"You know me too well," he murmurs and kisses my neck.

"I do," I say and close my eyes. Then, I let my doubts dissipate, and try to just enjoy him for this moment we have together, taking what he can give me.

Hoping it's enough.

# CHAPTER EIGHTEEN

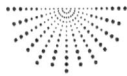

## JON

INDIA'S BODY is so responsive to me that I can't get enough of her. The sex is great – better than great. It's fucking amazing.

I love the way she looks when she's lying naked beneath me, and how she moans when I'm eating her, how she moves eagerly when I thrust inside her, how she loses control when she comes, her body arcing, her nipples hardening into tight buds.

Seeing her in the throes of pleasure because of what I'm doing to her is everything I imagined it would be. My own pleasure seems all the more intense somehow, knowing that it's been hard for her to just let herself go despite all her fears.

When we're both spent and I'm lying on top of her, I'm reluctant to pull out and end this moment where our bodies are still joined and we're drunk on pleasure.

I kiss her cheeks, her nose, her chin, and then her mouth, trying to soak it up before I have to move, take off the condom, and let the moment pass. I break the kiss and stare into her eyes, looking for a sign that she's finally over her reluctance. Her body is responsive, but it's her mind I want to see respond to me.

"That was so good," she whispers, and runs her fingers through my hair. "You can do that anytime you want."

I smile. "You said that once before, and then you asked Chris how much your stocks would be worth if you cashed them in now."

She glances away, guiltily.

I turn her face back and meet her eyes. "Don't be mad," she says softly. "I wanted to know what they were worth if things didn't work out between us and I felt I couldn't stay."

"I'm not mad. I'm surprised and worried. I can't imagine Pacifica without you at the helm of technology. You're an expert now in this field, you know."

She says nothing for a moment and looks into my eyes.

"I'm not going anywhere."

"Good," I say, but there's still this tiny sliver of doubt inside of me that she might just up and leave if she feels unsure of what we have together. I'll have to work hard to prove to her that while I won't say her word, I'll show her its meaning.

I try to put my doubts to the side so I can enjoy her in the current moment.

Reluctantly, I pull out of her body and remove the condom, tying it off and throwing it into the trash can by her bed. Then, I roll back on top of her, taking her hands in mine and pinning her beneath me, not letting her escape the way I know she wants to.

"I really should get up and pee," she says, giggling when I lick her neck and nibble on her earlobe.

"It can wait," I say, refusing to let her up.

"It's for the health of my lady parts," she says, stifling a laugh as I bite her shoulder playfully.

"Well, in that case," I say and roll off, letting go of her hands. "Don't want to threaten the health of your lady parts."

I watch her get up and walk to the bathroom, admiring her curvaceous butt and narrow waist. She disappears behind the bathroom door and I hear her peeing, and smile to myself. Hopping up, I follow her inside. She's sitting on the toilet, crouched over, a wad of tissue in her hand.

"Jon!" she says while I stand in the doorway and watch her.

"India!" I reply. "I just ate you and fucked you. I've seen a woman pee before."

Her eyes widen. "Please, give me a moment!"

She waits until I leave before finishing. I stand outside the door and shake my head at her. When she's done and I hear the toilet flush, I come back in the bathroom and take my place at the toilet to take a leak. I catch her watching in the vanity mirror. She's not used to the familiarity between us.

"Do you have absolutely no sense of shame?" she asks, and while I can hear humor in her voice, I know she means it.

"None. You'll have to get used to me being here," I say. "Being myself."

I flush and then wash my hands at the dual sink, watching her in the mirror.

"It's just a real change," she says and runs her hands over her hair. "You have to give me time to adjust."

"Immersion therapy works best, I find," I reply and pull her into my arms once my hands are dry. She slips her arms around my neck and smiles up at me.

"Patience works, too."

I bend down and kiss her. "I'm an impatient man, India. I want you now. Fully here and now with me."

"I'm here."

"Good."

We kiss again and then she leaves the bathroom and returns to bedroom.

I smack her butt playfully as I follow her. "Now I have to cook supper for you."

"Hey!" she says with a laugh. "No spanking."

"Aww," I say and grab her, tickling her. "I like the way your butt jiggles when I give you a love tap."

"I'm not a bad girl," she says and tries to squirm out of my arms. "I don't need a spanking."

"You were a very good girl and deserve an orgasm."

"I already had two," she replies, laughing again when I squeeze her, my fingers at her ribs.

"You'll get a guaranteed two more when I'm finished cooking and we're ready for round two."

We kiss, lingering over it. I could fuck her again right now, the way my body feels.

But then I hear her stomach rumble and feel pity for her.

"Time to eat food." I let her go and together we dress. "I'll eat *you* again later."

I cook for India, making my signature chicken marsala, with Marsala wine, cremini mushrooms, and fresh fettuccini noodles. I love to cook, and was in charge of chow for my team when I was deployed in Iraq during the last two years of my military service.

"You're good at this," India says, helping me with the preparation and cooking by keeping my glass of wine topped up. I do the rest, not trusting her with a chef's knife. I've seen her injured fingers when came in one day after having cut herself chopping onions.

While the chicken is simmering in the wine-mushroom sauce, we sit together on the patio overlooking the bay and enjoy the nightfall.

"This is my favorite time of the day," she says wistfully. She's sitting on my lap on one of her huge deck chairs, her head leaning back beside mine. We're staring at the horizon where the sun has set and the sky is a deep purple-orange.

Once the meal is done, we eat our supper on the patio by lantern light, toasting the success of the meal and talking about Pacifica and what's next on our agenda.

It seems completely natural for us to do this – mix business with pleasure. We move flawlessly between talk of Pacifica and enjoying each other's touch. After cleaning up and returning to the porch, we spend more time talking about Pacifica and our plans for the future. Around nine thirty, when there's a pleasant lull in the conversation, there's a knock at the door.

"What the fuck?"

India glances at me. "No one comes over to my place without texting me first," she says and grabs her bag from the office.

"Oh, crap," she says when she has her phone in hand. "It's Marina."

I stand there, watching her panic. "Just answer the door."

"She'll freak if she finds you here."

"I've been here before," I reply.

I go over to the door while India stands there like a deer in the headlights. I open it and there stands Marina, her cell in her hand.

"Hey," she says.

"Hey," I reply. "Come on in. India and I were just talking about Pacifica."

"I figured you were here when I saw your car."

Marina comes in. India's standing there, her phone in her hand.

"Sorry," she says and shrugs helplessly. "My cell was in my bag in my office and I didn't hear your texts."

"Obviously," Marina says. "I just came over to check on you since you didn't answer. You always answer."

"Thanks for being concerned," India says.

"It smells really good in here," Marina says and goes to the kitchen. There's a container of leftover chicken marsala in the fridge and I'm surprised at how free Marina feels to just barge into India's house and check out her food. "What's this?" she asks.

"Chicken marsala," I reply. "I cooked tonight."

"You cooked?" Marina asks, eyeing me.

"I did," I said. "I'm renowned among my former Army buddies for my grub-cooking skills"

"Do you want a glass of wine?" India offers and holds up her own glass. Her voice wavers, and I know she's nervous.

Marina glances from me to India. "No, that's fine. I'll go."

She turns and heads out the door and I can see India panic.

I grab India and stop her. "Nice seeing you, Marina," I say.

Marina turns back and glances at us once more. I can tell she's really fighting not to say something about me being there alone with India.

"We'll talk later," she says to India and makes the phone sign with her hand.

"Sure," India replies, forcing a smile.

The door closes and India turns to me, her eyes wide. After we hear the car's engine, India bursts out laughing.

"Oh my God," she manages between laughs. "What the hell just happened?"

"Busybody Marina just happened." I go to India and pull her into my arms. "I think the cat's out of the bag now. You'll probably get an urgent call from her warning you off. You better practice your response."

"I know what she'll say." India wraps her arms around my neck. "She'll say you're totally wrong for me and that I should be meeting the new man that MATCHED found for me."

"Yeah, another pencil-necked professor," I say with a laugh.

"Hey, my dad is a pencil-necked professor," she replies, punching me playfully in the shoulder.

I pretend to wince. "But he's really nice," I reply.

"He is," India says and adjusts my collar.

"But you don't want someone like your father," I reply.

"He is too much of an egghead for me."

"That's right. You want a man of action." I grin at her, pulling her against my hips. "Speaking of which, I want to get some more."

She smiles up at me, a coy look in her eyes. "You're insatiable."

"I am."

I kiss her and soon, she's forgotten all about Marina's little trip to check on her.

LATER, we're lying together, basking in the afterglow of our mutual orgasms when India rolls over and lies on top of me.

"So, are we going to be out as a couple? I mean at work?"

"People already suspect," I reply. "If you want people to know, you can let them know. If not, I'm fine with it."

"You don't care?"

"Not at all," I reply and run my fingers down a strand of her hair. "I don't care if they know or if they only guess. It doesn't matter."

She nods and sighs. "I'll play it by ear."

Then she rolls off and gets up, grabbing her dress and thong, and walking to the bathroom for her ritual after-sex pee. I lie on the bed and listen as she finishes and washes her hands. I don't feel a need at the moment, so I stay on the bed.

She dresses and leaves the bathroom, taking the hallway to the living room. I wait for her to return, but she doesn't, so I get up and pull on my boxer briefs.

India is in the living room, and she's reading texts, her hand over her mouth.

"What's up? Marina already working on you?"

She glances at me and holds her cell out.

I take it and read the text. Just as I thought. Marina's at work.

*MARINA: It felt suspiciously like you and Jon were together when I was over there earlier. What's going on?*

I hand it back to India. "What are you going to say?"

"I'll tell the truth," she says. "That you came over to talk about some upcoming business and made supper. It was nice. That's true."

"Okay," I say, narrowing my eyes at her. "That's not the entire truth. But like I said, I'll leave it up to you what to reveal."

She nods and types on her cell then hits send. She hands it back to me so I can see what she's written.

*INDIA: Jon wanted to go out for dinner and talk about Pacifica's upcoming contracts before he goes out of town. I didn't feel like going out so he offered to cook. It was nice.*

"That's not really true," I say and hand her back the cell. I can't help but feel a bit impatient with India because she won't stand up to Marina. "I never offered to take you out for supper."

She makes a face. "I know..." I hear a little ding, indicating an incoming text. She checks the cell.

"Huh," she says, and hands the cell back to me.

*MARINA: Don't forget what I said about him. He can't commit to any one woman. You have to decide whether what he can give is enough for you. I know you want someone you can rely on – someone who knows what he wants and it's you.*

"That meddling little –" I stop before I say 'bitch.'

"Jon," she says and takes the phone back. She texts a response and sends it. Then she hands it to me.

*INDIA: Jon is who he is. Any woman with him has to accept him for what he can give. If she can't, she has no right to be with him.*

I read it over and glance at her. "You mean that?"

"I do," she says and takes in a deep breath the way you do

before you leap out of a plane with only a parachute on your back. "I'll do my best to take you as you are. We'll see where this goes. It may go nowhere. Or it may go somewhere. I'm willing to give you a chance."

Her cell dings. She reads Marina's text and then sends off a reply, gets another response and sends another reply. Then, she hands the cell back to me.

*MARINA: I hope you know what you're doing. I have a great guy lined up for you if you want to check out his profile on MATCHED. You could come to my party on Saturday. Mid-thirties, wants to settle down, Assistant Professor of Biology at Stanford, lots of publications. Six feet three, built, dark hair and eyes. He's a hunk. You won't regret it.*

*INDIA: I can look after myself. But thanks for the offer. I'm going to take it easy for a while and just focus on other things besides finding someone through MATCHED. I'm sure you have other female Stanford grads you can use to test it.*

*MARINA: K sug, you know I love you.*

*INDIA: Back at you! <3*

I smile and shake my head before handing the cell to India once more. "It's quite the insight into how your mind works, seeing your conversation with Marina. She obviously thinks she knows what's best for you and it isn't me."

"No, she's made that very clear." She stuffs her cell into her bag.

"You're so afraid of her that you won't just tell her the truth?"

She sighs and sits on the sofa. I sit beside her, my arm around her shoulder.

"It's just that she thinks she's this great matchmaker because she had success with a couple of our friends. So she thinks she has an instinct for people who belong together. She doesn't think you and I belong together."

"She's wrong. We obviously want to be together."

"No," she says and shakes her head. "She means forever-together. You know, love and marriage and babies. The whole shebang."

I nod. "What about her? Why is she still single?"

India leans her head against my shoulder. "I don't know... She says she hasn't met her match yet. But she totally believes she will. She's the eternal optimist."

"You have to put yourself out there," I say and run my hand over India's hair, which is down and soft, flowing over her shoulders. "She's so busy matching other couples up that she's denying herself."

"She'll find someone."

I think of Marina, with her black hair in her signature pigtails and her dark-rimmed Harry-Potterish glasses. She looks so bookish and geeky that it's hard to imagine her with a man. She looks like she's ready to play some LARPG.

For the rest of the evening, we never talk about work. Instead, we spend some time watching Netflix, and then it's late and I should really go home and hit the sack if I'm going to get up early and get ready for my trip.

Now comes the moment when I have to leave and I don't know what India will think about it. Will she want me to stay?

"I have to go," I say and kiss the top of her head. "I have the early-morning flight to Washington tomorrow. I have to pack and get some shut-eye."

"Okay," she says and kisses me back when I kiss her. "You're back on Monday night?"

I nod and pull her onto my lap. "Yes, and I want to come right over and drive you crazy with lust. At least four times."

She smiles and nuzzles her face in the crook of my neck like she's still a little embarrassed.

"I'll be waiting with bated breath for your return."

We sit for a moment, enjoying each other's warmth and then I get up, picking her up as I do, and she slowly slides down my body until she's standing on her tiptoes.

"You're going to make me want to stay for another hour," I say with a chuckle.

"No, you should go," she says and runs her fingers through my hair. "Do your packing and get a good sleep. Text me when you can."

"I will."

I kiss her again and then go to the bedroom to gather the rest of my clothes. I dress while India watches me from the doorway, leaning on the doorjamb, her arms crossed. When I'm finished, she follows me to the front door, where I slip on my shoes. We embrace, kiss once more and say goodbye.

I hop into my car, and drive off, watching her wave to me in the rear-view mirror.

A completely successful night.

While I'll miss her, I'm looking forward to a weekend with the guys from my old Army unit. I know I'll have a great time with them and we'll get some real work done on the security business they're thinking of starting.

Still, it will be great to return on Monday and drive right over here from the airport to find her waiting for me.

Ready and willing.

# CHAPTER NINETEEN

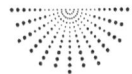

## INDIA

I FEEL good yet sad when Jon drives away and I'm alone in the house. It's not that I expected Jon to stay the night.

Well, to be truthful, I would have been impressed if he *had* stayed, and simply got up an hour earlier to go to his place and pack before going to the airport.

I want him in my bed.

But it's probably for the best that he goes home and gets a decent sleep. There's no telling what he might do if he stayed with me – probably wake me up an hour early for a nice slow morning fuck. Then he'd be in a rush to pack and get to the airport.

So, I take in a deep breath and go back out on the patio to watch the stars blinking over the ocean while I finish my nightly cup of hot tea. Marina got me in the habit when she was hugely into Harry Potter and went on an all-things-British jag, drinking tea like a proper Brit, eating British food and even using strange-sounding British words like jumper instead of sweater, fizzy drink instead of soda, and crisps instead of potato chips.

Marina is such a geek. Which is why the two of us got along so well. It's strange to think that of all my friends and acquaintances, Marina would be the one to develop a dating app. It's hard to square the idea of her knowing so much about romance, considering she's only had one boyfriend and they broke up a couple of years earlier. She's been single ever since.

But she's an analyst, even if only in psychology. She understands what makes people tick. To her, we're all emotion machines with algorithms we follow. She thinks she's cracked the romance algorithm, but sadly, I think her algorithm flopped.

I've always told her to match herself with someone, but she says it's impossible. A matchmaker can never match themselves. While they see others clearly, and can tell who works with whom, they can't see themselves clearly.

"But your algorithm should work, right?" I protested.

"I don't like any of the matches it's made for me." She shrugged like it wasn't a bad thing. If it didn't work for her, why the hell would she think it would work for anyone else?

So, poor Marina needs a matchmaker for herself. There aren't many dating apps that target geek girls, so until she meets someone with an algorithm as good as she was at matching people – or at least, an algorithm as good as we all *thought* she was – she'll stay single.

I'm beginning to doubt her ability to match people at all, considering how poorly she's done for both Jon and me.

Maybe those couples we all knew were freak accidents.


THE NEXT DAY, I wake late and luxuriate in the freedom of sleeping in without worrying about going in to work. I'll go in later this afternoon for a couple of hours to catch up on work I missed while my mom was first in the hospital.

While I'm enjoying a morning coffee in my pajamas on the patio, watching ships in the harbor, I get a text from Jon.

JON: *Flight was delayed, and now we're stuck in Denver for three hours. How did you sleep?*

I smile and text him back, glad that he texted me to re-establish our connection.

INDIA: *I slept like a baby. I guess I really needed to have dinner cooked for me.*

JON: *It wasn't the chicken marsala you needed. ;)*

I laugh and imagine him texting me, grinning.

INDIA: *I needed what you had to give.*

JON: *You did. I'm warning you. There's a lot more where that came from. Be prepared.*

I laugh out loud at that.

INDIA: *Oh, believe me. I have a pretty good idea what I'm in for.*

JON: *Good. I have plans for the night of my return. Keep it open, okay?*

INDIA: *It's open. Talk later. I'm going in to work soon.*

JON: *Hey, what happened to when the cat's away, the mice will play?*

INDIA: *I'm the cat as well, you know...*

JON: *You are the cat's meow, to quote my grandad.*

INDIA: *GROAN*

JON: *Later.*

I smile at the cat emoticon he sends me and sit imagining him in Denver's airport, seated in the first-class lounge, texting me.

I ARRIVE at the office and spend an hour finishing up a couple of reports I got from one of our suppliers. It's dry technical stuff so I need an extra cup of coffee to make it through. I take my bag and go down the street to my favorite local coffee shop on the next block. I've been going there for years, and they know me behind the counter, and start preparing my coffee when they catch sight of me outside the door.

It's busy this morning, as usual, and so I stand in line. When I arrive at the till, my coffee is ready without me having to order it, and when I move over to pay, I bump into someone. Before I can even say 'excuse me,' I glance up into the face of my ex.

*Blaine.*

He's grinning down at me, that old familiar quirk of a smile that used to make my knees weak.

Mr. Seduction, Marina always called him.

"Still like brown sugar instead of white?"

I finish stirring and slip the lid on my take-out cup, a jolt of adrenaline flowing through me.

"Still do." I finish paying and smile at the cashier. Then, I step away and turn to Blaine. "What are you doing in town?"

He glances around, apparently pleased to be back. "I'm back to open an office in San Francisco. Decided to visit my old haunts. Fancy meeting you here."

"Yes," I say, struggling for words. I'm just so totally shocked to see him that I'm at a loss. I stand there, coffee in hand, staring at nothing, wondering what I'm going to do if he's back and starts to hang out again with our old friends. Who are all still my friends.

"So, how are things? I talked to Marina this morning. She told me you're still with Pacifica. I hear it's doing pretty well. Congrats."

"Thank you," I say, trying to be polite. "Where's your office going to be?" I'm busy thinking through what this means. I hope he's not going to be in this neighborhood. The last thing I need is to see him every day.

"Just down the block. I love this area of the city and have a great space in a building with the entire top floor to myself. I'm meeting with some developers to work on a new media project. We should definitely go out for a drink later. What are you doing tonight?"

I open and close my mouth. "I'm doing something with Marina," I say, wracking my brain to think of what we were supposed to do this weekend. It's Saturday. She wants me to come to her place. She wanted to match me with some Stanford professor of biology at her party, but I said I wasn't interested.

"You going to her party, too? She invited me, seeing as I was in town."

"Yes," I say, kicking myself. Now, how do I get out of it? I'll have to call Marina and say I'm sick or something. I do *not* want to go to the party if Blaine will be there.

*No way.*

I know he'll be all over me, probably hoping he can luck out and seduce me for the night. I was such a doormat with him.

Not anymore.

"Marina said you're still single."

"She did?" I say dully, trapped in this nightmare of having lied to Marina about Jon.

"Yeah, she said she's trying to match you up with some Stanford types but isn't having much luck."

He smiles down at me, his eyes suggesting he's both amused at my bad luck in the love department, and hopeful that he can take advantage of it.

*Bastard...*

Although my heart was broken when he left, it was probably for the best. If I thought Jon was a rake and rogue, Blaine is even worse. As Marina called him, 'Mr. Seduction' says all the right words and makes all the right promises, but he has none of the follow-through.

At least Jon doesn't make promises he can't keep.

233

"What about you?" I ask, wanting to get a dig in if I can. "Any luck in the true romance department?"

"No, sadly," he says and takes in a deep breath, glancing around the store like he's a conqueror. "Just a lot of beautiful women as notches on my belt. Haven't found my one true love yet. Still looking."

"Maybe Marina can match you with someone. She's trying to match Jon."

"Ha!" he says with a guffaw. "Good luck. I'm hard to match. Besides, I'm not on the market to buy just yet. Still kicking tires." He waggles his brows in this really crude way. I know what he means by 'kicking tires.' More like smacking butts.

How the hell did I ever think I was in love with him? He's a total, *total* jerk.

I was good to be rid of him.

It's then that my spine stiffens and I smile back at him. "There's lots of tires if that's your goal. Kick away. I may see you at Marina's tonight. Now, I gotta go."

"Yeah, save a dance for me," he says and holds up his cup of coffee. "For old times' sake."

"I don't think so," I say and step out of the store and onto the street. "I'm not a tire to be kicked, Blaine. I'm past the test-drive stage."

"Hey, don't be like that," he says as I start walking down the street. He follows me and takes hold of my arm, stopping me. "We ended on good terms, right?"

"Good terms for you."

"You had a chance to come with me. I wanted you to come with me, but you said no."

"Because you wouldn't clarify what I'd be to you. I wasn't going to upend my entire life unless it was for keeps."

"India, we're not going to get into that old argument..."

"No, we're not," I say and pull away. I want to say something back that's cuttingly sarcastic, but I'm not fast enough on the draw.

Instead, I'm totally creeped out by Blaine, now that I have some distance between us and can see him for what he is – a blowhard jerk who is in love with his own self-image.

I head down the street and duck into the building, glad to be rid of him. I get back up to the office and lock myself in. After plopping down in my chair, I remove my cell from my bag and check my messages.

There's one from Marina.

MARINA: *Guess who's back in town?*

INDIA: *Mr. Seduction.*

MARINA: *You know? How? Did he contact you?*

INDIA: *He went to the coffee shop and we ran into each other.*

MARINA: *OMG can you believe it? He's back in town and is opening an office here. I guess he'll be in SF for a while.*

INDIA: *Unfortunately.*

MARINA: *What? You've been pining away for him for over a year. Aren't you glad to see him? He asked me about you and how things were. If you were seeing anyone. He probably wants to get back together with you.*

INDIA: *He told me he's still at the 'kicking tires' phase of relationships. I'm past that. He had his kick at my tire and went looking for a better model.*

MARINA: *Maybe he realizes he isn't going to find a better model. Maybe he realizes that you were the best model and he regrets leaving you. Why else would he go to that coffee shop? He was hoping to run into you, I bet.*

INDIA: *It was purely an accident. Anyway, he can take his huge ego and shove it, as far as I'm concerned. Not interested.*

MARINA: *Wow. That sounds pretty final.*

INDIA: *Ya think?*

MARINA: *Why do I get the feeling you're mad at me?*

I pause and take in a deep breath. I'm not mad at Marina. I'm mad at myself for not being more truthful with her. Maybe things wouldn't have come to this if I had been.

*INDIA: I thought I was still in love with Blaine, but when I saw him today and heard him talk, I realized he's nothing but a spoiled rotten boy in a man's body. He's still just as much as narcissist.*

*MARINA: A very gorgeous successful one.*

*INDIA: Doesn't change the spoiled rotten boy part.*

*MARINA: The very gorgeous part can be pretty enjoyable if you can overlook the rest.*

*INDIA: I don't have time to waste.*

*MARINA: What about my latest match for you? You won't change your mind and come to my party?*

*INDIA: I don't think so. I'm really not interested in seeing Blaine again and I don't feel up to meeting anyone new. Sorry.*

*MARINA: You said you'd help...*

*INDIA: Maybe in the future. I'm just tired of looking, I guess.*

*MARINA: You've had three dates. That's hardly onerous. Some people take twenty or thirty dates before they find their match. That's industry research, not just me talking out my ass.*

*INDIA: Like I say, maybe later.*

*MARINA: Okay, sug. If you change your mind, you know where I live.*

I put my cell away, disheartened and wishing Jon were here to cheer me up. I'd be able to look forward to us being together instead of spending the evening alone.

I spend the rest of the afternoon in the office, working on the technical specs of our latest drone. Around six, I get a text from Jon.

*JON: Hey, babe. How are you? I'm in my hotel after checking in.*

*INDIA: I'm just leaving work. What are your plans?*

JON: I'm having dinner with the guys and then it's the convention all day tomorrow. We're going to do some paintball after we do the wrap at the convention. I'll be busy but I sure wish you were here. You'd probably be bored with all the former-soldier talk and bullshit, though.

INDIA: No doubt!

JON: What are you doing tonight? You and Marina getting together?

INDIA: Nah. Staying home. She's having her usual MATCHED party and I told her I wasn't interested in meeting anyone else for a while.

JON: That's good. Cause I'd be jealous as hell if you went on a date.

INDIA: Just jealous?

JON: Probably insanely jealous. Fly back home and stop you jealous.

INDIA:

INDIA: What about you? Not going trolling for pussy tonight, I hope...

JON: Nah, the guys are all happily married so we're going to sit around the hotel bar and shoot the shit.

INDIA: Good, because I might have to get a new phone number if you were.

JON: No worries. Not gonna happen.

INDIA: I wish you were here tonight.

JON: I could call you later and we could do some phone sex...

INDIA: I've never done it before.

JON: First time for everything. We could do a session of Facetime so I could watch you.

INDIA: That sounds so desperate.

JON: I am, I am! Call me at ten your time. It'll be 1:00 here. I should be back by then. I'll make sure I'm back.

INDIA: Okay...

JON: *It'll be fun. I'd love to watch you make yourself come.*

INDIA: *I'll be embarrassed.*

JON: *No, no! You can't be embarrassed! There's nothing to be embarrassed about. Men fantasize all day long about watching beautiful women get themselves off. Seriously fantasy material. Spank bank material.*

INDIA: *Spank bank?*

JON: *You know – spank the monkey?*

INDIA: *???*

JON: *Masturbate. Beat the meat. Bleed the weasel. Buff the banana. Bop the weenie. Flog the log. Jerkin the gherkin. Pump the python.*

INDIA: *OMG*

JON: *Choke the chicken.*

INDIA: *Choke the chicken?*

JON: *There are many names for the practice, some as old as mankind itself. Believe me, men in uniform are often housed in cramped and crowded quarters with little or no privacy. We come up with names and techniques that allow a man to get a certain degree of relief. Watching a real live woman doing it is pretty much the greatest thing ever to most men.*

INDIA: *It's such a private thing. Isn't it embarrassing for you to have me watch?*

JON: *Not at all. In fact, it's hot. Extra hot if I do it while watching you do it while watching me.*

INDIA: *Men...*

JON: *You love us.*

INDIA: *I'm speechless.*

JON:

JON: *Facetime me later. 10:00 your time.*

INDIA: *Okay. Later.*

JON: *I'll be waiting.*

I put away my cell and smile, enjoying our texting. I have a little buzz from the idea of phone sex – or should I say Facetime sex. I've never done it before, so it'll take some courage on my part to try it.

I'd love to watch Jon, but the idea of him watching me... I'm a little shy about it, but if it will bring us closer together when we have to be apart...

I spend a couple more hours at work, then close up the office after eight. I grabbed a sub sandwich earlier to quell my hunger, but I feel like some popcorn. I'll probably open up Netflix on my Apple TV and watch something new. Maybe a movie or another episode of the latest television show to come online.

My evening planned until I call Jon at ten, I drive back to my house and park, then go into the house, happy that I'll be talking to Jon soon. I put my sub in the fridge and go to my room to get out of my clothes and into the shower. When I'm done, I wrap a towel around me and go out to my bedroom to search for some pajamas – I'm seriously planning to be a total couch potato tonight.

Then I hear something in the other part of the house.

I wrap my towel more tightly around me and wonder if it's the ice machine. It sometimes makes a funny sound when it starts up. When I round the corner, I see Blaine standing in the kitchen, fixing himself a glass of water.

"Oh my God!" I cry out, startled. "What the fuck, Blaine? What are you doing in my house?"

He holds up his keys.

"I forgot I had these. I knocked on your door but you were in the shower and couldn't hear me."

"So, you just let yourself in?"

"Yeah, I came around the side of the house and heard the shower running so I knew you were home."

"Blaine, that's breaking and entering."

"No, it isn't, India. Not if I have keys."

"You said you'd lost those."

"I found them when I unpacked."

"Well, you weren't invited in and I didn't give you permission to come in. You should go."

"Oh, come on, India," he says and puts his glass down on the counter. "Don't be like that. Don't you feel the way I feel? I'd be happy to just walk right back in where we left off." He steps closer and I step back.

"I wouldn't be happy," I say and hold my hand out to stop him. "Please leave."

"I thought I'd stop by and pick you up. We can go to Marina's together."

"I'm staying home," I say and stand my ground. "You go ahead."

"Aww, come on," he says and steps even closer. I glance around, looking for some kind of weapon. I'll use it if I have to.

He sees me staring at the butcher block filled with knives.

"India," he says and puts his hand over his heart. "I'm crushed. I'd never force myself on you."

"I hope not," I say and relax a bit. "You should go. Please tell Marina I'm sorry but I'm not coming tonight."

"I was already there. Her party's a bust. There were no unattached women so I decided I'd come by here and stay for a while. We could have a drink, talk."

I shake my head, wanting him to leave as soon as possible.

"No. Please leave."

My heart is racing that he had the nerve to come in the house on his own while I was in the shower.

Sure, we were lovers. Maybe if Jon and I weren't together, I might have been open to having coffee with him or even a drink. But to have him violate my personal space like this...

It's totally creepy.

"Don't look at me like that," he says, and now he looks angry. "I'm not a rapist."

"I didn't mean to imply –"

"But that's exactly what you're implying. Do you think *I* have to resort to forcing women to have sex with me? I don't have to, India. They practically throw themselves at me."

"Women are raped all the time by men they know, Blaine." I back away a step; I can almost feel his anger radiating off him.

"I don't have to force women," he says, his eyes moving over me from head to foot. "They volunteer."

Then my cell rings. I glance at where it's sitting, on the island in the kitchen. He does as well.

"You gonna get that?"

I nod and go over, glad to be able to do something. It's Marina.

"Hey, there," she says, sounding all chipper.

"Hi," I reply. "What's up?"

"It's really dead here so I thought I'd call it a night and come over with some beer and we can watch some Netflix like old times."

"What about all your dates?"

"They're all matched up and gone."

I glance over at Blaine. "Sure," I say, glad that she'll come to my rescue. "Blaine is here for a visit but he was just leaving."

"Oh, he's there? He was here for a while and I told him you weren't coming so he left. I didn't realize he was going to your place. Do you want me to leave you two alone?"

"No, no," I say quickly. "Come on by. We can munch on popcorn and watch Netflix."

"Okay, I'll be right over."

I end the call and Blaine is standing there, his arms crossed, smiling.

"I'm crushed you prefer Marina over me. Have you turned to pussy instead of cock?"

"Blaine!" I frown and go to the door, opening it and pointing to his car in the driveway. "You can go now. Marina is on her way over."

"All right, all right," he says and I can tell he's angry that I'm kicking him out. I'm sure he figured he'd be able to just walk right back into my life and into my bed. How convenient for him. How arrogant to believe it could ever happen.

Blaine goes to the door and passes by me, trying his best to brush up against me.

I try to avoid him, holding my towel around my bust, and step back. "Later," he says and gives me the once-over before turning to his car.

Then I remember the key and hold out my hand. "My key?" I say firmly.

He stops and frowns.

"If you insist," he says and starts digging in his pocket. He returns and drops the house key in my outstretched palm.

When he gets back to the car and hops in, I heave a sigh of relief. I was sure he wouldn't rape me, but he might have made a very physical pass at me, which would be embarrassing and upsetting.

I close the door and lock it once I see that he's driven down the street. Then I go check each window and the sliding doors off the kitchen, living room, and bedroom. I no longer feel safe and can't wait for Marina to get here.

SHE ARRIVES within fifteen minutes with two buckets of movie theater popcorn she bought at the local theater on the way to my place. She also has two big plastic glasses filled with soda and a bag of Twizzlers.

It's going to be a girl's night in.

Of course, it's only then that I check my watch and realize that I'm going to be with Marina when Jon is expecting me to call him for some Facetime sex.

"Here you go," she says and hands me the popcorn while she carries the drinks and candy. "I got one tub with butter and one plain because I know you hate the butter."

I air kiss her and take my tub and drink, and we go to the living room where I have my Apple TV hooked up, ready to go.

"So are you doing okay?" she asks once we're on the sofa. "With Blaine being back, I mean. Are you tempted to get back with him?"

"Not on your life," I say, giving her a look of horror. "He dumped me with barely a thought."

"That's not true, India. You know he asked you to come with him."

"He did, but as what? His main squeeze? I'm not going to move across the country on that."

"It was your choice. He asked. He wanted you to go with him."

"There was no choice. Give up on Pacifica just when we were making a big push to expand? Go with him to Manhattan with nothing but some money in the bank and an idea of what to do with it?"

"But he came over here. That suggests he's interested."

"He may be, but I'm not. Definitely not."

"Okay. By the way, Jon agrees with me. I told Jon he was here and Jon seemed to think Blaine might want you back."

"What?" I sit with my mouth open while Marina is flipping through movies on Netflix. "You talked to Jon tonight?"

"We texted. I wanted him to know I was shutting the party down early, in case he was coming tonight." She turns to me and gives me a guilty look. "I didn't know he was out of town."

"You told him Blaine was here?"

"Yeah, I texted him right after Blaine left. He was really shocked to hear he was back in town and that he wanted to see you."

"You told him Blaine was coming over to my place?"

She nods, her hand in her bucket of popcorn. "I don't think he likes Blaine."

"He *hates* Blaine. He held back his criticism, but I could always tell he disapproved of him."

"Men, right?" Marina shovels some popcorn into her mouth. "Can't live with them. Can't live without them."

"You do," I say and sit back, wondering what Jon will say about Blaine being back in town and that he wanted to see me.

I'm horrified that Jon will be in Washington thinking of me being alone with Blaine. That's the last thing I want. I don't want Jon to even imagine I'm interested in Blaine. For a while after Blaine left, I was sad that things didn't work out. Jon used to give me pep talks —most of them about how I was better off without Blaine and that he was a first-class jerk who didn't realize what a gem he'd had in me.

I set my alarm on my cell for nine forty-five so I can remember to call Jon and let him know that I'm not alone. We'll have to put off doing a Facetime sex session until another night. I hope he's not too upset. I know he's looking forward to it.

Marina and I watch a movie on Netflix and I almost forget about the time. Luckily, my cell chimes to notify me of an upcoming event and so I excuse myself and go to the bathroom. I have to be careful not to alert Marina that I'm texting Jon.

I hate the deception. One of these days, when I feel more secure about Jon and my relationship, I will tell her. But right now?

I'm trying to avoid confrontation.

I slip to the bathroom and take my cell with me, having

tucked it into my hoodie pocket. Once I'm alone with the door closed, I take out my cell and open Facetime.

Jon comes on the screen. I can see his hotel room in the background – the typical art above his bed, the headboard and the row of throw pillows. He's sitting on the end and smiles when he sees me.

"There you are," he says. His expression is unreadable. Not happy, but not angry.

"I can't talk now," I say in a half-whisper. "Marina's over."

"Hmm..." he says, and raises his eyebrows. "Marina?"

"Yeah. She invited herself over and brought popcorn and Twizzlers. I guess she felt bad about me being all alone on a Saturday night."

"She texted me something about Blaine being in town. What's up?"

I shrug. "Nothing. He's in town to open an office in San Francisco. He popped by earlier. He left and now Marina's here."

"Are you okay?"

"I'm fine. Look, I'm sorry about this but I better go. Marina will wonder what's taking me so long."

Jon frowns. "Are you sure everything's okay? You're not having second thoughts, are you?"

I shake my head. "Why would you think that?"

"Well, you did ask Chris about cashing in your shares, and Blaine is back so..."

"No," I reply, trying not to raise my voice. "It's just I don't want a confrontation with Marina to top off a rather bad day overall."

"Okay. I'll hit the sack earlier than I planned. Maybe we can do some Facetime fun tomorrow night." Then his eyes brighten. "Send me a pic of your tits and pussy. I'll choke the chicken while looking at you."

"Jon!"

"Do it now. While I watch. Show me your stuff, babe."

I take in a deep breath and then lift my pajama top and show him my breasts. I hear a soft groan and I close my eyes, embarrassed to be doing this.

"Now your pussy," he says and I can hear the desire in his voice.

"I can't believe I'm doing this," I mutter and stand up, pulling down my pajama bottoms and holding the cell low enough so he can see.

"Spread yourself for me," comes his voice.

"Jon!"

"Do it," he commands. "I want to see your clit."

I do, cringing but smiling at the same time.

"That's it, Jon. Call me tomorrow night. I'll make a point of staying home all evening. Alone." I raise my eyebrows meaningfully.

"Deal. Talk later," he says and then blows me a kiss. I blow one back and then our call ends. I imagine him leaning back and taking his erection in hand, beating off – choking the chicken – while he looks at our video feed.

I adjust my pajamas and take in a deep breath, running the water to fake Marina out. When I finally get back to the living room, Marina shoots me a glare over her bucket of popcorn.

"What happened? I was going to send in a search and rescue team."

"My stomach's a bit off," I say, and, as much as I want the popcorn, I push the bucket away to stay in character. "I'll just have a few Twizzlers."

She turns back to the screen and together, we spend the next couple of hours watching *Crouching Tiger, Hidden Dragon*.

Don't ask me why. It was Marina's pick.

# CHAPTER TWENTY

## JON

I sit on the edge of my bed, hand pumping my cock, and replay India's video feed. I stop it so I can look at her spread pussy while I finish, groaning while I spill, wishing I was buried deep in her body instead of in my hand.

I recover, clean up all the evidence of my solitary confinement, and then lie back on the bed and watch some late news before I turn off the flat screen.

When I finally can't keep my eyes open, I switch the TV off and lie in the darkness, wondering what India's doing and expecting that Marina will be staying until at least three o'clock my time. I have to get up early and meet Chris for a run before the final session at the convention. Otherwise, I might consider calling her back once I think she's alone.

Instead, I fall asleep soon after the light goes out and wake up to my alarm.

When I do finally open my eyes, the sun is streaming in from the cracks between the curtains and I can see motes of dust floating in the air. I roll over and wonder what India's doing now.

When Marina texted me to ask if I was coming to the party, I was shocked to learn that Blaine was back in town.

I read over our texts from earlier.

*MARINA: Why would he locate an office in San Francisco of all cities? It must be because of India. I think he still has a thing for her and realized it after being separated from her this past year.*

*JON: Or it might be because he wants access to Silicon Valley's finest techies?*

*MARINA: I have it on good authority that the first thing he did was go to Pacifica's office to see India. I think she was the reason he came back. I think he's going to make a play for her.*

*JON: Well, he broke her heart so I don't think she'll take him back.*

*MARINA: That was her choice. She could have gone with him, but she didn't because she knew he couldn't commit to the relationship. She didn't want to go all the way across the country with a man who couldn't say the word, let alone commit to it.*

*JON: Exclusive?*

*MARINA: Yep. It's India's bottom line with men. Exclusive or nothing. I had a great choice for her tonight but she turned it down. I wonder if she wasn't hoping to hook up with Blaine again and that's why she turned her MATCHED date down.*

*JON: Maybe she thought your latest match was a wash. Like the other three...*

*MARINA: Maybe she's hoping Blaine will see the light this time. To come all the way back to San Francisco to open an office to be closer to her... That's a pretty big commitment.*

*JON: You're reading too much into it. There's no proof he came back because of her.*

*MARINA: There's more proof that he did.*

*JON: Whatever. I gotta go. Meeting some colleagues for drinks. Later.*

*MARINA: Have fun with your buds. I'm sure India is having fun with Blaine. He said he was going over to her place for a visit.*

*JON: He's going to India's place?*

*MARINA: Yeah, he said that's where he's going now.*

*JON: Okay. Talk later.*

*MARINA: Later.*

I don't want to think Blaine returned to San Francisco because of India. If she truly isn't over him, she might be tempted to think things could work out between them. Marina seems pretty convinced that Blaine wants her back.

*The bastard...*

I sit in my chair at the desk in my hotel room and debate with myself whether to stay in Washington for the rest of the day and return home tomorrow as planned, or whether I should just catch the next flight out. Being out here while Blaine is there with India is going to drive me crazy.

I check out the available flights to San Francisco and decide to pack up and go back today. I know I wouldn't enjoy myself, thinking of India and not being able to be with her. It's probably stupid of me, but it's taken years for the two of us to get together. I don't want to blow it by playing paintball with some old Army buddies I haven't seen for years when I should be with India.

I SEND a text to my buds indicating there's a personal emergency back in San Francisco that I have to deal with and I have to take a raincheck on the day. They send their regrets and hope that everything works out, without asking for any details. They'll have a great time without me anyway.

I quickly pack up and take an Uber to Dulles airport, go to the ticket counter at Virgin to get my ticket changed. I'm able to get a first-class ticket to San Francisco. There's a non-stop flight leaving in an hour so I'm good to go.

I sit in the lounge and wait for my flight, reading some news headlines and eating breakfast while I wait for my flight.

When it's just about time to leave, I send India a text, just to check in.

JON: *Hey, how are you today?*

There's no response and so I figure she's in the bathroom or maybe still asleep. It's only six a.m. back in San Francisco. While she's an early riser like me, she probably stayed up late last night with Marina watching movies.

I give up waiting and collect my bags and head to the departure gate when our flight is announced. I'm one of the first people on the flight and get set up in my seat, which is nice, a window seat. There's a screen and remote, plus ports for computers and phone charging. I'll be able to focus on work for five hours straight and keep my mind off India and what's happening with Blaine, and hopefully get up to speed on a few projects Pacifica's working on.

I don't get a text from India during the flight and wonder what's up. The time passes slowly, but finally, our flight lands and we disembark and I catch a taxi to Pacifica's offices. It's now almost one o'clock and when I climb the stairs to the office, I expect to find someone there, but it's not who I expected.

India and Blaine are in her office. The door's open, so it's not like they were trying to hide or anything, but I get a total shock to see him there, standing in front of her desk. She's sitting behind it, her laptop open.

When she sees me, she looks totally shocked. Of course, I didn't text her to let her know. I felt a bit stupid for coming back early because of my concerns.

"Jon," she says, frowning. "You're here."

"I am," I say and lean into her office, giving Blaine a nod when what I'd really like to do is punch his lights out. "I came back early. We've got that meeting on Tuesday with Baker and his group. I wanted to make sure I was prepared."

She nods, but the expression on her face suggests she doesn't believe my story, which I made up on the spot. I'm totally prepared for our meeting with Baker and his group. I've been ready for two weeks and India knows it.

"Hey, Blaine," I say and nod again in his direction. "What brings you to San Francisco?"

"Setting up an office just down the block, actually. I missed San Francisco."

"Are you moving back?"

He shakes his head. "Part time. I'll spend half my time here, half in Manhattan until things get set up."

"Cool. Good to see you." I point down the hall. " I got some work to do." I raise my eyebrows at India. "Come to my office when you're free."

She nods and then turns to Blaine. "Blaine was just leaving."

"Don't leave on my account, if you two want to catch up." I don't mean it, of course, but I want to appear charitable even if I want to kick his ass down the stairs and out of the building.

Then I walk across the hall to my office and put my things down, then sit behind my desk, opening my laptop so I at least appear to be working. In the corner of my eye, I keep track of India's office and see her stand up and talk to Blaine. He stands close to her, his arms folded, and talks to her. She's standing with a frown on her face and I wonder if she's mad that I've turned up unexpectedly.

Was she planning on getting some afternoon delight with Blaine in the office? There's no one else here, so they could have been fucking like bunnies. She didn't expect me to show up – that's for sure.

Something like jealousy roils in my stomach. It's the first time

I felt like this since... since the night at the convention when Marina invited a date to our team function.

I'm jealous.

I hate the idea that India might consider getting back with Blaine.

I want her to myself. All of her for me and me alone.

I don't want to even think about her with someone else.

Finally, Blaine leaves and India comes into my office. I remain seated behind my desk and let her lead the way.

"So, why are you back?" she asks and sits at the chair across from me.

"Disappointed?" I can't help but say, my tone a bit too acid.

"Why would you say that?" She frowns, crossing her arms.

"Well, you and Blaine were..."

"We were what?"

"Alone in the office. On a Sunday. With me out of town..."

She stands and I wonder if I've gone too far.

"Are you insinuating that there's anything happening between Blaine and me?"

"Not insinuating. Asking."

"There's nothing between us except ill-will on my part and arrogant assumption on his."

That makes me feel better. It also makes me feel like a bit of a heel.

I lean back, exhaling, not realizing that I was holding my breath and was so tense.

"So, you're not happy to see him?"

She shakes her head. "Not even a bit. In case you forgot, he left me."

"He asked you to come."

"As a business partner. And a fuckbuddy. Nothing more. It wasn't good enough for me."

I nod. I already knew that. I wanted to hear her say it.

"I came back because I was worried that you were getting back with him."

"What on Earth gave you that idea?"

"Marina said—"

"What did Marina say?"

I take in a deep breath. "Marina said that she thought Blaine realized what he lost when he left you. I figured if you still felt the same way about him, you might want to get back together with him."

"You figured wrong. I despise him."

I get up from behind my desk and go over to where she's standing, clearly upset that I would consider the idea.

"I'm sorry. I felt insecure because you asked Chris about cashing in. Then Blaine shows up and I was worried that you were planning on leaving Pacifica and going with him instead."

She sighs audibly. "I wanted to know what would happen if we did this thing and it ended badly. That's all."

"It's not going to end badly, India. This is what both of us have wanted for years."

She frowns, so I pull her against me, my arms around her waist. She rests her hands on my chest and looks up into my eyes.

"Is this what you've wanted all these years?" she asks, her voice soft.

"It is. I just didn't know it. I didn't know if it was possible. I always wanted you. But I wanted Pacifica to succeed and I was afraid that if I pushed you, you and I would end badly and both the relationship and the business would suffer. Now, I'm not worried anymore. We've known each other for five years, India. I feel like I know your mind."

"And yet you worried that I might get back with Blaine?"

"That's just natural male jealousy."

She shakes her head and plays with my collar. "I don't want Blaine. He couldn't commit to me but he expected me to be his fuckbuddy and business partner and upend my life for him and his business plans." She looks into my eyes. "I'm willing to give you and us a chance. I've already given my all to Pacifica."

"You have. We've both given our all to Pacifica. The thought of losing you to Blaine—"

"Was a fantasy all of your own concocting."

"And Marina's doing," I say. "The thought of losing you to Blaine made me realize that I couldn't stand it. I want you, India. I've wanted you for years. I'm sorry I've been such a dick and have never told you how much. And I'm not going to make the same mistake that Blaine did and not commit to you."

I bend down and kiss her, and the kiss is passionate from the start and only gets more intense.

My body responds to the feel of hers against me, the soft mounds of her breasts, her belly and her buttocks beneath my hands.

I break the kiss, because I have more to say.

"I know I've been hesitant to say the word 'exclusive,' but I'm not any longer. I realize I don't want you to look at anyone else, be with anyone else, or even think of anyone else. I want you and you alone. I love you. I want us to be exclusive."

She smiles, and there's moisture in her eyes. "I love you."

We kiss again, her arms slipping around my neck. I feel a swell of emotion, realizing that this is what I really wanted all along, but didn't want her to say no to me. If we did nothing, and just kept imagining being with each other, what we have wouldn't be put to the test.

Now, we're willing to put it to the test and I know what I want – I want it to work. More than anything.

If she needs me to say the word, I can say it with no hesitation.

We break our kiss and she pulls out of my arms, and I'm

surprised, but I wait for whatever it is she's going to do. She goes to the door and closes it then turns the lock.

When she comes back to me, my body is ready for her, and I know what she wants by the expression in her eyes.

She wants me and I want her.

Of course, it's at that moment that India's cell rings. It's in the pocket of her hoodie and she pulls away from me and groans when she pulls it out and checks the caller ID.

"Marina," she says, her voice exasperated.

"Man, she has the absolute worst timing."

"Should I answer it?" she asks, holding the phone to show me.

"Go ahead, answer her. That way we can get back to our regularly scheduled programming."

India grins. "I was thinking what's happening is more like a special Breaking News report. India and Jon love each other."

I laugh. "No, that's old news. I just didn't realize it until now."

She answers.

"Hello, Marina..."

She listens to Marina for a moment.

"No, Blaine just left. I'm at work and Jon's filling me in something he's been working on."

She listens some more.

"No, I don't think anything's going to happen with Blaine. That was over a year ago. He made his choice and I made mine."

There's another pause and so I pull her against me, against my hips so she can feel my erection. She closes her eyes for a moment, and grinds against me.

"Yeah, Jon came back early. He wanted me to help him with a big project he's been wanting to give me for a while now."

I have to hold back a guffaw at that and lean closer to nibble on her shoulder, pulling down the hoodie neck as far as I can. She stifles a giggle and makes a face.

"Sure," she says and checks her watch. "Yeah, I'll be there in an hour like we planned."

I squeeze her, not wanting her to leave. "Hey," I whisper.

She waves me off. "Talk later. Bye."

India ends the call and puts the cell on my desk. Then she slips her arms around me again.

"I'm meeting Marina for coffee. We made plans with the girls earlier. Sorry."

"Aww," I say and pull her back into my arms so she's resting on my body. "I was hoping I could eat with you tonight. Eat *you*," I say, grinning. I'm disappointed that India is going to leave, but at least we have this thing between us settled. I can wait. "Remember, I have this big project to give you."

"Oh, yeah?" she says and rubs herself against me in a very erotic way. "What can you give me in, say..." She checks her watch. "Thirty minutes?"

"A lot," I reply and grab the bottom of her hoodie before pulling it over her head. She's wearing a lacy bra with a front closure. I unfasten it and her beautiful breasts fall out, her nipples hardening in the cool air. "A lot."

I bend down and take one nipple between my lips, sucking it into my mouth while my hands stroke down her back to her butt. She moans softly and that's all the reward I need.

I pull back and look in her eyes. Nothing and no one has ever felt like this for me. This is more than lust, although it is that as well.

"I love you," I say to her, my chest tightening with emotion.

"I know," she says and runs her fingers through my hair before slipping them around my neck again.

"I want you to be mine, and no one else's. I can't imagine not being with you. Not now. Not ever."

Then we kiss again and the emotions are roiling inside of me – love, lust, need, want, possession.

This is love.

# CHAPTER TWENTY-ONE

INDIA

"You're going to have to tell her, you know. Eventually."

Jon and I stand side by side in the executive washroom when we're finished. I'm brushing my hair, trying to look less disheveled before I leave for brunch with the girls.

"I know. I'll play it by ear."

"You're going to have to tell people at the office. I mean, they already suspect, but they should know."

"I know. We'll let them know when the time feels right." I turn to Jon, smiling. "You seem pretty insistent on letting everyone know about us."

He smiles and pulls me into his arms once more. Immediately, my body responds to the feel of him in my arms, even though I've just finished coming twice in rapid succession.

"The cat is, or should be, out of the bag. I don't have any doubts, India. Do you?"

He holds me tightly, his gaze on mine, waiting.

"Of course, I don't have any doubts," I say softly.

"We have to just do it," Jon says. "In the end, you have to jump."

We kiss and finally, my doubts are gone.

I jump.

I LEAVE Jon and drive to the restaurant where Marina and the girls will be waiting for me. I'm running late and am a bit flustered, my stomach still all butterflies because of what's happened between Jon and me.

He finally felt able to say the words. I feel a bit stupid now, doubting him. Making him say the word, but I wanted to know that if we did this thing, we would do it with eyes wide open and aware of the risks to our business, which we both love so much.

But I love Jon and finally, I think he really does loves me.

I enter the restaurant and see the girls sitting in the corner booth. They all glance at the door when I enter and wave. I smile back, wondering how Marina will take it when I tell her that Jon and I are a couple and that's all there is to it. No protests and no complaints.

I sit beside Jill and smile when the waitress comes by with a carafe of coffee. I turn my coffee cup up and am happy to get a cup. I need something to calm my nerves. "You're late," Marina says in her domineering way. "What's up? I thought you'd be happy to see Blaine back."

"Really?" I say, shaking my head in surprise. "He broke my heart, Marina. Why would you think I'd be happy?"

"Because he came back to be close to you, in the hopes you two could get back together again. That's why. I told him you hadn't been with anyone else since and he thought –"

"He thought wrong," I say and pour more sugar into my cup.

Just then, Jon walks into the restaurant. I see him out of the corner of my eye, and then Marina glances over.

"Well, look who it is," she says.

I frown. What's he doing here?

Probably wanting to show solidarity with me when it comes time to break the news to Marina.

"Hello, ladies," Jon says and stands at our booth. "I was just passing by and thought I'd crash your party. Can I join you?" He looks me in the eyes. "Scoot over."

I do, but am speechless for a moment.

"So, what are you talking about?" he asks and picks up a menu.

"We were talking about Blaine being back in San Francisco."

"Yeah, he was by earlier. Luckily, I think he got the message and left."

"What message?" Marina asks, her eyes narrowing.

"That India is taken and not interested in him," Jon says, and he turns his cup up happily as the waitress comes over with the coffee again. She pours and then drops a few creams off before leaving us alone.

To stunned silence.

"What do you mean, she's taken?" Marina asks, her expression priceless – a mix of shock and awe. I imagine it matches mine.

"India has something she wants to tell you. Right?"

Jon looks at me, meets my eyes, his expression expectant.

I take in a deep breath and stare Marina down. "I don't want to hear any criticism. Not one word of negativity. Seriously."

She makes this face somewhere between insulted and angry. "Why would you say that?"

"Jon and I are together."

For a moment, there's silence as the three of them glance between Jon and me.

Then, Jill turns to Lara and they high five each other.

When Jill turns back, she has a huge grin on her face. "We *knew* it."

"What do you mean?"

"We knew you two were in love," Lara says, smiling at Jon and me. "You two were the only ones who didn't know, apparently."

Jon laughs and slips his arm around me. I'm still shocked, but I'm enjoying the expressions of glee on her and Jill's faces.

"You really thought that?"

"Oh, God, India. It's so clear that you two belong together," Jill says. "You guys are amazing together."

Jon glances down at me and pulls me closer. "We are."

His eyes are warm. I feel a thrill go through me at how serious he is.

I turn to Marina, who is sitting there, straight-faced.

"You're not going to say anything?"

"Nope," she says, and there's no indication of her emotions, except that her hands are folded on the table and her head is tilted sideways.

"I figured you'd protest and tell me that we're making a mistake, and that we're totally wrong for each other. You've been telling me that for the past five years."

Then she reaches into her bag and pulls out a white envelope. She hands it to me, and then sits back, her arms still folded, her face unreadable.

I take the envelope, which is old and looks worn, like she's been carrying it around for ages. I open it carefully. Jon peers at it, curious. Inside is a folded letter. I open the letter and see it's from MATCHED.

*MATCHED ANALYSIS:*

. . .

*SUMMARY:*

CANDIDATE: *Ward, India Louise*
    *Candidate: Thorson, Jon Anders*

MATCH POTENTIAL: *97%*

"WHAT?" Jon says and takes it from my hands. He reads it over and now I lean in and read it too, noting that we were almost perfect on every score on the questionnaire. The only one where we didn't score perfect points was trust. Jon and I were twenty-five percent different in our ability to trust, and both of us were low. But the difference wasn't enough to knock us down from Perfect Match to Very Good Match.

The analysis goes on to suggest that for the couple to overcome the differential in trust, they should have obstacles placed in their path that they need to overcome together, in order to learn to trust. That would build trust between them and pave the way for the couple to be together.

"I'm low on trust?" Jon asks and looks to Marina for an answer.

"Oh, yes," Marina says and takes the questionnaire summary back. "According to my questionnaire, you're afraid of being hurt so you only date – and I say 'date' loosely – women who are not interested in relationships. Who only are interested in fun and excitement."

"When did you do this?" I ask, taking the questionnaire from Jon's hands and reading it over once more.

Marina smiles. "When we began work on the app. We had the first run at our algorithm and I had you both do the test questionnaire. Remember that first one? It matched the two of you up from all the other candidates we had in the system. All the other iterations of the questionnaire have been just getting the technical bugs out of the app's algorithms. The questionnaire has been the same all along."

"What about the bad dates you fixed Jon and me up with?" I ask.

"Yeah," Jon says. "They were like every other woman I would normally date, but none of them were serious matches for me. I wouldn't consider *any* of them as commitment material."

"They were the worst matches for both of you, but ones that you both would have chosen yourselves," Marina says to me, her expression pointed. "Jon wasn't into commitment so he looks for women who aren't into it either. He knows you are, so he picks women who are not like you. The two of you have been dancing around each other for five years because neither of you were ready."

"Why didn't you just tell us?"

"You wouldn't have gone for it. You wouldn't have believed it because you had both convinced yourself you weren't the right match for each other. You thought he was superficial and glib about relationships, and he thought you were too serious. I had to force you each to see how good the other person really is by putting you with someone who really *is* wrong for you."

She smiles, the biggest smile I've seen on her face for a long time.

"You manipulative little..." I say, at a loss for an appropriate insult that also shows how impressed I am, but I can't think of one. "All these years you've been pushing us apart!"

"No, I haven't. When you and Jon first became friends, I thought you two would get together. But you both held off, giving all these excuses why. I knew neither of you were ready. I merely parroted back all the arguments you were already making and they were enough to keep you from committing to each other."

"You never once said you thought we should be together. *Ever.*"

"If those arguments could keep you apart, neither of you were ready," she said. "But I knew. When I developed the questionnaire and saw the results, I knew it was real, but your fear of commitment meant you had to learn to trust each other. The only way to do that was to force you two to face up to your feelings."

"You are so conniving..."

"It worked." She smiles.

"All this time, I've wanted to talk to you about Jon, but I was afraid you'd shoot me down," I say.

"You had to grow a backbone and realize it was more important to be happy with Jon than be on good terms with me. I can take it. Besides," she says and takes a sip of her coffee, smiling like the Cheshire Cat, "I'm damn good at this."

I can't help but smile back at her. Beside me, Jon is shaking his head in amazement.

"You are. Here I thought MATCHED was a flop. We were so confused, wondering why you matched Jon and me with such bad dates."

"Nothing helps clue you in to a perfect match like a bad one. You remember my latest matches for you both? They got together at the party and are very happy together now. They were perfect matches for each other but terrible matches for you guys."

She winks at me, grinning at the two of us like she owns the world.

"Genius," Jon says.

I sit and think about everything for a moment while the waitress takes our orders.

"So? Are you happy?" Marina asks when the waitress leaves. She looks between us, her smile huge.

Jon and I hold up our cups of coffee. "Very happy." Jon bends down and kisses me and I kiss him back, cupping his face with my hand. It feels good to be able to show him affection in front of everyone.

I no longer care what anyone thinks. The only people who matter are Jon and me.

"Good," Marina says and holds up her coffee cup. "My work here is done."

# CHAPTER TWENTY-TWO

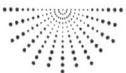

JON

*TECH CRUNCH DISRUPT, Berlin*
*December 5$^{th}$*

WE FIST BUMP while the announcer is warming up the crowd, introducing us as the dynamic duo behind the multimillion-dollar tech startup firm Pacifica, which just landed huge contracts with the US Defense Department to provide satellite tech and software coverage for the modern battlefield.

India's excited to be here and give the presentation. I'm excited as well, because this time, we're doing it together. She looks amazing in her black dress and heels, her hair down, her face fresh and smiling. I'm dressed in matching black, shirt and slacks.

We're a pair.

Our tag-team presentation, we call it, is perfect – just like our relationship. We've rehearsed this for a couple of weeks and have it down pat. When the announcer finally calls out our names, we walk on the stage together to a roar of applause. India starts the video while I begin delivering the presentation. We each have our own sections, and the presentation goes seamlessly, cutting from the image of our satellite in the production facility and then on the top of a Falcon 9 rocket, being delivered into orbit. India talks about the modern battlefield and the importance of communication for the soldiers and decision-makers. She tells the story of her brother and how he lost his life in an ambush that our technology could have seen beforehand, and possibly prevented.

The crowd is riveted as she tells the story of Steven's death and of the founding of our company, Pacifica, and how it went from my parent's garage in Pacifica, CA to a multimillion-dollar tech company in Palo Alto – and now, the Dulles Technology Corridor just outside of Langley, Virginia.

When the presentation is over and the lights come up in the auditorium, there's a loud and appreciative round of applause and even some cheers as we bow to the crowd and then walk off the stage, shaking the hand of the announcer in the process.

When we're finally behind the curtain, I grab India and kiss her. I'm overwhelmed with how successful we've been these past few months since we decided to come out to our staff and friends.

We shocked none of them in the process.

We were the last to know, it seems. But that's all in the past. Since then, we bought a place in Virginia. Now, we divide our time between Palo Alto and D.C., so we can be closer to Washington and our primary contractor – the US Government. We have a place on the coast very much like India's bungalow. We wanted it to reflect both our tastes and provide us with access to the beach.

Now that our presentation is finished, we have a week off and are taking a cruise in the Mediterranean as soon as we can get to the airport and catch our flight to Rome. After a night in a local hotel, we'll take a Viking cruise from Rome to Barcelona and then fly back to Virginia.

Life is good.

In the car back to our hotel in Berlin, we discuss the convention and how our presentation was received.

"It went well," India says and smiles, taking a drink from her bottle of water.

"It went fantastically well," I reply, needing at least one superlative to describe it. "Our timing was perfect."

She nods and smiles at me, her cheeks flushed, her eyes bright.

At that moment, I realize once again just how much I love her. I lean over, taking her hand and kissing her.

"I love you, India," I say, taking her hand and kissing her knuckles.

"You've told me that more than a dozen times today already," she says, smiling up at me, her eyes narrow. "What is it you want? There must be something you're shooting for to say it so many times."

"Can't a man just tell the woman he loves that he loves her?"

"Yes, but a dozen? That's high even for you. What's up? We already had sex twice today."

"Only twice?" I grin at her, because I'm thinking we'll probably fuck one more time before we crash tonight. Both of us are exhausted, but I'm hyped. "I want to run you a nice bath and pamper you. We have that outlandish hotel room with the jet tub. We should take advantage."

"Sounds perfect."

I kiss her one more time and then we drive through the streets of Berlin in silence, watching the pedestrians on the sidewalks with interest. Once back at the hotel, I do exactly what I've planned – running her a nice warm bubble bath while she pours us a couple of glasses of wine. I pour in some bubble bath, then turn on the jets. I go out to the main room, and India and I toast each other.

"To us," I say, holding up my glass of red wine.

"To us and Pacifica," India replies.

I nod, correcting myself. "To us and Pacifica. May our partnership and relationship be successful."

We both drink and I wrap my arm around her shoulder. Together we stand at the window and watch the fading sunlight and the city lights blinking on in the city below our hotel room. We stand like that for a few moments and then I pull her into my arms and kiss her. The kiss is intense and my body warms to her, my dick thickening, my mind going to thoughts of us fucking after the bath is finished.

India glances around my shoulder.

"Jon," she says, her voice sounding hesitant. "How much bubble bath did you put in the tub?"

"I don't know," I reply, frowning. "A couple of big squirts. Why?"

"Oh my God," she says and puts down her glass of wine before running to the bathroom.

As I watch, bubbles start frothing from under the door. "What the fuck?"

"Oh, you put in too much!" She opens the door and a wall of bubbles falls out of the doorway and into the room.

She pushes her way through the bubbles to the tub and turns off the jets.

"Holy shit," I say, following her inside. I can barely see her through the white bubbles. We grab towels and start flapping them, trying to burst all the bubbles. For the next five minutes, we flap and slap and flop towels around, until most of the bubbles have been burst and are just faint soapy traces on the carpet and bathroom counter.

When we're done, we stand and look at each other.

Then we burst out laughing.

India's leaning against the counter and I'm standing beside the tub, wiping my eyes.

"We can still have a bath," I say, and I start to undress. She nods and undresses as well. Soon, we're both naked and we step into the huge oval tub and sit across from each other. The water is warm and fragrant and even without the jets, it's relaxing.

I take India's foot in my hands and start to massage it, kissing the sole of her foot before sucking on her little toe.

"Mmm," she murmurs, leaning back, watching me. "That feels a bit kinky. Do you have an unreported foot fetish?"

"The only fetish I have is for your entire body and mind."

She smiles coyly. "They're yours."

I put her foot down and then I crawl on top of her, my arms on either side of her shoulders. I float just above her, my body between her spread thighs, my erection pressing against her belly.

We kiss and when the kiss is finished, we lie in each other's arms and savor the moment.

"This is nice," she says, and I nod in agreement.

"It is," I reply. "Six months ago, who would have thought we'd be here now doing this?"

"Marina, apparently. And everyone else assumed we already *were* doing this."

"I was so angry when she had the nerve to invite an outsider to our team meeting after the convention. And for it to be a date for you, and a totally wrong man for you? I was livid."

"He was so totally wrong for me," she says, and we both laugh at the memory. "I can't even remember his name, but he told us how great he was. That I do remember."

"Total pencil-neck. Skinny neck, big head."

She grins. "As opposed to a small head and thick neck?"

"Exactly," I say and tense my upper body, trying to make my muscles pop. "In contrast, I have a big head *and* a big neck."

She laughs out loud at that. "You do have a big head," she says and presses her groin up against me, wrapping her legs around my hips.

"I do," I reply and press the head of my erection against her.

Those are the last words we speak for a while, and our last sounds besides moans of pleasure.

LATER, after we've dried off and are wrapped in the hotel bathrobes, we lie on the king-sized bed and feed each other fruit from the gift basket TechCrunch sent us to welcome us to the conference. She pops a grape in my mouth and I chew, then I hold a chocolate-dipped strawberry out for her to nibble on.

"Get me one of the candied pineapple pieces," I say and she digs into the basket, searching for the non-existent candied pineapple.

It's a ruse to get her searching through the bottom of the basket, where I've deftly hidden the brilliant five-carat diamond engagement ring.

"I don't see any candied pineapple," she says, sounding slightly frustrated.

"Keep digging. I think there's a red box of it."

She searches, moving items out and pushing aside the stuffing. Then she finds the small red box.

"Here it is," she says, and frowns. "It's awfully small."

When she sees the inscription, she realizes what it is.

"Cartier?" she asks, glancing up at me. "What's this?"

"Open it," I say, barely able to hold back a grin.

She does and, of course, inside is the ring. It's a simple solitaire, five carats, flawless.

"Jon!"

She stares at the ring, her hand over her mouth. Then she looks in my eyes.

"Are you serious about this?"

I nod solemnly. "Yes," I say. I pull her into my arms and we lie together while she continues to stare at the ring. "I've never been more serious in my life."

Then, because she's continuing to stare at it, I take the box out of her hands and remove the ring. I take her hand and slip the ring on her finger.

"India, you are the love of my life. I can't imagine not spending the rest of my life with you by my side as my partner, as my lover, as my wife. I love you. Will you marry me?"

She examines the ring on her finger. Then she looks up at me, her eyes filled with tears.

"Yes," she whispers, and throws her arms around my neck. "Yes, of course I will. I love you."

We kiss and, despite the fact that we've both only recently had mutual orgasms, my body and mind can't get enough of her. Less than six months earlier, I was afraid I'd lose her. I couldn't imagine letting her go.

Now, I never have to.


THE END

# S. E. LUND NEWSLETTER

Sign up for S. E. Lund's newsletter — she hates spam and will never share your info:

http://eepurl.com/1Wcz5

# ABOUT THE AUTHOR

S. E. Lund writes erotic, contemporary, new adult and para-normal romance. She lives in a century-old house on a quiet tree lined street in a small city in Western Canada with her family of humans and animals. She dreams of living in a warm climate by the ocean where snow is just a word in a dictionary.

Other Books by S. E. Lund:

~

## CONTEMPORARY EROTIC ROMANCE: THE UNRESTRAINED SERIES

The Agreement: Book 1
The Commitment: Book 2
Unrestrained: Book 3
Unbreakable: Book 4
Forever After: Book 5
Everlasting: Book 6
Drake Forever: Book 7
Endless:Book 8

~

**THE DRAKE SERIES** (The Unrestrained Series from Drake's Point of View)

Drake Restrained

Drake Unwound
Drake Unbound

∾

**THE BRIMSTONE SERIES**
If You Fall: Book One in the Brimstone Series

**THE MR. BIG SERIES**
Mr. Big Shot: Book One

∾

**Military Romance / Romantic Suspense**
**THE BAD BOY SERIES**
Bad Boy Saint: Book 1
Bad Boy Sinner: Book 2
Bad Boy Soldier: Book 3
Bad Boy Savior: Book 4

∾

**PARANORMAL ROMANCE:**
**THE DOMINION SERIES**
Dominion: Book 1 in the Dominion Series
Ascension: Book 2 in the Dominion Series
Retribution: Book 3 in the Dominion Series
Resurrection: Book 4 in the Dominion Series
Redemption: Book 5 in the Dominion Series

∾

*For More Information:*
www.selund.com
selund2012@gmail.com